Apprentice Spellbinder

The large reptile lunged to its feet, long neck outstretched, flat head weaving back and forth.

The song that came to Bhaldavin's lips was one of the first he had learned. Rising clear and true above the angry hissing of the draak, the mesmerizing notes of the song flowed sweetly on the air. Ten seconds... fifteen...

Suddenly his voice broke and the song was destroyed. He turned and ran.

The draak shook its head and gave chase.

Also by Marcia J. Bennett
Published by Ballantine Books:

WHERE THE NI-LACH

SHADOW SINGER

BEYOND THE DRAAK'S TEETH

Marcia J. Bennett

A Del Rey Book

BALLANTINE BOOKS • NEW YORK

Dedicated to
Monte, Eileen, and John

With special thanks to
Dawn for Gringers
And to
Scott for Barl-et-Bara

Prologue ⟨

T*HEON SAT ON THE EDGE OF THE DOCK REPAIRING A* tear in his net and muttering to himself, cursing the hot day, baby draak who liked to chew on fishing nets, and Hansa, his boatmate, who had promised to help him with the net, but who had found more important things to do elsewhere.

He straightened, easing tired neck muscles by rolling his head from side to side, then he glanced out over the docks. The morning catches were all taken care of and almost everyone had left for town. There were a few, like himself, who had stayed behind to repair boats, nets, and sails, but the majority of fishermen who plied the river waters in and around Natrob had long since called it a day.

He bent back over his net and started to weave a new piece of line into place. Suddenly he saw movement out of the corner of his eye and turned to look at the shore just a few meters away. There was a man standing deep in the shadow of the trees that overhung the water.

Theon shaded his eyes with his hand. "Hello. Who's there?"

"A friend, Theon."

Theon dropped the net and jumped to his feet. "Gringers! What are you doing here?"

"Come talk with me and I'll explain."

"Sure! Just a minute. Let me put this net away."

Theon gathered up the netting and threw it into the bottom of the nearby boat, then hurried to the shore, excitement stirring. Gringers. Here. And looking for him. Gods, he had never thought to see the man again, not after their last argument.

He stopped before Gringers and took a deep breath, trying to remain calm. "It's been a while," he said, his glance darting over the handsome, dark-haired man whom he had once dared call friend.

"Two years," Gringers said.

Theon licked at dry lips, suddenly conscious of his appearance: hair uncombed, sweat-stained tunic, a gaping hole in the knee of his pants.

"What brings you to Natrob?" he asked, trying to sound casual.

"Last year's crop of spidermoss."

"Oh." Theon hesitated. "You're not alone then?"

"Hardly."

"Seevan's with you?"

Gringers nodded.

Theon grimaced. "My luck."

"Just stay out of my uncle's way, and everything will be all right."

"How long will you be here?"

"One week at least. Seevan's gone downriver to Port Cestar to meet with a new dealer for spidermoss."

"Why didn't you go with him?"

"I have other business to attend to."

"What kind of business?"

"Something that concerns you, friend—if you are interested."

Theon frowned. "I thought that after what happened, you wouldn't want to . . ."

"What happened two years ago is not important now."

Theon shook his head in confusion. "Does that mean I'm forgiven for stealing from your uncle?"

"It means that I want us to start over again. As friends."

Theon tried to read Gringers's expression, but the man gave nothing away. Theon nodded, accepting. "Friends it is."

"Good! I'm glad," Gringers said, clasping Theon's hand. "Now I have a favor to ask."

Suddenly wary, Theon withdrew his hand, but gently so as not to offend. "What kind of favor?"

"Do you remember Diak?"

"The old man with the dream of finding Barl-gan?"

"Yes."

Theon nodded. "I remember him. He was always going on about a diary he'd found. Said it proved that the stories about the Ral-jennob were true, that men did come from another world. Everyone thought he was crazy."

"He's not crazy. The diary told the truth about the First Men, the Ral-jennob. The box proves it."

"Box?"

"The box. Remember, I showed it to you. Diak found it with the diary. Well, now he's found a way to make it work."

Theon was curious in spite of himself. "What's it do?"

"It's like magic, Theon. It makes pictures in your mind. I've seen for myself the man called Barl, leader of the First Men, and I've seen the great ship that brought men to Ver-draak—well, part of the ship; it was awash in a large body of water. And I've seen men and women working with strange-looking tools, building a city they called Barl's Holding. It has to be Barl-gan!"

Theon looked skeptical. "Who else has seen this box work besides you and Diak?"

The excitement faded from Gringers's face. "A few. We were careful to whom we showed it."

"Seevan?"

Gringers hesitated, then nodded. "Yes, he's seen it."

"What did *he* think of it?"

"He called it evil and wanted it destroyed, and he named me a fool for meddling with things I didn't understand."

"What happened to the box?"

"Nothing yet. Diak left and took it with him. When the time is right, I'll go after him and together we are going to look for Barl-gan."

A clammy chill skittered down Theon's back. He pulled his sweat-soaked tunic away from his body and realized that more than tree shade was making him cold. He had a sudden premonition that Gringers was headed into great danger.

He looked his friend straight in the eyes and tried to make his voice steady. "What has Diak's box to do with the favor you want from me?"

Gringers laid a hand on Theon's shoulder. "Two years ago you told me that your brother owned one of the Green Ones, a Ni who had come to him as a child. Does he still have him?"

"Yes. Why do you ask?"

"If Diak and I are to reach Barl-gan, we'll need a draak singer."

Theon frowned. "Why not borrow one of Seevan's?"

Gringers shook his head. "You weren't with us long enough, Theon. If you had stayed and rafted with us a year or two instead of just a few months, you would know better than to even suggest such a thing. Draak singers are too few now to waste on the kind of expedition Diak wants to make. Seevan would never hear of it."

"Even if you offered him part of whatever it is you and Diak hope to find?"

"Even then."

"Too bad, because I don't think my brother's Ni is going to do you much good. He's a halfwit. He makes noises but no way could they be interpreted as singing."

"Perhaps he could be trained," Gringers suggested.

"I doubt it."

"I want to see him, Theon. It's important to me. Can you arrange it?"

Theon turned to look out over the water. "What's in this for me?" he asked finally.

Gringers chuckled. "You haven't changed, I see."

"Did you expect me to?" Theon responded, turning around.

"No," Gringers said, smiling. "You are as I remember you: keen-witted, sharp-tongued, and as sly a customer as ever I've run into—and a man who would make a good addition to our expedition."

Theon sputtered a moment, then the full meaning of Gringers's statement came through and he stood there in open-mouthed surprise. "Are you asking me to come along with you?"

"Why not? You once told me that you wanted to travel, to see other places, to become rich and famous."

"Rich?"

Gringers nodded. "Diak believes that finding Barl-gan will be worth a lord's ransom. You can be a part of it if you want to be. Interested?"

Theon answered without hesitating. "Yes. I'm interested."

"Good! Then now all we need is a draak singer!"

Chapter 1 🖋

*B*HALDAVIN'S HEAD SNAPPED BACKWARD, PAIN EXPLOD-ing in his face. He slammed hard against the ground and for a moment or two he was too stunned to react to the danger approaching.

Warm wetness flowed down from his nose to his lips. The taste of blood stirred him to his senses and he opened his eyes. A blurred figure stood over him. An inarticulate cry escaped his lips as he rolled away from the reaching hands.

Panic filled him as he scrambled to his feet. He blinked and tried to focus on the figure shambling toward him. It was a man. Enemy to the Ni-lach. To be captured was to be killed.

Move! his mind roared at him. He turned, saw the body of water just a few steps away, and made a desperate dive for safety. No man could outswim one of the Ni-lach.

There was a splash as the warm lake water closed over him. He started swimming underwater, but something was wrong; he felt uncoordinated. Something dragged at his right ankle, and his left arm...

He opened his eyes and saw the emptiness of blue-green water where there should have been an arm. His scream was drowned as water swirled into his mouth and down his throat, choking him. His instincts for survival sent him kicking toward the surface.

He erupted out of the water in a cloud of bubbles. A moment later he felt a sharp tug on his leg. Before he could recover his breath, he was being drawn through the water, facedown, by a rope attached to his ankle. He had to fight to turn himself over.

As soon as his face cleared the surface, he flicked his hair out of his eyes and looked in the direction of the shore. The man stood there, legs braced, hauling hand over hand on the rope.

Bhaldavin fought against the rope, but was pulled into the shallows as easily as if he were a fish in a net. He groped the bottom frantically, searching in vain for a rock he could use as a weapon. The man waded into the water and grabbed hold of him, but he kicked and flailed so violently that the man lost his balance and fell back into the water.

Strong arms closed around Bhaldavin as he went under, forestalling any attempt to break free.

The man floundered a moment, then got his legs under him. As he stood up, he accidentally kneed Bhaldavin in the stomach.

Caught upside down in the water, Bhaldavin took in water instead of air. He choked and spat up water, and was still choking as the man carried him out of the shallows and laid him down on the ground.

The man knelt over Bhaldavin and began pushing on his back. "Breathe, Little Fish. Come on, breathe. You'll be all right. You just swallowed some water."

Bhaldavin coughed a few more times, then breathed easier. The man stopped pushing on his back.

"Little Fish?"

Bhaldavin knew the lake was just a few paces away. He thought about making another break for freedom, then remembered the rope at his ankle and the strength in the hands that had hauled him ashore. He remained motionless, unable to understand why the man had not already killed him.

The man turned Bhaldavin over onto his back; his hand came to rest on Bhaldavin's chest. "Little Fish, you all right?"

Bhaldavin felt his heart beating strongly against the man's fingertips.

The man slapped Bhaldavin's cheek lightly. "No playing, Little Fish. Open your eyes. You're safe now."

When Bhaldavin failed to respond, there followed a second, harder slap.

Bhaldavin gave up playing dead and cautiously opened his eyes. The first thing he saw was the man's smile.

"Hah!" the man laughed. "You were trying to fool Garv."

Startled by the man's good humor, Bhaldavin allowed himself to be drawn to a sitting position.

The man reached out and wiped at the blood that dribbled from Bhaldavin's nose. "You made Garv angry, Little Fish, so he had to hit you. Garv has told you time and time again not to touch his knife. You could hurt yourself."

Bhaldavin studied the man as he spoke. Garv had brown eyes and shoulder-length dark brown hair. His beard was short and unkempt. He was big through the shoulders and heavy in the stomach; his wet clothes, patched many times, clung to him.

Confused, Bhaldavin sat quietly while Garv coiled the draakhide rope attached to his ankle.

Garv finished looping the rope and stood up, pulling Bhaldavin to his feet. "Come, Little Fish, I still have some fish to catch, and you must behave yourself until I'm through."

Bhaldavin heard Garv, but his attention was elsewhere, for suddenly he became aware of his own body. Not only was he lacking an arm, but the length of his legs and the proportions of his body were not as he remembered. Gone were the youthful contours of a twelve-year-old; what he looked upon was the body of an adult Ni!

Disbelief and fear chased through his mind as he turned on the man. *What has happened? What have you done to me?* The words roared through his mind, but he couldn't give them sound. He swallowed convulsively, fighting for control.

The man saw his distress and stepped close. "What's wrong, Little Fish? You going to be sick?"

Tremors shook Bhaldavin; his legs were not going to hold him up. Waves of darkness reached for him.

The man caught him before he fell. "No more fishing today," he mumbled. "Garv will take you home now, Little Fish. Close your eyes and rest. You are safe with Garv."

Bhaldavin lay quietly on a bed inside Garv's small cabin; his green hair lay wet and tangled on his shoulders. He was hot, sweaty, and restless—and he was feeling lost and alone.

He used his fingers to trace the lines of bone and muscle in a body he didn't recognize and tried to make sense out of the impossible. He reached over and touched the stump of his left arm, trying to remember the years that separated him from the youth he knew himself to be. But it was difficult to think, his head hurt so.

The day was warm and still but for the chirring of insects and the trilling of distant birds. He looked out through the open doorway and thought about freedom, but the man who called himself Garv sat on another bunk

near the door, whittling a spear, and he didn't feel up to
testing the man's reflexes by attempting an escape.

He glanced around the room. There was a small table
with two chairs in the center of the room, a large kist at
the foot of his bed, and a washbasin sitting on a wide
shelf across the room. Clothes, rope, fishing poles, nets,
baskets, and drying racks all hung from wall pegs around
the room. The one small window in the room was over
the washbasin. A narrow side door near the hearth was
barred with a stout branch.

Bhaldavin couldn't remember ever having been in a
man dwelling before. Did they all live like this? he wondered. Ni homes were more open and often built high in
the strong branches of aban trees where there was safety
from draak and gensvolf, and his people took great delight
in carving decorations for their homes. Seldom did a chair
or table go without some kind of ornamental scroll-work,
and the walls were often as not covered with lacy grass
weavings that could be decorated with seasonal flowers
and spices.

Bhaldavin sensed that he was far from his home, not
only in time but distance. He glanced at the man, then
closed his eyes and concentrated, trying to remember
something of the past few years, but it all was lost in the
darkness. His only clear memories were of his parents,
his small brother and sister, the time before the war, and
then the running and hiding—the war itself.

Bhaldavin drifted off to sleep, his last thoughts centered on the sadness in his mother's eyes as they left their
tree home that last day, the same day the Sarissa entered
the Deep.

Bhaldavin was afraid as he crouched beside his father
and peered out through the bushes. He saw the Sarissa
moving in their direction; he heard them call to one another.

He turned to his mother. Her crystal eyes were round

with fear as she looked at him. Baby Telia started to cry. His mother pressed her tight to her bosom, trying to keep her quiet; but silence didn't matter any longer because the enemy knew they were there.

There were other Ni hiding in the bushes around them. Bhaldavin knew some of them. Like his own family, they had come from the small Ni villages just north of the Sarissa capital of Annaroth.

Bhaldavin turned to his father, who held young Dhalvad. Kion claimed that greed drove men to hunt and kill the Ni-lach, but Bhaldavin's mother said it was much more than that. She said that men's souls were not like those of the People, that they were stunted by envy and a failure to believe in the continuity of life. She said that the Ni-lach were feared because men could not hear the songs of life or sing them and believed in nothing but their own might.

But if they kill us, Bhaldavin thought angrily, our songs will be lost to them and they will have to fight the draak alone. He shook his head. The war didn't make any sense. Surely the Sarissa could not be so shortsighted. Perhaps after living so long under the protection of the Ni-lach, they had forgotten what it was like to plant, harvest, and hunt without the help of the Draak Watch.

Bhaldavin felt his father's eyes upon him. Kion's light green hair had come loose from its braiding, his winged eyebrows were drawn down into a scowl, and his narrow lips were tightly pressed in frustration—for in trying to lead his family to safety, he had managed only to lead them into a trap.

Kion touched Bhaldavin's shoulder. "Be ready," he whispered. "If we're separated, go north to Val-hrodhur. You'll find sanctuary there."

Bhaldavin gripped his father's arm, chilled by the thought of separation.

Suddenly someone among the hidden Ni cried out and everyone started running, to scatter as the men charged the bushes along the river, shouting and waving their swords and taking aim with bows and arrows.

Bhaldavin's family was caught in the wild scramble, but they finally broke free. His mother ran in the lead, Telia clutched in her arms. Bhaldavin stayed at her heels, running close beside his father, who carried young Dhalvad.

More men appeared. Some Ni were captured and others were cut down as Sarissan swords spilled Ni blood without regard for age or sex.

Bhaldavin stumbled and almost fell. Heart racing, he caught his balance and tried to catch up with his father, who began to drop back.

Kion pushed Dhalvad into Bhaldavin's arms, then slapped him on the shoulder. "Follow your mother!"

Bhaldavin was too terrified to question or disobey. He shifted Dhalvad's weight to one hip and kept going.

"Run, Bhaldavin!" Kion yelled. "Run!"

Bhaldavin started awake, his heart pounding. He looked around the confines of Garv's cabin and remembered where he was. His thoughts went back to his dream.

No. Not a dream. Reality.

The Sarissa had declared war on the Ni-lach and had driven his people from their homes. His father had brought them to a place of supposed safety, but the men had followed.

The taste of fear he had felt that day was still with him. He brushed the stump of his arm. *What happened after I started running?* he wondered. *What happened to my parents? Why can't I remember?*

He sat up, frustrated in his attempt to remember beyond those frightening moments when he had run from Sarissan weapons. He looked across the room to the front door; it now stood closed. The man snored softly from the other bunk.

Bhaldavin waited for his eyes to adjust to the darkness,

then he tried to untie the rope attached to his ankle cuff. But the cording had been wet and dried so many times that it had become welded into a solid knot.

He gave up and quietly gathered the rope in his hand. He had to leave, with or without the rope. He was almost sure Garv wasn't one of the Sarissa, a member of the ruling class among men, but Sarissan or not, Garv was still a man and, therefore, his enemy.

Garv snored on as Bhaldavin moved silently past him. When he reached the door, he found it bolted with a long wooden bar that was going to be difficult to raise using only one hand.

He set his rope carefully on the floor and moved to the middle of the door. He placed his hand under the center of the bar and lifted. He felt the right side come free, then the left.

Suddenly the bar tilted to the right and Bhaldavin lost his hold. He jumped backward as the bar clunked to the floor.

The noise woke the man.

Bhaldavin dove for the door handle and jerked the door open just as Garv heaved himself off the bed. He was five or six running steps out the doorway when he came up against the end of the rope, which had become entangled with the bar. He fell hard, knocking the air from his lungs. By the time he recovered, Garv was standing over him.

"Where you going, Little Fish? It's not morning yet."

Garv pulled Bhaldavin up and took him back inside. After lighting the candle that stood in the center of the table, he untangled the rope from the bar and pushed Bhaldavin back onto the bed. He then tied the ankle rope to one of the posts at the bottom of the bed. With another piece of cord, he lashed Bhaldavin's arm to the right-hand post above his head.

"No more wandering!" Garv admonished, pointing a finger in Bhaldavin's face. "Go to sleep now. Garv will tell you when it's morning."

Angry words trembled on Bhaldavin's lips, but some inner warning cautioned him to silence. There was something definitely strange in the man's behavior. The way he talked to himself and his *little fish* made Bhaldavin nervous.

Bhaldavin turned his head to the side and closed his eyes, swallowing his anger. There was an old Ni saying that it was better not to pull the gensvolf's tail without first counting its teeth, meaning that if Garv *was* mentally unbalanced, it would be foolish to antagonize him.

Garv blew out the candle flame and returned to bed, mumbling to himself.

Bhaldavin waited for Garv to settle down, then he tested the rope at his wrist. He found it secure; there would be no escaping that night.

Chapter 2 🗡

*B*HALDAVIN WOKE THE NEXT MORNING TO THE SOUND OF Garv's voice. The man's running conversation with himself continued as he prepared breakfast.

Garv wielded his knife with practiced skill. Within minutes he had filled two dishes with nabob roots cut into bite-sized pieces, over which he poured a hot, white gravy.

Garv looked up and grinned at Bhaldavin. "Little Fish hungry?" he asked, as he shambled toward the bed.

Not waiting for an answer, he reached for Bhaldavin's arm and pulled him to a sitting position. He placed a wooden plate of roots and gravy on the floor next to Bhaldavin's feet, then took his own plate to the small table and sat down.

"Little Fish will feel better if he eats something. Then we will go to the lake for a little while. Garv needs fish for trading."

Bhaldavin looked down at the orange roots swimming in the gravy. He was hungry, and he liked nabob roots both cooked and raw, but the gravy had a strange smell that made him hesitate.

Garv looked up from his plate. "Eat, Little Fish. It's good."

Bhaldavin picked up the plate and set it on the bed. Garv hadn't supplied him with any kind of eating implement, so he stirred the mixture with a finger and tasted it. It was salty but edible. He fingered all the nabob out of the gravy, then lifted the plate and drank the remains.

Garv continued to talk, not once pausing to give Bhaldavin time to answer a question. When he finished eating, he came and took Bhaldavin's bowl, rinsed it along with his own, and set both on the hearth to dry. Then he returned and patted Bhaldavin on the shoulder.

"Little Fish ready to go now?"

Bhaldavin moved out from under Garv's hand, but the big man seemed not to notice as he bent to unfasten Bhaldavin's ankle rope. Garv coiled the rope in one hand, then turned to pick up his fishing net and pole.

Garv's cabin was set off by itself in a patch of overgrown bushes only a few paces from a tall stockade wall. Garv led Bhaldavin along a narrow dirt path on the inside of the wall until they came to a small gate that was guarded by a single man.

"All quiet today, Garv," the man said as Garv approached. "No draak in the area."

Garv nodded and walked on, strangely quiet.

Bhaldavin looked at the gate guard as he passed, and for a moment their glances locked. Was it pity Bhaldavin saw in the man's face? Or disgust? He couldn't tell.

A fifteen-minute walk brought Garv and Bhaldavin to a large backwater fed by the nearby river. Garv led Bhaldavin along the riverbank, then cut to the right down a well-worn path overhung with vell vine draped from tree to tree. When they reached the edge of the water, Garv tied the free end of Bhaldavin's rope to a loop in his belt and waved him back away from the water.

"Little Fish rests today. Garv doesn't want you getting sick again. You can help Garv fish tomorrow."

As Garv settled down with his pole, Bhaldavin moved as far away from the man as the rope would allow and walked back and forth in what appeared to be aimless wandering, but his eyes were busy searching the ground for something he could use either as a weapon or a means of freeing himself from the rope.

Finally he found a small rock that had a sharp edge. Sitting down, he turned away from Garv and began to work on the rope. But the draakhide was tough and resisted such a poor cutting edge.

Giving up, he threw the rock into the water. He was frustrated and growing impatient.

Garv turned and glared at him. "Garv can't catch any fish if you chase them all away. Throw another rock, and I will tie you up."

For a few minutes Bhaldavin actually contemplated an attack on the large man, but Garv seemed to be extraordinarily alert, turning to check on his captive whenever Bhaldavin moved.

Deciding to try one more tack, Bhaldavin went to the edge of the water and sat for a while, hoping that the water, as it soaked through the draakhide, would loosen the knot. It didn't. Glaring at the offensive knot, he moved back from the water's edge and lay down, his back to Garv. Anger and self-pity brought a lump to his throat. He hated himself at that moment, his crippled body, his ineffectiveness. He felt awkward and clumsy, and he knew that it would take him a long time to feel at home with his new body.

By late afternoon Garv had caught twelve large stoa and seven good-sized brekel. Satisfied with his day's labor, he put his catch in his net bag and called Bhaldavin from the shallows.

Bhaldavin was wading knee-deep in the water and pulling up handfuls of a bottom weed called seena. The dark green leafy fronds were edible raw, and Bhaldavin was hungry. Stuffing several pieces in his mouth, he gathered another handful, but waded ashore as Garv began to coil the ankle rope.

Garv met him at the edge of the water. "What you want that for?" He slapped at Bhaldavin's hand, trying to make him drop the grass. "Throw it away. It's no good."

Bhaldavin turned to the side and stepped back, trying to protect his small gather. Suddenly he came up against the rope and fell, half-in, half-out of the water. He sat up and flicked water from his face.

Garv stood looking down at him, frowning; then he shrugged. "Little Fish wants seaweed, he can have it. Come. Stand up! It's time to go now."

Garv pulled Bhaldavin to his feet and turned him back toward the path leading to the stockade. As they walked, Garv spoke about the fishing that day, his plans for tomorrow, and the upcoming trade fair to be held the next month. His words spilled out in an unending waterfall of sound. Bhaldavin wondered if the man ever stopped talking.

The guard at the gate had been changed. The new man nodded to Garv and asked how the fishing had gone.

Garv just nodded and walked on, eyes straight ahead, his hand on the back of Bhaldavin's neck, guiding him down the pathway they had walked that morning.

Bhaldavin glanced up, wondering at Garv's silence when confronted by other men.

When they reached the cabin, Garv took Bhaldavin inside and fastened the end of the rope to his bedpost; then he took a sharp knife from a shelf high on the wall and left to clean the fish.

Bhaldavin dropped his gather of grass at the foot of the bed and looked out through the open doorway. Garv was working right outside the door, where he could keep an eye on the room and its occupant.

Bhaldavin glanced quickly around the room, searching

for something with which to cut the rope, but found nothing.

He turned and glanced out through the doorway, deciding to bide his time. Escape should not prove too difficult, he thought, if I plan properly. His failure to escape the night before had been his own fault. He had been in too much of a hurry and had not thought things out.

He sat down on the floor and began to pull the grass apart so it could dry. As he worked, he tried to recall something of the past few years, anything that would give him a hint as to where he was and how long he had been Garv's *little fish*.

His loss of memory worried him. Why, if escape looked so easy, hadn't he attempted it before? Perhaps he had, he thought. Why couldn't he remember?

He was startled from his thoughts by the door banging closed behind him. He turned as Garv crossed the floor and set the gutted fish on a large wood platter on the table.

Garv came over to inspect the grass Bhaldavin had spread in the corner. "What does Little Fish want with smelly grass?"

Bhaldavin took a small piece of grass and put it into his mouth.

Garv's dark eyebrows lifted in surprise as Bhaldavin chewed on the grass. "Little Fish likes to eat seaweed?"

The man went to a knee beside Bhaldavin and took some of the grass, sniffed it, and put it into his mouth. He spat it out seconds later.

"Garv doesn't like your seaweed, Little Fish. You want it, you can eat it, but don't make yourself sick."

Rising, Garv left Bhaldavin and went to start a fire in the hearth, which filled a good portion of one wall of the cabin. The other walls were made of solid oak logs.

Bhaldavin watched Garv for a few seconds, then returned to his own work, lifting and separating the grass to speed the drying process. He listened to Garv move around the room behind him, but ignored the man's muttering, knowing now that he wasn't expected to answer.

A few minutes later, Garv stepped around the small table and tripped over Bhaldavin's leg. Cursing loudly, he caught Bhaldavin by the arm and propelled him onto the nearby bed.

"Little Fish stays there, out of Garv's way," he growled. "No more playing with smelly grass."

Time passed. Bhaldavin lay quietly on the bed watching Garv busily preparing supper. It seemed impossible that he had no memories of the man beyond the previous day.

He lifted a lock of hair from his shoulder and straightened it out until it reached his stomach. He knew that Kion would be shamed if he saw it so long and unkempt, for only Elders or Seekers ever wore their hair so long, and he certainly had no right to claim either title.

Thoughts of his father stirred thoughts of his home in the Deep, filling him with sadness. He closed his eyes, trying to relieve the burning pressure of tears that ached for release; but the tears wouldn't come because the memories behind them were locked in his past, where he couldn't reach them.

A sudden knock on the door startled Bhaldavin.

Garv was checking the fire to see if the coals were ready to use. Before he could stand up to see who was there, the door swung open and a small clean-shaven man stepped through the doorway. He had dark hair and a hooked nose that was accented by a pair of lively brown eyes.

"Hello, Brother."

Garv smiled widely. "Theon! I thought you would be gone for another week!"

"My plans didn't work out." Theon glanced at the fish lying on the table. "Am I invited for supper?"

Garv nodded. "There's more than enough."

Theon set a small backpack down next to the nearest bed. "What are you having besides fish?"

"Nabob roots in gravy and spice bread."

Theon rolled his eyes. "Should have known. That's all you ever eat. I'm going to have to teach you to cook something else, Brother. A man can survive on food like that, but sooner or later it's going to drive him crazy."

Garv went to the table to cut and debone the fish. "Sit down, Theon, and tell me about your trip."

"First let me say hello to Little Fish."

Theon walked over to Bhaldavin's bed and sat down on the edge of the bunk. "And how are you today, Little Fish?"

Did the man expect an answer? Bhaldavin wondered. Or was he like Garv, only talking in order to hear his own voice?

"Little Fish was sick yesterday," Garv said, taking the pan of fish over to the fire. "I think Chagg should look at him."

Theon caressed Bhaldavin's arm from shoulder to fingertips. "Chagg can't do anything for him, Garv. You know that."

Theon's hand moved up Bhaldavin's naked side, sending chills coursing up and down his spine. Uneasy, Bhaldavin edged away.

"How about letting Little Fish go home with me tonight, Garv?" Theon asked. He placed a hand on the other side of Bhaldavin's chest, near the stub of his arm. "It'll give you a chance to go into town without worrying about him."

"I have no money for town," Garv responded without turning.

"I have. You can borrow some."

Theon pushed Bhaldavin back onto the bed. Bhaldavin got his arm in between himself and Theon as the man leaned down over him, but Theon was stronger than he looked and Bhaldavin couldn't push him away.

As Theon's lips touched his, Bhaldavin panicked and tried to twist away.

Suddenly Garv was there. He caught Theon by the back of his shirt, dragged him back away from Bhaldavin, then literally threw him across the room.

Theon hit the floor rolling and came up against the far wall with a thud.

"I told you before," Garv yelled, pointing his finger at Theon. "Leave Little Fish alone!"

Theon sat up, grimacing and rubbing an elbow. "Oh, come on, Garv. I wasn't hurting him."

"No, but you scare him. He doesn't understand what you want."

Theon shook his head as he got to his feet. "I'm just teasing him, Garv. A little teasing never hurt anyone."

Theon glanced at Bhaldavin, then turned as Garv moved back to the cooking fire. "Oh, by the way, Garv, I have someone who would like to meet Little Fish, a friend of mine. He's been looking for a draak singer."

Garv answered without turning. "Little Fish can't sing."

"No," Theon agreed. "But if he could be taught to sing, he might be worth a lot of money. My friend said he would go as high as one hundred marks if he liked what he saw."

Garv shook his head. "Little Fish is not for sale."

"Think about it, Garv! It would mean—"

"No! Your friend can't have him. He's mine."

"All right. All right. Forget it," Theon muttered. "Keep him for a pet, but you're a fool if you don't get better use out of him. We could be making good money with him right now if you'd have let me set things up. There are few enough of his kind around these days. There would be plenty of people who would pay just to see him!"

Garv stood and pushed past Theon to go to the table. "No. Little Fish stays here with me."

Theon looked at his brother's back, then glanced at Bhaldavin, who lay with his back to the wall, as far away from the two men as he could get.

"Simpleminded and lackwit. You two make a good pair," Theon growled softly as he picked up a bucket and started for the door. "Garv, I'm going for some water. Do you need any more wood for the fire?"

"There's some stacked around the corner of the house," Garv replied calmly, as if he had completely forgotten his show of temper only moments ago.

Theon returned with the water and firewood and washed for supper. Garv set the table for himself and Theon, then fixed Bhaldavin's plate and placed it on the floor near the bed. Taking Bhaldavin by the arm, he pulled him down to sit beside the plate.

"You let him feed himself now?" Theon asked, surprised.

"He's messy," Garv said, returning to the table, "but I can always sweep the floor, and he eats better if I leave him alone."

Bhaldavin noticed that Garv spoke differently now that his brother was there, and he questioned his first assessment of the man's faculties. Perhaps Garv was not the complete simpleton he had first appeared to be.

He picked up his plate and held it on his lap. He glanced up, but the two men were busy with their own food. He sampled the spice bread and cooked fish, then proceeded to devour the nabob roots.

"Garv, he's going to make himself sick gulping food like that," Theon observed.

Garv turned to look just as Bhaldavin put several fronds of grass in his mouth.

"What's he eating now?" Theon asked.

"He likes seaweed," Garv said. He watched Bhaldavin a moment, then returned to his own food.

Bhaldavin watched the two men while he finished the slab of bread on his plate. The nabob roots and gravy were oversalted this time, making him thirsty.

Theon caught Bhaldavin watching Garv drain the last swallow of water from his cup. "Thirsty, Little Fish?" He poured another dipper of water into his own cup and took it to Bhaldavin.

Garv turned in his seat. "Don't let him have the cup, Theon. He's broken all the others I have. These are my last two."

Theon knelt and placed the cup to Bhaldavin's lips. Bhaldavin leaned away, wary of the man's closeness even though he realized that he had little to fear from Theon as long as Garv was around.

"Come on, Little Fish, drink if you're thirsty, or I'll take it away," Theon warned.

Bhaldavin looked at the cup. The need to wash the saltiness from his mouth drove him to take a chance. His hand closed over Theon's as he pulled the cup to his mouth.

"You want more, Little Fish?" Theon asked after Bhaldavin had emptied the cup.

Bhaldavin locked glances with Theon, and for a moment they both stared. Startled by the strange look that suddenly crossed Theon's face, Bhaldavin dropped his glance to his plate.

"You know, Garv," Theon said, "for a moment there it was almost as if he understood me."

Garv stood up and began clearing the table. "Little Fish understands sometimes."

Theon caught Bhaldavin by the chin and forced his head up. "Garv, come over here."

"Why?"

"Never mind why. Just come look. There *is* a difference in his eyes."

Garv came and bent over Bhaldavin. "I see no difference."

"I do. Look! He's watching us."

Bhaldavin pushed Theon's hand away, disliking the man's touch.

"And look at that. He doesn't want to be touched. That's new too!"

"He's afraid of you," Garv said.

"No. It's more than that. It's not fear I'm seeing, it's more like hate." Theon turned on his brother. "Have you been mean to him lately?"

Garv frowned. "You know I wouldn't hurt Little Fish."

"Not intentionally, but . . ." Theon looked at Bhaldavin again. "Then what's happened to him? He *has* changed. I can see it in his eyes."

Bhaldavin heard the suppressed excitement in Theon's voice and wondered what would happen if he spoke to the man. Would escape be easier or harder if they realized he was not the fool they thought him?

"Garv, how long have you had Little Fish? Fifteen years now, isn't it?" Theon said. "Remember, you brought him back from Port Cestar the same year that I started working with Hansa on his boat."

Garv nodded.

"I remember how surprised everyone was to see you that morning, getting out of the boat carrying one of the Green Ones," Theon continued. "Hansa had his eyes on him from the minute you entered town, but once he realized Little Fish had no mind left, how quickly he lost interest."

Theon continued to talk, but Bhaldavin wasn't listening. He had realized that a number of years had passed— but fifteen? He was stunned. How could he have lived so long without knowing, without being aware of his surroundings? It seemed impossible. Yet the truth was there for him to see, his unclothed body testimony to the years he couldn't remember.

He leaned back against the bed, sick with the knowledge that so much time had elapsed. Where were his parents? His sister and brother? Had they survived the war?

A worried frown appeared on Garv's face. "Shut up, Theon," he said. "Something's wrong with Little Fish."

Garv leaned down and laid a hand across Bhaldavin's

forehead. "Head hurt again, Little Fish? Garv has something to make it feel better."

As the big man went to the kist across the room, Theon pushed his face close to Bhaldavin's, his brown eyes searching the crystal-gray ones before him. "Little Fish? *Do* you understand what we're saying? Gods! It doesn't seem possible after all this time, but . . . If you understand me, Little Fish, nod your head. Come on, I *know* you understand. I can see it in your eyes."

Bhaldavin felt confused, and for a moment he forgot the part he had been playing. He almost nodded; then suddenly Garv was there, pushing the spout of a wineskin toward his mouth.

"Drink this, Little Fish. It'll make your headache go away."

Bhaldavin turned his head, the sickness that churned in his stomach pushing upward.

A large hand closed on the back of his neck. "Drink," Little Fish!" Garv commanded.

"Garv, maybe he's not thirsty," Theon said. "Why don't you let me talk to him a little longer. If he—"

"No! You can talk to him tomorrow. He's going to sleep now."

"Garv, I'm not going to do anything to him," Theon protested. "I just want to talk to—"

Bhaldavin folded over and began retching, spewing pieces of nabob root and fish into Theon's lap. Theon cursed and jumped away as Garv knelt beside Bhaldavin and held him until the retching spasms passed. The seizures were so violent that Bhaldavin also lost control of his bowels.

"Gods, what a mess!" Theon cursed as Garv picked Bhaldavin up and carried him toward the door.

"It's your fault," Garv growled. "You upset him. You clean up the mess here while I wash him off. There's water in that bucket over there."

Theon had the mess on the floor cleaned up by the

time Garv returned with Bhaldavin. Garv snatched a blanket from one of the beds, wrapped it around Bhaldavin, and led him over to the hearth, where he made him lie down; he fastened the rope at Bhaldavin's ankle to one of the table legs.

"Garv, may I stay the night?" Theon asked quietly.

"I guess so." He pointed to Bhaldavin's bed. "You can use that bunk."

Theon looked at his brother a moment, then went over to the pile of grass strewn on the floor.

"What're you doing?" Garv asked, as Theon began to pick up the grass.

"Throwing this stuff away. It's probably what made him sick. You'll have to begin to watch what he eats, Garv."

"I watch," Garv said defensively.

"I know you do, Garv. I just meant that if Little Fish is more alert now, you'll have to keep a closer eye on him. Are you going fishing tomorrow?"

Garv nodded and returned to the task of cleaning the supper dishes.

"Mind if I come along?"

"You talk too much. You scare all the fish away."

Theon smiled. "I'll be quiet, Garv. I promise."

"What about Hansa? Won't he look for you?"

"He's doing some repair work on the boat. He said it would be three or four days until he's ready to go out again."

The heat from the coals soon warmed Bhaldavin. He closed his eyes and listened to the men talk, their voices blurring into a soothing rumble of sound. In the back of his mind he knew he should remain awake and make plans for an escape while the men slept, but exhaustion won out and he fell asleep.

Chapter 3 ✍

*B*HALDAVIN WOKE HUNGRY THE NEXT MORNING, BUT Garv gave him only one piece of bread and a fresh kansa for breakfast. The yellow fruit was ripe and juicy, and Bhaldavin looked longingly at the bowl of fruit sitting on a nearby shelf.

Garv untied Bhaldavin's ankle rope and began coiling it up. When finished, he set the rope on the table and went for his net and pole.

Bhaldavin cautiously sidled toward the bowl on the shelf, but as he reached for a second fruit, Garv turned, saw what he was doing, and came over to slap his hand away.

"No, Little Fish, no more this morning. Garv doesn't want you getting sick again."

Theon appeared in the doorway. "Oh, let him have another, Garv. It won't hurt him." He pulled his tunic over his head and tucked it into his pants, then sat down to put on his sandals. "You about ready, Garv?"

After Garv and Bhaldavin went out, Theon took several fruits from the bowl and stuffed them into his tunic pocket, then hurried to catch up with the other two.

Beyond the stockade gate, they followed the narrow trail that led along the river. The overhanging vines and bushes that enclosed the path on both sides made the trail dark with shadows. When the trail widened slightly, Theon moved up beside Bhaldavin.

"Here, Little Fish," he called, tossing one of the kansa he had brought from the cabin. "Catch."

Bhaldavin caught the yellow globe, and before Garv could interfere, he took a large bite.

Garv glared at his brother, but Theon had eyes only for Bhaldavin, who was busy making the fruit disappear as fast as possible.

Theon reached out and grabbed ahold of green Ni-lach hair, forcing Bhaldavin to look him in the face. "So I wasn't dreaming last night. Our *little fish* has awakened. You know that I'm talking to you, don't you, Little Fish? How long have you been fooling Garv? And why?"

Garv caught Theon's wrist. "Let him go, Theon! You'll frighten him."

"I doubt that!" Theon snapped, twisting out of Garv's hold. "Little Fish isn't afraid of me. Look at him. Look into his eyes, Garv. He's watching us and he understands. Damn it, I said look!"

The sudden snap and crackle of underbrush put an end to the argument. All three turned just as the head of a large blue draak appeared over the top of the bushes alongside the trail. Wakened from sleep by the angry voices, the large reptile lunged to its feet, its long neck outstretched, its flat head weaving back and forth.

Though land draak were lighter in build than their water cousins, each of their four legs was the equal of three men locked breast to back, and though ungainly looking, they could move quickly.

Garv and Theon thought of no one but themselves as they ran downtrail, diving for safety among the trees and bushes. Neither man saw Bhaldavin fall, entangled in the rope Garv had dropped.

The draak was upon Bhaldavin before he could kick free of the rope.

The song that came to Bhaldavin's lips was one of the first he had learned; at first his voice cracked, but then the high trilling notes rose clear and true above the angry hissing of the draak.

The draak's head dipped down as if to scoop Bhaldavin up, then the open jaws closed and the draak straightened to its full height and stood quietly listening.

Bhaldavin hurriedly began to untangle the rope about his legs; he worked quickly, unsure how long he could hold the draak. The mesmerizing notes of the song known as "Ara-vol" flowed sweetly on the air . . . ten seconds . . . fifteen . . .

He stood up and began backing away, the coil of rope caught in his hand. Suddenly his voice broke and the song was destroyed. He turned and ran down the dirt pathway. The draak shook its head and gave chase.

Draak were known to have poor eyesight, but their hearing was keen, and as Bhaldavin sought safety in the heavy underbrush along the trail, the draak followed, crashing through the bushes as easily as Bhaldavin might have waded through grass.

Using all the skills he had learned in the Deep, Bhaldavin searched for a place to go to ground. Climbing a tree was out of the question because the draak was too close behind.

Suddenly the rope he carried caught around a branch and tore out of his hand; he ran only a few more steps before he was brought up short. He dove for cover under the branches of a kansa bush and crouched motionless as the draak lumbered closer. It took a few more steps, then stopped, confused by Bhaldavin's sudden disappearance. Its head wove back and forth as it waited for its quarry to make another noise.

Bhaldavin flinched as something brushed his shoulder. He turned to find Garv lying beside a fallen tree. There was a narrow culvert beneath the tree that led down to the edge of the river, and Garv, motioning to Bhaldavin to follow, edged back into the culvert. Bhaldavin came up against the rope and shook his head, pointing to the problem. Garv quickly drew his knife. Carefully he moved up beside Bhaldavin and began to cut the rope.

The draak moved a step closer and pushed its head down among the bushes, its long tongue snaking in and out as it snuffled the air.

Bhaldavin held his breath, waiting for the draak's head to swing in his direction. He could smell it now, the mud and grass that clung to its thick scaly hide carrying the odor of rotten dewbird eggs.

Garv sawed frantically on the rope, his harsh breathing audible in the morning silence. Suddenly the rope snapped, throwing Garv back against several branches.

Alerted by that small sound, the draak thrust its head down farther still and finally saw its prey.

Garv scooted backward, pulling Bhaldavin headfirst into the culvert.

Unable to take his eyes from the gaping mouth and sharp teeth snapping at his legs, Bhaldavin felt himself slide, then his head struck something hard and he fell into darkness.

"... believe me or not, Gringers. I swear, I heard him. He was singing the draak!"

"Are you sure, Theon?"

"Yes, damn it! I was there. I heard him."

"But how? You told me he wasn't trained."

"I didn't think he was," Theon said fiercely.

Gringers raised his hand in a placating gesture. "Easy, Theon. Relax. Losing your temper isn't going to—"

"I'm not losing my temper," Theon grumbled, lowering

his voice slightly. "I'm just trying to tell you that since the last time I saw him, Little Fish has changed!"

"Changed how?"

"It's his eyes. Before it was like looking into twin pieces of gray glass, but now there's a feeling of presence there, as if he's really aware of what goes on around him. When he wakes up, look into his eyes and you'll understand what I'm trying to say."

"*If* he wakes up," Gringers said softly.

"Let's think positive, all right?"

"Sorry. Theon, is there a possibility that your *little fish* has been faking all this time?"

"For fifteen years?" Theon snorted. "Impossible!"

"How do you explain the changes in him then?"

"I can't explain it, unless..."

"Unless what?"

"Last night I noticed that he had a bruise under one eye. If Garv had hit him hard enough, perhaps such a blow would knock him back to his senses."

"It's a possibility, but you told me that Garv would never do anything to hurt him."

"Not intentionally. Garv treats Little Fish with a gentleness you wouldn't believe. Oh, I've seen him slap the Ni a couple of times, but only as one would slap an erring child. The only time I really ever saw Garv angry with him was that time he wandered away from the cabin and ended up in town walking around stark naked. Garv hit him with a stick a couple of times and made sure he wouldn't wander off again by putting that rope at his ankle; the same rope that nearly cost him his life this morning."

"Tell me again what happened," Gringers prompted.

"Garv and I were arguing, not paying attention to how loud we were getting and where we were. Suddenly a draak appeared. It must have been sleeping by the riverbank. We were caught off guard and we ran. I was halfway back to the stockade when I heard Little Fish start to sing. I stopped to look back and saw him facing the draak in the middle of the path and singing it to a standstill. For a minute I thought he was going to be able to control it, send it away or something. I was so shocked by what was happening that all I could do was stand and stare. Then he stopped singing and the draak turned on him.

"He made a run for the bushes just like we had, but the rope Garv had tied at his ankle got tangled around a bush. If Garv hadn't cut him free, the draak would've had our *little fish* for dinner."

Bhaldavin lay quietly, listening to the two men talk. He had wakened to their voices and the smell of meat cooking. He cautiously opened his eyes. The shadowed room was small; the only exit was the open doorway to his right. He was not in Garv's cabin.

There was soft padding beneath him and a light blanket covering him. He pushed the blanket aside and sat up. A sharp pain exploded in his head and he dropped back.

As the darting pain gradually receded, he opened his eyes once more and slowly let his glance wander the confines of the dark room. There was a single stool on the other side of the room and a small table near the bed. Pieces of clothing hung from wall pegs near the door.

Bhaldavin prepared himself against a return of pain and carefully rolled to his side so he could see out through the doorway. The room beyond was lighted with an oil lamp sitting in the middle of a table; a window showed that it was dark outside.

A broad-shouldered, dark-haired man sat with his back to the doorway. Theon, who sat facing the door, was using his hands to emphasize the size of the draak and how close it had come to having Bhaldavin for a meal.

Out of Bhaldavin's line of vision a door opened and closed. "Is he awake yet?" a new voice asked.

"No, Chagg, not the last time we looked," Theon responded.

"If he doesn't wake soon, he may never wake."

"Do you want to see him again?" Theon asked.

"I might just as well while I'm here."

Chair legs scraped across the floor as Theon and Gringers pushed away from the table and followed Chagg into the next room.

Chagg was a thin, gray-haired man. The lantern he carried into the room cast a ruddy glow to his features. He set the lantern on the table and nodded when he saw that Bhaldavin's eyes were open. "Good, he's awake. Theon, bring me that stool, will you?"

After he sat down, Chagg placed his fingers at Bhaldavin's throat, then lifted Bhaldavin's eyelids one at a time.

Bhaldavin endured the examination quietly, fearing that if he moved, the pain would return.

He glanced at Theon, then at Gringers as Chagg continued his examination. Gringers approached barefooted; he wore dark brown knee-length pants, a sleeveless tunic that laced from midchest to neck, and a leather band that held his dark hair away from his face. His dark eyes and red-bronzed skin were striking. Kinsa bloodlines, not Sarissa, Bhaldavin noted, thinking how strange was mankind's custom of naming themselves according to facial features and coloring or the places they lived. The Nilach thought of themselves only as the People.

Gringers moved closer, studying Bhaldavin with great interest, noting the stump of his arm, the bruise under his eye, and the crystal-gray eyes that met his glance boldly.

Bhaldavin stared at Gringers only a moment or two before a sudden tremor of uneasiness touched him; it started at the back of his neck and skittered down to his stomach. Gringers's fathomless black eyes drew him in, demanding entry into his thoughts and commanding instant obedience.

He fought against the pull and broke contact, shuddering as the strange cloak of ownership the man had tried to wrap him in slowly dissolved. Who is this man?

he wondered. He had known few men in his lifetime and had no way to judge them, yet he felt Gringers was above the ordinary. He sensed raw power in the tall man, a belief in self that bordered on arrogance.

Chagg touched Bhaldavin's head. Bhaldavin flinched.

"Ah, tender there is it?" Chagg murmured.

"Yes," Bhaldavin answered softly.

That one simple word brought three very different responses. Gringers raised a quizzical eyebrow; Chagg swore softly; and Theon sat down on the edge of the bed, his eyes alight with the knowledge that he had been right about Bhaldavin.

"You can talk!" Theon exclaimed. "And in trader. Why? Why haven't you spoken before this?"

When Bhaldavin didn't respond, Chagg leaned closer. "Answer him," he said firmly.

Theon quickly pulled Chagg away. "Easy, let's not frighten him." Theon turned back to Bhaldavin. "Little Fish, tell me, how long have you been able to talk and understand what's happening around you?"

"My name is Bhaldavin, *not* Little Fish." Bhaldavin's voice sounded strange to his own ears. It was much deeper than he remembered it. And it was raspy, rusty from nonuse. He cleared his throat.

An uneasy smile touched Theon's face. "All right... Bhaldavin it is. Will you answer my question?"

Bhaldavin wasn't sure he wanted to cooperate with men who so obviously looked upon him as a piece of property, but he finally decided that silence hadn't served him very well and that he couldn't lose anything by talking to the men.

"I remember nothing of the past fifteen years," he began. "I don't know where I am, nor how I got here. The last I remember is running from the Sarissa. They were killing all the Ni-lach who lived in and around the Deep."

"How old were you at that time?" Theon asked.

"Twelve."

"Do you remember what happened to your arm?"

"No."

Theon glanced at Chagg. "Amnesia?"

"It's possible. The shock of seeing his people killed, the loss of his arm—either would be reason enough for him to want to forget what happened. The mind can be very protective."

"But why would he suddenly snap out of it?" Theon asked.

"A natural healing process, or perhaps some stimulus from the outside."

"Are you a draak singer, Bhaldavin?" Gringers's voice was low and lacked the harsh tone Bhaldavin heard in Theon's and Garv's voices.

When Bhaldavin failed to reply, Theon pressed him. "I heard you trying to sing the draak on the trail, Little Fish. *Were* you a draak singer once?"

"No."

"But I heard you!"

"I was young when the Sarissa declared war on my people. My father had just started to teach me to sing draak. I wasn't very good yet."

"Little Fish!" Garv's deep voice startled everyone.

Theon stood up as Garv pushed past Gringers. "Little Fish was talking!" Garv boomed. "I heard him!"

"Yes, Garv," Theon said, catching Garv by the arms. "He can talk. We were just asking him some questions about—"

"Why didn't you talk before, Little Fish?" Garv demanded, ignoring his brother.

"He couldn't, Garv," Theon tried to explain. "He didn't even know who he was. There was something wrong with his mind."

Garv leaned down, peering into Bhaldavin's face. "Garv always gave you wine when your head hurt, Little Fish. Does your head hurt now?"

"A little," Bhaldavin answered hesitantly.

"The draak almost got you this morning. But I found a place for us to hide. You remember that?"

"Yes. I remember."

Glowing with excitement, Garv turned to Theon. "He talks, Theon! He talks!"

"Yes, we know. Now calm down."

Gringers put a hand on Garv's shoulder, pulling him away from the bed. "Why don't you go home now, Garv. We'll take care of Little Fish for you. He'll be safe here in Theon's cabin tonight and—"

"No!" Garv knocked Gringers's hand aside. "Little Fish is mine."

The smile had dropped from Garv's face. Jaw outthrust, he glared at Gringers. "Little Fish goes home with me. Now."

Before anyone could stop him, Garv turned and grabbed Bhaldavin's arm, dragging him out of bed. Bhaldavin cried out as pain lanced through his head.

"Let him go, Garv!" Theon yelled. "You're hurting him. Chagg! Gringers! Help me!"

"No!" Garv roared as the three men broke his hold on Bhaldavin's arm and wrestled him toward the door.

"Garv, listen!" Theon cried. "Listen to me! No one is taking Little Fish. He still belongs to you. Damn it! Listen, you big oaf! He's sick. He can't go home right now. I swear, as soon as he's well, you can take him home."

Bhaldavin lay crumpled on the floor, pinwheels of light flickering before his eyes. He was aware of the men's voices raised in angry shouts, but they were drowned out by the loud ringing in his ears.

A door slammed and the angry voices faded. Naked feet approached and gentle hands picked him up and put him back in bed. Moments later something was placed at his mouth and he was raised carefully so he could drink if he wanted to.

The door opened and closed again. "Gringers, how is he?"

"I think he'll be all right, Theon, but one of us should stay close by for a while."

"You stay. I'm going to take Garv home."

"Will he stay there?"

"I think so, now that I've reassured him that his Little Fish won't be taken away from him."

Gringers gestured to Theon and stepped away from the bed. He kept his voice low as he spoke. "I think we're going to have to move fast, Theon."

"What do you mean?"

"How long before Chagg tells someone about your *little fish*? You know as well as I what any of the Reach lords would give right now to have a functioning draak singer in their possession. If not for the dangers found in the swamps, they'd have had every one of our singers years ago!"

"Do you think Chagg could be bribed to keep quiet?"

"It's too late for that. I saw the gleam in his eye as he left. He plans to be well rewarded for the information he carries. Who will he tell first?"

Theon hesitated, thinking. "Probably Laran. He runs the Council."

"How long before Laran will act?"

Theon shook his head. "I don't know. Not tonight. Tomorrow maybe. He's not the kind to let chances slip away, not when money is involved. He'll be here, if only to check things out. We might be able to put him off a day or two if we can get Little Fish to keep his mouth closed."

Theon glanced down at the bed. Bhaldavin's eyes were open and he was listening.

Gringers's glance followed Theon's. "We need him, Theon. When you first told me about him, I wasn't sure it would work out. But seeing him has changed my mind. We'll have to get him out of here as soon as possible. Once we're into the swamps, they'll not try to come after him. But we may need some help getting him out of here. Can we count on your brother?"

Theon nodded. "If I ask him in the right way, yes."

"What happens when he finds out he can't have his *little fish* back?"

"I'll worry about that when the time comes. Garv isn't too hard to handle if you do things right."

Chapter 4 ⫷

*B*HALDAVIN LOST COUNT OF THE NUMBER OF MEN WHO
entered his room the next day. Warned to be silent
should anyone ask him questions, he watched the parade
of visitors through crystal eyes shaded by dark green eye-
lashes and wished himself elsewhere.

Several of the men did try to speak to him, but most
came only to look. Though he had lived with Garv on the
fringe of their town for over fifteen years, he had been
no more to them than a stray pet nida with neither song
nor wit to stir their interest. Now all that had changed
and he had become the center of attention.

One of the most important men to visit him was the
man called Laran. "Show him that you can speak or sing,"
Theon had said, "and by the end of the week you'll find
yourself wrapped in chains and sold to the highest bidder."

"Is this Laran an Elder among your people?" Bhaldavin asked.

"If by 'elder' you mean 'leader,' the answer is yes,"
Theon responded. "We of Fisherman's Landing have

learned that life runs more smoothly if there's someone in charge. For us that someone is a five-man council—officially. All decisions concerning local squabbles, trade, and defense are settled by Council law in what we call hearings. And Laran, who is head of the Council, takes it upon himself to carry out those laws—usually in his own way. That means that if any money is to be made, he'll make sure the scales always balance in his favor."

Bhaldavin shook his head. "I don't understand."

Gringers moved out of the doorway between the main room and the bedroom. "He means that once Laran is sure you are a full-fledged draak singer, he'll take you from Garv and sell you to one of the Reach lords for enough money to make everyone in Fisherman's Landing rich for a year."

Theon frowned. "Of course, Laran will make sure that half of the selling price goes into his own pocket. Garv would be lucky if he ended up with his original buying price."

Theon glanced at Gringers. "We intend to see that that doesn't happen."

Garv, who had been listening quietly, reached over and patted Bhaldavin's leg. "Don't worry, Little Fish. Garv won't let Laran take you away."

"Theon, why don't we leave right now?" Gringers suggested. "Before Laran moves against us."

"Have you looked outside lately?" Theon asked. "Step to the door and take a peek. There are two men sitting on the porch across the street and another two stationed down near the stockade. We are going nowhere without Laran knowing."

"Then there's no sense in waiting, is there? Tonight?" Gringers raised one eyebrow in question.

"I think so," Theon agreed. "If we wait any longer, I'm afraid we'll lose our *little fish* to Laran's dung-eating servants!"

Theon glanced at Bhaldavin to see if he was following

the conversation. Bhaldavin met his glance with a calmness that belied the growing realization that being Garv's pet or Laran's property was all one and the same to him.

Theon dropped onto the stool next to the bed. "This is probably all confusing to you, isn't it, Little Fish? Too much is happening too fast for you to understand it all. Well, don't worry, we'll take good care of you. If anything—"

"Don't talk down to him, Theon," Gringers said sternly. "He understands what's happening. Don't you, Little Fish?"

Coldness settled in Bhaldavin's stomach. It was almost as if the man could reach into his mind and know his thoughts. He turned from Gringers to Theon; he felt more comfortable talking to the smaller man.

Bhaldavin had learned much since first morning light, for Theon had answered his questions freely, but there was one subject Theon had brushed over, and now Bhaldavin wanted to know more. His plans for escape made it imperative that he know what these men were planning to do with him and whether or not there were any Ni in the area to whom he could go for help.

"You spoke twice of needing a draak singer," he began. "Why?"

"Gringers and I are planning a trip somewhere and we need a draak singer to ensure we get there safely."

"There are no other draak singers in this area?"

"Not anymore. The Ni left the Reaches shortly after the Sarissa declared open season on the Ni."

"Open season?" The trader term was new to Bhaldavin.

"Hunt to kill." Theon hurried on when he saw the effect his words had on Bhaldavin. "Not that any of that was done here! The Sarissa don't rule the Reaches—not yet, anyway. Their war with your people was none of our doing. In fact, it all happened so fast that by the time we heard about it, it was almost over.

"The disappearance of the Ni-lach is referred to as the Leaving," Theon continued. "It was as if someone among the Ni suddenly gave the order for everyone to abandon home and work and leave the area. Some of us were aware of the smaller numbers of Ni seen in town each day, but it wasn't until the Draak Watch failed to show for work one morning that anyone grew worried. By then it was too late to do anything to stop the Ni, not that we could've done much had we tried."

"What do you mean?"

"Most of the Ni left during darkness. Once into the heavily forested lands beyond the river holdings, they simply vanished. A few men did try to follow them, but no one had any luck. Several men even failed to return. The mass exodus lasted about a week, if I remember right. Some claimed that the Ni left the Reaches because they feared the Sarissa War would grow to include them, but whoever started that rumor was a fool, because the Ni were all gone by the time we first heard about the war. There simply was no way they could've known what was happening in Annaroth before we did."

Bhaldavin remained silent. If Theon had never heard of Ni-lach Seekers, he was not about to offer any information on the subject.

Ni-lach Seekers were gifted with the ability to move from place to place through the power of their fire stones, shards of the great crystal called the Tamorlee. Teachers and travelers, they gave freely of their knowledge to any who asked, but their most important task was the recording of all they discovered, to augment the wisdom held within the Tamorlee so that future generations could use it for growth. Knowledge feeding knowledge until there was a perfect understanding of life—that was the one true law of the Ni.

Bhaldavin's grandfather had been a Seeker, and after his death the fire stone he had carried was given to his son to keep until another in their family was Seeker-born.

Bhaldavin's father had hoped that one of his sons would turn out to be a Seeker, but Bhaldavin had not yet reached the age of testing when the Sarissa War broke out.

Bhaldavin was startled from his thoughts by Gringers.

"Was there a Draak Watch where you came from, Bhaldavin?"

"There is a Draak Watch wherever there are Ni. It means our survival."

"And ours," Theon agreed. "Without the Watch we have become easy prey for draak. We of the Reaches were the first to realize what it was going to mean to live without the Watch: crops overrun, fences and ponds destroyed, workers killed or frightened off. The Draak Watch had become such a part of our lives that no one could remember a time when they weren't there. We've tried to fight back, to build defenses against the draak, but it hasn't been easy. The Reach lords have lost a lot of valuable cropland because there's simply too much territory to protect by fire watch alone. The Sarissa were fools to make war on the Ni, no matter their reasoning!

"Several of the Reach lords did manage to hang on to a few of the Watch by using bribery and coercion, but the Green Ones didn't last very long. Within a year all of them had either died or escaped. Since the Leaving there has been a standing order that any sighting of Ni within the Reaches be reported immediately to the Reach Lords Council at Cambrian. At one time it was hoped that some of your people would return, but it was a false hope. A few, like yourself, did turn up in the slave markets in Port Cestar, but all attempt to work with them failed."

"Work with them?" Bhaldavin asked.

"Breeding programs. It was Lord Farrel's idea, I believe." Theon shrugged. "He said it would be just like raising gensvolf cubs. Capture the adults, breed them, and then train the young. Except it didn't work. The Ni parents-to-be weren't very cooperative; some committed suicide rather than enslave themselves and their unborn."

Bhaldavin turned his face to the wall, shocked. Words his father had once spoken came back to him.

What man doesn't own, he will try to buy. What he can't buy, he takes. It's their way, my son. Man is like an unwelcome weed in the forest; he cannot be destroyed by pulling him up and throwing him away, because, like all weeds, he will just take root somewhere else. So we must learn to live with him. I sometimes think of man as tangle vine, which is deadly to the unwary, but useful to those who know how to tame its coils.

But it is they who sought to tame us, Father, Bhaldavin thought, and those who would not be tamed were killed. Oh, Father, what am I to do?

Laran arrived in the afternoon. He was a big man, much like Garv in stature and coloring, but where Garv was slow-witted, Laran was quick, his dark eyes alive with schemes.

The man was full of questions, and he didn't like it when Bhaldavin refused to answer. Theon, who was present during Laran's visit, made excuses for Bhaldavin's silence—perhaps the blow to the head the day before, or the shock of waking to a strange world, or the feeling of being lost among strangers.

Laran cut Theon off with a wave of his hand. "Enough! He might be frightened and disoriented, but from what Chagg said, he *did* speak—and I *want* to hear him. Now!"

Theon glanced at Bhaldavin and gave an almost imperceptible nod. Laran didn't miss that byplay. He looked down at Bhaldavin, one eyebrow cocked. "Well? What about it? Can you talk?"

"Yes," Bhaldavin answered.

"And sing?"

"A little."

A slow smile spread across Laran's face. He reached out and patted Bhaldavin lightly on the shoulder. "That's all I wanted to know, Green One."

Laran turned to Theon. "We have some talking to do, you and I. I suggest we get started."

Theon grunted noncommittally and headed toward the doorway. Things had not gone as he had hoped. Laran was no man's fool, and it was going to take more than fast talk to outmaneuver him.

Before the door closed behind the two men, Bhaldavin got a glimpse of Gringers and Garv seated at the table in the next room. They were playing some kind of dice game. Gringers looked up as Theon and Laran emerged from Bhaldavin's room.

"I'll be out for a little while," Theon told Gringers. "Don't let anyone else in until I get back."

The door to the bedroom closed, leaving Bhaldavin in darkness. A moment later he heard the outside door shut. He waited a few minutes, then left the bed and walked to the bedroom door where he stood and listened.

Garv and Gringers were talking, but the words were too indistinct to make out.

He moved away from the door. Theon had said no more visitors, which meant that for a while he would be undisturbed. If he could work fast enough, it was just possible that he could be gone by the time Theon returned.

Hours passed. Eventually a small amount of daylight filtered through a crack in the west wall of the room, giving Bhaldavin just enough light to see what he was doing. His fingers were sore from prying at the half-rotted floor boards, but he wouldn't give up. He had already loosened three boards to a point where he knew he could wrench them up out of the way when the time came. One more board and the hole would be wide enough to allow him to slip out and under the floor. The crawl space below offered him plenty of room to maneuver.

The smell of damp dirt wafted up from below as he continued to work, using the handle of a spoon as a wedge. Suddenly something stabbed a finger. The board snapped back into place as his hand jerked back in reflex. The solid thump of wood against wood was clearly audible.

He froze. Though the door was closed, he could hear someone moving around in the next room. He tasted blood as he explored the cut with his tongue; the wound was shallow and of little consequence.

He wiped his hand on his tunic and returned to work, determined to escape before Theon returned. As he bent over, his empty sleeve brushed the floor. Late that morning, Theon had brought him an old tunic and a pair of thigh-length pants. The clothes were frayed, but clean. He had put them on with Garv's help.

It was strange, he thought, but with the stump of his arm covered he felt less vulnerable; his visitors that afternoon hadn't stared at his maimed body, but had looked him in the face, eyes alight with curiosity—and sometimes with fear, which baffled him. He didn't feel at all threatening.

He carefully wedged the floor board up, bracing it with his knee. He then reached down and under, searching for the sharp object that had cut him. He found a shard of stoneware caught in a crack; he worked it back and forth until it finally came free.

Suddenly the door behind him opened and light flooded the room. Startled, he jumped and lost his hold on the board. It snapped back, catching his arm.

"I thought I heard something in here," Gringers said. "What in the name of Cestar's Eyes are you doing?"

Bhaldavin tried to pull his arm free, but before he could do so, Gringers was upon him, jerking him backward by the hair. He cried out as his arm scraped between the two pieces of planking; he felt as if his skin was being stripped away.

Gringers caught him by the tunic front and thrust him up against the nearest wall. Bhaldavin struggled to break free, but his resistance earned him only a stinging blow to the face.

Gringers crushed Bhaldavin between himself and the wall. "Don't fight me, Little Fish," he growled, laying his forearm across Bhaldavin's throat. "You can't win."

Bhaldavin gasped in pain as Gringers caught his arm at the wrist and slammed it up against the wall, pinning him securely. Suddenly fear and rage gave Bhaldavin strength, and he kicked out, catching one of Gringers's legs.

As Gringers lurched to the right, Bhaldavin wrenched free and brought his arm up and around, slamming his elbow into the side of Gringers's face, knocking him down.

Numbing pain shot up Bhaldavin's arm as he darted around the fallen man and headed for the doorway.

Gringers rolled to his feet and lunged at Bhaldavin, catching him by a pant leg and slamming him hard against the floor. Bhaldavin fought instinctively, kicking at Gringers's head. The man grunted in pain, but somehow blocked another kick with his forearm. He rolled away as Bhaldavin scrambled to his feet; then he too had regained his feet and stood between Bhaldavin and the door.

Bhaldavin feinted to the left, then broke to the right. Gringers grabbed the back of Bhaldavin's tunic, then turned and swung him into the wall.

Bhaldavin hit the wall with his good shoulder and bounced back into Gringers's arms. Gringers drove him back against the wall again and held him.

"Stop it. Stop it, Little Fish," Gringers snarled. "You're only hurting yourself."

"No!" Garv's bellow of anger was deafening.

Gringers turned just as Garv plunged into the room and grabbed him around the waist. He swore and began hitting Garv in the face as the big man lifted him from his feet. A solid blow to the nose finally broke Garv's hold.

Gringers turned as he dropped, caught Garv by an arm, and hauled him up and over his side. The floor shook with the impact of Garv's body. Whirling around, Gringers threw himself on top of Garv, pinning the large man to the floor.

Suddenly Theon was there. He threw himself into the battle, and soon he and Gringers had Garv immobilized.

"What happened?" Theon demanded, panting with the effort of holding Garv still. "Did Garv start this?"

"No!" Gringers snapped fiercely, glaring at Bhaldavin, who stood with his back to the wall. "He did!"

Nose streaming blood, Garv yelled incoherently at his brother.

It took them minutes to bring Garv under control and longer to get him out of the room.

"Go and wash the blood from your face, Garv," Theon commanded, pushing Garv out of the doorway. "Then bring me some fresh water. I'm going to need it to clean Little Fish off."

Garv eyed Gringers warily as he shuffled toward the other room. "You don't touch Little Fish again," he warned. "Or I'll kill you."

"Go on, Garv," Theon yelled. "Do as I told you!"

He watched until Garv was out of sight, then turned to inspect Bhaldavin. When he saw the blood dripping down Bhaldavin's arm, he stepped closer. "What a mess," he muttered as he bared the arm. "Come on, Little Fish, sit down. Let me see the damage."

Gringers crossed to the bed. "How bad is it?"

"Not too bad," Theon replied. "He's lost some skin, but nothing that can't grow back." He shook his head. "What happened?"

"I heard something from the other room. I came in to see what he was doing and found him working on the floor boards. He got his arm caught and he fought me as I pulled him away. Then Garv came in and the fight started. I don't know what we're going to do about him."

"Garv? Don't worry. I'll handle him. Just remember, keep your hands off Little Fish. Garv is the most gentle of souls unless angered, and the one thing that can really set him off is someone touching Little Fish."

Theon indicated Bhaldavin. "Stay with him a minute.

I'm going to need something to cover his arm. How about you? Are you all right?"

Gringers stretched and winced. "Garv nearly cracked my ribs, but I guess I'll live. See to the Ni."

Theon left and returned a few minutes later with a pan of water and a roll of cloth bandage. During the time he was gone, Gringers stood quietly watching Bhaldavin.

Uneasy under Gringers's silent scrutiny, Bhaldavin kept his eyes downcast. As Theon began to work on his arm, he clenched his jaws against the pain and turned from the light.

Theon tried to be gentle, but he could feel the tremors in Bhaldavin's arm as he applied a disinfectant. "Almost over, Little Fish. We'll wrap it up and let nature do the rest. Gringers, there's a flask of wine sitting on the floor behind the front door, and some cups on the shelf over the fireplace."

Theon had finished bandaging Bhaldavin's arm by the time Gringers returned. The two men shared a drink, then Theon refilled his cup and handed it to Bhaldavin.

"Drink, Little Fish. It'll help dull the pain."

Bhaldavin ignored the offering by closing his eyes. He hated Gringers for ruining his escape, and he hated Theon for the kindness and sympathy he was showing. All he wanted was to be left alone.

"Little Fish?" Theon said.

"Never mind," Gringers said. "Don't push him. He's angry right now and sulking. He'll get over it."

"Yes, in time," Theon agreed, "but we don't have a lot of time. We're going to have to move tonight, and the way he's acting now, it means we'll have to secure him if we don't want to lose him."

Gringers glanced at Bhaldavin, then gestured toward the other room where they could talk privately.

Theon nodded, then pushed Bhaldavin back onto the bed. "Lie down for a little while, Little Fish. Try to get some rest. You're going to need your strength tonight." He stood up and started for the door. "We all are."

Chapter 5 ✒

"IF YOU DON'T LEAVE HERE TONIGHT," THEON YELLED, getting up from the table, "Laran is going to walk in here tomorrow and take Little Fish away from you. You have no choice, Garv. You have to come with us."

Garv scowled down at his empty plate. They had just finished eating supper, and Gringers had left to bring his boat to the western edge of Fisherman's Landing, away from prying eyes.

"I want to stay here," Garv said.

"Stay here then," Theon snapped. "But don't look to me for help when Laran confiscates Little Fish, because I'll be gone."

Bhaldavin sat across the table from Garv. He flinched as Theon's hand came to rest on his shoulder.

"And what about Little Fish, Garv? You aren't even thinking of him," Theon said reproachfully. "Laran intends to sell him to the highest bidder and you know that will mean one of the Reach lords. Once they have their hands on him, he'll be lucky to last out the year. He'll be beaten and starved into submission. Is that what you want for him?"

Garv mumbled something.

"What?"

Garv shook his head. "Little Fish is mine. The Reach lords can't have him."

"And how are you going to stop them? You can't and you know it. The only way you're going to be able to keep Little Fish is to come with us."

Garv raised his head and looked at Theon. "Where?"

"I already told you. The swamps. Gringers has invited us to stay with him on his raft."

"I don't like the swamps. Too many draak there."

"There's nothing to be afraid of, Garv. The rafters know how to handle draak, and they have a few draak singers among them. We'll all be safe there."

Garv glared at Theon. "I'm not afraid!"

"I know you're not, Brother. I didn't say that you were. I only said that if you want to keep Little Fish, you'll have to come with me to Gringers's raft."

Theon came around the end of the table and slapped Garv on the shoulder. "Come. Don't scowl so! We won't have to stay in the swamps forever. If everything works out as I hope, we'll be on our way to a place called Barl-gan by the end of the warm passage."

"Barl-gan?" Garv repeated. "Where is that?"

"I don't know for sure, but Gringers has a map—well, not a map really, but directions. He believes there's great treasure to be found there. It has something to do with the First Men. I don't know much about the old legends, but Gringers has studied them, and he's sure that the treasure to be found in Barl-gan will make us all rich, rich enough to buy and sell any one of the Reach lords!"

Barl-gan translated to Barl's Hold. Bhaldavin searched his memory for a reference, but came up empty. But then, if Barl-gan was part of man's past, there was little reason for him to know anything about it. Though he had lived within a day's march of the coastal town of Sadil, Bhaldavin suddenly realized that he was appallingly ignorant of men's social structure, their beliefs, and the inner needs that drove them.

Several times that evening Theon had spoken about a great treasure, his eyes lighting with greed. The concept of being rich, as expressed by the small man, was not within Bhaldavin's grasp. To be rich with health, knowledge, family—that he could understand. But to be rich with things that could only buy another's obedience was alien to all he had ever been taught.

Time passed. Theon grew restless. "Gringers should've been back by now," he grumbled.

Garv looked up. He had combed and was plaiting Bhaldavin's hair, a task Theon had suggested to keep his brother's mind and hands occupied. "Maybe he got lost," Garv offered.

"In Fisherman's Landing? I doubt that. It's more likely Laran or his men are responsible." Theon went to the front window and looked out into the darkness. "Come on, Gringers! Where are you?"

Garv finished with Bhaldavin's hair and patted him on the shoulder. Bhaldavin looked up. "Thank you, Garv."

Garv smiled. "It's good to hear Little Fish talk, isn't it, Theon?"

Theon turned and glanced at Bhaldavin, his frown striking in contrast to the childlike innocence on Garv's face at the moment. "Yes, it's nice he can talk, but unless we get him out of here soon, it won't matter one way or the other. Laran will have him, and we'll be left with nothing but promises."

Theon crossed the room and picked up the two bundles he had readied. "I think it's time to leave, Garv. Once outside the stockade, I know a place where you and Little Fish will be safe until I can find Gringers. Here," he said, handing the bundles to Garv, "you carry these. I'll take Little Fish."

Garv frowned as Theon took down a length of rope from a wall peg near the door and proceeded to loop it around Bhaldavin's chest and over his arm. "What are you doing to him?"

"We don't want to lose him in the dark, Garv," Theon explained, keeping a wary eye on the big man. "I'm not hurting him. The rope isn't even tight. It will just give me something to hang on to if he starts acting up."

Theon pulled on the single braid falling down Bhaldavin's back. "You *will* behave yourself, won't you, Little Fish?" He pulled a little harder, forcing Bhaldavin's head up. "Believe me, Green One, life as a pet to one of the Reach lords would kill you, but only after you were driven insane. Your only chance for life lies in cooperating with us. Do as we tell you and give us no trouble, and perhaps, just perhaps, you can earn your freedom. Freedom. That is what you want, isn't it?"

Bhaldavin met Theon's glance without flinching. "Yes."

"Good! Then we have grounds for bargaining. It's a start." Theon barred the front door, then took hold of Bhaldavin's rope. "Garv, put out the lights. We'll wait for you by the back door."

Theon guided Bhaldavin across the main room into a small kitchen. They reached the back door just as Garv extinguished the last light.

"It's been a good home," Theon mumbled to himself. "Gringers, you'd best be right about this Barl-gan. If you aren't—"

Theon's threat was cut off by a knock on the front door.

The sound of heavy footsteps told Theon that Garv was responding to the knock. "No, Garv," he hissed softly. "Don't answer the door!"

But it was too late. Garv had drawn the bolt. The door swung open. Theon peeked through the kitchen doorway and saw two men on the doorstep, one holding a lantern.

"Going to bed so early, Garv?" Laran asked, pushing past the big man.

Theon cursed softly and opened the back door a crack, then closed it quickly, shooting the bolt into place. "They're out back too," he whispered.

Laran and the other man were in the main room now, looking around. "Where's Theon?" Laran demanded, stepping toward the bedroom door.

Before Garv could reply, Theon burst out from the kitchen, dragging Bhaldavin along beside him. "Get them, Garv! They're here to take Little Fish!"

Theon slammed into the man with the lantern, knocking him back away from the front door. The lantern fell and smashed against the floor.

Laran shouted for his men and lunged toward Bhaldavin. Garv moved to intercept him and caught Laran around the waist, knocking him off-balance and onto the small dining table. One of the table legs gave with the combined weight of the two men, sending them crashing to the floor.

Theon jumped to miss being caught in the tangle of legs as Laran and Garv rolled over and over, each seeking a stranglehold on the other. Bhaldavin wasn't as lucky and had his legs kicked out from under him. Theon lost his hold on Bhaldavin's rope as he fell.

Fear constricted Bhaldavin's throat, and the moment or two he was down on the floor felt like an eternity. Someone stepped on him; booted feet swung close to his face; burning lamp oil raced across the grass mat toward him.

Theon tried to haul Bhaldavin to his feet, but Laran's companion interfered, catching Theon around the chest and tossing him outside.

Bhaldavin rolled away from the burning mat and finally managed to regain his feet. A loud pounding erupted on the back door. He began backing toward the open doorway, his attention on Garv and Laran.

Suddenly Garv bellowed in anger and lurched upward, breaking Laran's hold. He started toward Bhaldavin, but had taken no more than a step or two when Laran jumped him again.

Bhaldavin thought he saw the flash of a knife in Laran's hand, but the dancing firelight made it difficult to be sure.

Something caught at Bhaldavin's rope. "Come on, Little Fish, move!" Theon yelled. "Garv! Let's go!"

Theon thrust Bhaldavin out into the front yard, not waiting to see if Garv followed.

Two men appeared around the side of the house. Theon pushed Bhaldavin away from him and turned to face the men, his knife raised. One man skidded to a halt in time to save his life; the other man couldn't stop and took Theon's first thrust in the stomach. He screamed and fell away just as the second man closed in, his own knife raised.

Bhaldavin wasn't interested in the outcome of the battle and turned to run—straight into the waiting arms of another of Laran's men. He fought to keep his feet as the man tried to wrestle him to the ground.

"Be careful with the Ni, Barry!" someone yelled. "Don't hurt him!"

Bhaldavin bit down on the arm snaking around his neck. His attacker swore and struck out. Bhaldavin saw the man's fist and ducked, but he didn't move fast enough. The fist caught him on the jaw, knocking him sideways. Before he could recover, the man's weight descended on his back, pushing him to the ground. Something sharp stabbed across his forehead as the man pushed his face down into the grass.

Suddenly the knee in his back was gone; the hands holding him down were ripped away. He rolled over and saw Gringers straddling him, the knife in his hand dripping blood. The man who had attacked him lay on the ground a pace or two away.

Something wet and warm dribbled down his forehead into his eyes. He shook his head, trying to clear his vision.

Gringers left Bhaldavin where he lay and, like a night shadow, flitted around behind the man who had Theon backed up to the outside wall of the cabin. He moved so quickly and quietly that Laran's man wasn't aware of his danger until too late.

As the man fell, Laran and Garv appeared in the doorway, silhouetted against the burning cabin. They struggled chest to chest for possession of the knife in Laran's hand.

Laran brought his elbow around and caught Garv in the face, breaking Garv's hold. Faster than the eye could follow, Laran brought his knife down, driving it into Garv's left shoulder. Garv bellowed in pain and staggered back, pulling the knife from Laran's grasp.

Gringers leaped forward, confronting Laran and giving Theon a chance to reach his brother's side. Laran took one look at Gringers's face and saw his death. Choosing to live, he turned and ran, darting around the far side of the house. Gringers started after him, then halted and came back.

Unable to use his arm, Bhaldavin rolled onto his back and sat up; from there to his knees took a moment longer. He was almost to his feet by the time Theon and Garv approached.

"Are you all right, Garv?" Theon asked worriedly.

Garv grunted.

Gringers ran up and caught at Bhaldavin's rope. He saw the blood dribbling down Bhaldavin's face and wiped his hand across the place where the skin was welling blood. "You'll live," he said.

"Garv's been hurt, Gringers," Theon said.

"Bad?"

"His shoulder's bleeding."

Garv saw the possessive way Gringers held Bhaldavin's rope. "Little Fish is mine!" he snarled, pushing Gringers's hands away. "He goes with me!"

Theon and Gringers exchanged a look. Theon shook his head. "Let him alone. We haven't time to argue. Let's get going before Laran returns with reinforcements."

It took them only minutes to reach the western gate. Theon greeted the gate guard with a wave. "We want out, Kelly. Open up."

The guard stood within the glow of a lantern hanging from a hook in the stockade wall. "This late?" he asked, surprised.

"We haven't time to talk," Theon snapped. "Just open up."

The man looked suspiciously at the splotch of wetness growing down Garv's front. "What's going on?"

Bhaldavin heard voices coming from somewhere behind them. Theon heard them too and stepped toward the small side gate.

"Theon, wait," Kelly said. "Before you open that gate, you'd better tell me what has—"

Gringers interceded, his knifepoint ending the man's objections. "Just stand quietly and you won't be hurt," he said softly.

Bhaldavin turned and saw the flicker of torchlight down the roadway leading to the gate. Then he was being pushed along by Garv, who followed Theon through the gateway. Gringers brought up the rear.

"Where's your boat?" Theon asked, as they started down the narrow pathway into darkness.

Gringers took the lead. "Follow me. It's not far."

Gringers stayed on the dirt path for a short distance, then stepped off the trail near a large aban tree. Theon moved aside to let Garv and Bhaldavin go ahead of him.

"Hurry, Gringers," he said, glancing back. "They're going to try to follow us. I can see their torches."

"How many?" Gringers demanded.

"Can't tell. Just keep going!"

Blinded by the blood in his eyes and at the mercy of a jerk on the rope, Bhaldavin lost his footing and went

down. Garv never hesitated; he simply leaned down,
picked Bhaldavin up under his good arm, and kept going,
Theon urging him on from behind.

Bhaldavin struggled and demanded to be put down.
Garv ignored him and kept after Gringers, who reached
back and caught at Garv's sleeve in order that he not lose
him in the darkness. Theon, in turn, held tight to the back
of Garv's tunic.

Bhaldavin finally stopped fighting, closed his eyes, and
ducked his head, trying to avoid the branches that whipped
by his face. Suddenly he noticed the wetness on Garv's
tunic as it soaked through to his own clothes.

Bhaldavin felt a change in the air as they neared the
river. Suddenly Garv began to make strange sucking
noises, as if he couldn't get enough air. A moment later
he stumbled and went down to a knee.

Bhaldavin felt the big man shudder. The arm around
him slowly loosened, and he slid to the ground. Before
he could sit up, Garv keeled over and landed on top of
him. He knew a moment of panic as the big man's weight
pushed him facedown into the ground, then something
warm and wet gushed over him. The smells of blood and
urine were strong.

"Gringers!" Theon cried, hands anxiously pulling at
his brother. "Garv is down!"

"I'm here," he told Theon as he knelt over Garv. "Let
me look." Sensitive fingers quickly checked for life signs.

"Is he out?" Theon demanded.

"Not out, Theon," Gringers said. "I think he's dead."

"Dead?" Theon echoed. "But he can't be! He was
just—"

"He's dead, Theon. He must've been hurt more than
you thought. Come on, help me get him off the Ni. Hurry!
I hear someone coming."

Theon swore softly as he helped Gringers pull the hulk-
ing form off Bhaldavin.

"Are you all right, Bhaldavin?" Gringers asked as he drew Bhaldavin to his feet.

"Yes," Bhaldavin answered. He peered out of one eye and saw Theon kneeling by Garv's body.

"Dead," Theon mourned. "Dead because I can never let things alone."

"I'm sorry, Theon," Gringers said. "I know what he meant to you. But there's nothing you can do for him now. We can't take his body with us, and those who follow will be here soon. Do you stay here and bury him, or do you come with me?"

Theon didn't respond.

"Make up your mind, Theon! We left men dead back there," Gringers snapped. "Stay if you think you can brazen it out, or come with me. A raftman's life isn't so hard."

The sounds of pursuit grew near. Theon looked up and saw lights flickering through the trees behind them.

"Go on. Lead the way," he said. He stood up, his hand closing around Bhaldavin's arm. "Go! I'll take care of Little Fish. He's mine now."

Chapter 6 🖎

IT WAS DANGEROUS TO TRAVEL ANY WATERWAY ON VER-
draak in darkness, but staying in the vicinity of Fisherman's Landing that night would have proven far more
deadly had Laran and his men found them. Gringers led
the way to his boat and, when Bhaldavin and Theon were
aboard, pushed it off and guided it out into the river where
the current was strongest.

"How far are we going tonight?" Theon asked.

"There's a reasonably safe place about an hour downriver. We'll stay there the night and continue on at first
light. It should give us a good lead in case anyone decides
to follow."

"How long will we have to stay in Natrob?"

"Uncle Seevan should be about finished with the trading, so I'd say a day or two, no more than that. Why?"

"News travels with the wind. It won't be long before
everyone on the river is looking for us. The quicker we
are out of Natrob, the safer we'll be. What will your uncle
say when he sees the two of us?"

"We'll have to hide Bhaldavin for a few days, until we're well into the swamps. As for you, I doubt you'll be welcome on the Homeraft, but Seevan can't say very much if you stay on my raft."

Theon snorted. "If you believe Seevan will accept my presence among the Ardenol clan without saying a few choice words, you are as crazy as a skitter."

By morning Bhaldavin was stiff and sore, and grateful when Theon released him. The small man helped him strip, then rinsed Garv's dying gifts of blood and urine from his clothes and hung them to dry. After Bhaldavin had sluiced down, under the watchful eyes of both men, Theon rebandaged his arm and all three sat down to eat.

A short time later they got back in the boat and Gringers paddled them out of the side channel where they had stayed the night. A flat wooden platform perched high in the branches of an aban tree had served to keep them safe from night-wandering draak and gensvolf. Such platforms were scattered up and down the river and were known by all of those who plied the waters of the Obway.

Gringers's boat was cut and hollowed out from a single oro tree. Sharp wooden points extended from either end, and man-length spears with barbed heads were fastened along the gunwhales.

Before taking up his paddle, Theon leaned over and tied Bhaldavin's ankles together, then looped a rope carefully around his chest and arm.

"Is that necessary?" Gringers asked.

Theon looked up. "Yes, if you want to keep him. He's small and has but one arm, but he can move fast when he wants to. Am I not right, Little Fish?"

Bhaldavin turned and looked out across the river, not answering. Out of the corner of his eye he saw Theon give him a mock bow.

"Your pardon, Green One, I forgot. It's Bhaldavin now and not Little Fish. I'll try to remember."

Propped against a pack and tied, Bhaldavin watched the trees along the banks slip quietly by. The waters of the Obway were clear and fairly shallow, which explained why neither Theon nor Gringers seemed overly concerned about running afoul of any large water draak—the velnara, or water-kings, always migrated downriver to the deeper swifter channels leading to the sea. Only the young water draak stayed in the shallows and upland rivers, and often they could be frightened off by raised voices or splashing oars.

Land draak were far more threatening to man than their water cousins, because on land the two species were in direct territorial competition.

Thoughts about men and draak made Bhaldavin realize that of the two, men were far more dangerous to the Ni, because a draak could be controlled by any one of seven different songs, but what songs did one sing to touch the hearts of men?

The journey downriver took two days. Theon was quiet most of the time. Gringers respected the other man's grief and did not intrude upon his thoughts. Bhaldavin ignored both men and thought of nothing but escape.

It was late afternoon when they reached the docks of Natrob. Ra-shun was already low on the western horizon; Ra-gor, the smaller of the sister suns, was still overhead.

Gringers guided the boat past a line of stakes set at intervals around the docks to keep away all but the smallest of water draak. Theon threw a line around a dock post and pulled the boat up close to the dock. While Gringers secured the boat on the other end, Theon removed the pack from behind Bhaldavin's back and told him to lie down flat in the bottom of the boat.

"Why?" Bhaldavin demanded.

Theon jerked him backward by his hair. "Never mind why. Just do as I say."

Theon unrolled a blanket and flipped it out. Bhaldavin

started to sit up as it settled over him. Theon pushed him back down. "Stay down!" he growled. "Or I'll sit on you."

The boat rocked as Gringers stepped up onto the dock. "I won't be gone long," he promised Theon. "I want to talk to Seevan a few minutes, then I'll find us something to eat. Stay with the boat and keep the Green One hidden."

Time passed. Bhaldavin grew warm under the blanket. He rolled onto his right side and pushed his face into a gap between boat and blanket, where breathing was easier.

As the minutes crept by, Bhaldavin let his mind wander, his thoughts flitting from the moment he was knocked back to his senses by a blow from Garv's fist to the moment of Garv's death. Everything had happened so fast that he'd had little time to sort things out.

Though he was unable to move anything more than his head, fingers, and toes, escape was uppermost in his mind; but he realized that until Theon and Gringers let down their guard, he would have to play the docile prisoner. A cunningness born of fear and anger took control. He relaxed, feeling suddenly calm and clearheaded. He *would* escape these two men, and he *would* survive to return to his home to find out what had happened to his family. He *would*—or he would die trying.

It was growing dark by the time Gringers returned. "Any trouble here?" he asked Theon.

Theon climbed up onto the dock. "Two men stopped and looked me over, then moved off. What took you so long?"

"Seevan was busy. I had to wait until he'd finished talking to Sar Gainor, owner of the town mart. The trading hasn't gone as well as expected. Our crop of spidermoss is half what we harvested last year, and Seevan is having to do some hard bargaining just to get us the things we'll need for the rest of the season."

"But you did get a chance to talk to your uncle."

"Eventually."

"Did you tell him about me?" Theon sounded worried.

"Yes. He told me I was a fool to take you on, that you'd be more trouble than you're worth."

Theon snorted. "I love him, too. Did he say how soon before he'll be ready to leave?"

"Three days."

"Three! We can't stay here three days. Someone from Fisherman's Landing is sure to come downriver looking for us."

"I know, that's why we'll leave here early tomorrow morning. There's a spot a few days up the Brayen Channel where we can wait for Seevan and the others. I told Seevan I might go ahead."

"Did he ask why?"

Gringers stepped down into the boat. "He has other things on his mind right now and could care less what his crazy nephew is doing."

Gringers drew the blanket back and leaned down to release Bhaldavin's legs. "Theon, you take Bhaldavin up to the shore and wait for me. I'll take the boat over to the other side of the wharf, away from all the traffic. It'll make it easier for us to leave unnoticed tomorrow morning."

Bhaldavin was stiff, sore, and hungry, but he made no complaints as he walked beside Theon. Without Garv to act as a buffer between himself and the small man, Bhaldavin knew he would have to tread carefully, for Theon was unpredictable, his mercurial nature making him difficult to outguess.

The rafters' camp was deep in shadow by the time they arrived. Gringers chose a place away from the campfire's glare and left Theon to watch Bhaldavin while he went to get them something to eat and drink. Many of the rafters had not yet returned from town, so there were few there to bother them.

After supper, Gringers noticed Bhaldavin trying with

his one hand to massage his legs. He pushed Bhaldavin's hand away. "Here, let me."

Bhaldavin meant to object, but as Gringers's strong supple fingers worked their way up his leg, kneading out cramps and relaxing the muscles, he changed his mind.

"Feel better?" Gringers asked.

"Yes," Bhaldavin replied, unsure of how to take the man's ministrations. Until that moment, he had known nothing but pain and fear from the man.

"The ropes won't be forever, Bhaldavin," Gringers said. "Only until we know you can be trusted not to run away. You see, I have a dream. It lies beyond the Draak's Teeth. And with your help, that dream may just come true."

Bhaldavin could not see Gringers's face clearly in the dark. Curiosity stirred, and he leaned forward. "What is your dream?"

"To find man's beginning. An old friend of mine believes that if we can find a place called Barl-gan, a place where the First Men lived when they came to Ver-draak, we will uncover mysteries that will help us tame the land and all of its creatures and perhaps even tell us more about the Ral-jennob."

Theon laughed harshly. "We know all we need to know about them! If Diak's claims are true, and man did come here from some other world, then it was probably the Ral-jennob who did the bringing, dumping us here and leaving us to fight the draak alone. I say forget the Ral-jennob! Better to concentrate on the here and now and what we can build on this world. Anyway, the old legends are full of holes. I doubt half of them are true!"

"Perhaps. Perhaps not. But we won't know until we go and find out. If there really is a Barl-gan, it might mean a new way of life for all of us."

Bhaldavin knew little of man's past beyond the fact that they had settled the territories in and around the Enzaar Sea more than a thousand years ago and that their coming had changed the ways of the People.

He glanced up at the nighttime sky and saw the first
of the evening stars. Was it possible that men had come
from another world? Or were such thoughts just faran
smoke, dream dust that made one mad?

The light of false dawn touched the sky with a glow of
mint green, pushing back the darkness. Tied once more,
Bhaldavin sat in the bottom of the boat and looked out
at the haze of fog that overhung the dark waters. He
thought how peaceful and still it was there, before all the
fishermen and river traders began their day. It reminded
him of his own home in the Deep, a lush world of streams
and forests, birds and animals.

His thoughts were interrupted by fingers drumming
impatiently on the side of the boat. "What's keeping him?"
Theon said. "Come on, Gringers. Come on. It's time we
were out of here!"

Bhaldavin looked at Theon, but remained silent. Theon
had grown impatient and surly since Garv's death. He had
cuffed Bhaldavin twice that morning for not moving fast
enough.

Minutes passed.

Theon's head lifted at the sound of footsteps on the
dock. Bhaldavin turned and saw Gringers hurrying toward
them; he carried two small cloth bags.

"About time," Theon growled as Gringers reached the
boat and handed him the two bags.

"Makel is in a bad humor. He's in charge of all the
food being taken back to the lake and he wouldn't let me
have anything extra unless I paid him for it; then he wanted
to argue price! I should not have bothered. We could've
caught fish for the next week. Seevan would've seen I
got my share when they caught up with us."

"Fish for a week? Ugh!"

Gringers stepped down into the boat. "You're going to
have to change your eating habits, my friend. A large part

of your diet from now on will be fish of one kind or another."

"I know," Theon said, stowing the bags in the small hold in the prow of the boat. "What did you get from Makel?"

"Three packets of dried nida, some fresh vegetables, salt, and a few herbs."

"Wine?"

"Two bottles." Gringers reached for the mooring rope.

A deep voice cut the morning air. "Gringers! Hold a moment."

Gringers looked up. "Damn! It's Seevan. Theon, the blanket."

Theon pushed Bhaldavin down and quickly flipped the blanket over him, ordering him to lie still.

Bhaldavin did as asked, not because Theon had told him to do so, but because he believed his chances of escaping two men were much better than escaping the twenty or more he had seen in the rafters camp early that morning. He listened to the footsteps on the dock; there were more than one pair. They came to a halt next to the boat. All was silent for a moment; then a man cleared his throat.

"Leaving rather early, aren't you, Gringers?"

"I told you, Seevan, I might go ahead," Gringers replied calmly.

"So you did." Seevan paused. "And this is Theon, if I remember right. But perhaps we should call him *thief* and *murderer* instead."

"Who names me so?" Theon demanded loudly.

"A man by the name of Laran sar Vanden. He claims that you have stolen a draak singer from him, and that you killed three men while doing it. Do you deny the charges?"

Before Theon could answer, Gringers spoke up. "Is Laran here? In Natrob?"

"No."

"Then where did you hear such charges?"

"A boatman came downriver. He arrived here late last night and spoke with several men on the town Council. With him he carried a warrant for Theon's arrest. It seems the body of Theon's brother was found at the scene of the theft. The warrant also specifies an unnamed man who helped Theon escape." Seevan looked at Gringers. "A tall dark-haired man who came in his own boat."

Silence fell. All that could be heard was the cry of a loring bird somewhere in the distance, its lonely twirring call echoing upriver.

"Well, thief?" Seevan said. "What do you have to say for yourself?"

"My brother—" Theon gasped, a tremor in his voice.

"Before you go further with your show of disbelieving shock," Seevan said sarcastically, "would you be so kind as to remove that blanket. I'm most curious about the cargo you carry. Such a mound of goods must have cost you dearly."

"What we carry is none of your concern," Theon said.

"I am making it my concern. Remove the blanket!"

It was Gringers who leaned forward and pulled the blanket back, his face cold and impassive.

Bhaldavin looked up at the five men who stood on the dock. All were dressed much the same, with sleeveless cloth tunics and knee-length pants of supple leather. One wore sandals; the others were barefoot. Three of the men were dark-haired, like Gringers; the other two were blonds. All of them wore headbands to keep their hair out of their eyes.

One of the dark-haired men squatted down, his black eyes taking in every detail of the captive Ni.

Bhaldavin recognized Seevan, though he had never seen him; the facial resemblance between nephew and uncle was striking. But the eyes were different. Gringers's eyes held dark mystery, Seevan's glared with cold challenge, and the set of the older man's jaw spoke of a man who was seldom denied.

"Is he full-blood?" Seevan asked, glancing at Gringers.

"We believe so," Gringers replied.

Seevan stepped down into the boat and straddled Bhaldavin's legs. "Full-blood," he murmured, taking a closer look. "Young, fit." He glanced at Gringers again. "What happened to his arm?"

"We don't know," Gringers answered, resigned now to the fact that Seevan meant to take charge.

"Can he sing?"

"Theon says so. But he needs training."

Seevan nodded and stood up. "Training we can give him, if we can hold on to him." He held out a hand, and one of the men on dock helped him up out of the boat.

Gringers climbed up beside his uncle. "Seevan, does this mean you aren't going to turn us over to—"

"And have it known that my nephew is a thief and a murderer?" Seevan beckoned to two of his men. "Get your boat, load it up, and be ready to travel in ten minutes. You'll take the Ni with you up the Brayen Channel and wait for us on Ander's Island."

"Now who is the thief?" Theon demanded.

Seevan turned on the small man, eyes blazing. "You will be silent. If you value that worthless hide of yours, you'll do as I say. You'll go with the Ni and these men, and so be out of the way when the authorities come down to the wharf in another hour to check our boats. And you"—Seevan glared at Gringers—"you'll be here to answer any questions put to you. If anyone asks how long you've been here, you'll say three days. Word is being passed among the men, so no one will betray you. I myself will so swear if asked. As for how you make this up to me and the other men, that we will decide later. Agreed?"

Gringers glanced at Theon, then at Bhaldavin, his lips tight in anger. Finally he nodded. "Agreed."

Chapter 7 ⚡

THE BRAYEN CHANNEL WAS A WIDE, SHALLOW WATER- way that wound south by west. An island appeared in the channel late their fourth day out, its white, sandy beaches inviting the weary travelers to stop and rest.

Theon, who had chosen to take a turn at the paddles each day rather than face hunger if he did not, was in the bow and was the first out of the boat, splashing into knee-deep water. Ysal and Glar were right behind him and together they pulled the boat up onto the beach.

Ysal ordered Theon and Glar to take care of the packs, then he turned and untied Bhaldavin and escorted him to the dense stand of rilror pine in the center of the island.

"Draak ever bother you here?" Theon asked, following Ysal and Bhaldavin down through a wedgelike opening in the trees.

Ysal shook his head. "The fishing is poor here because of the shallow water, so water draak are seldom seen near the island."

"What about land draak?"

"They don't like to swim."

"They wouldn't have to. They could wade across without wetting their backs."

Ysal turned brown eyes on the small man. "They don't know that."

"You mean they won't even try?" Theon was surprised.

"You don't know much about draak, do you?"

"I know enough to run when I see one," Theon replied sharply. "That is all I need to know."

Ysal shrugged. "If you stay with us, you'll learn—or you'll die." He turned away. "I'm going to secure the boat. Start a cooking fire while I'm gone, and keep an eye on the Ni. Glar is already gathering wood."

Theon growled a curse under his breath, but did as Ysal ordered. After he had a good fire going, he sat down next to Bhaldavin, whose arm was still lashed to his side.

He looked at Bhaldavin and shook his head. "Living with these men is going to be an experience, one I could do without, I'm sure. And how about you? What do you think of these raftmen, Little Fish?"

Bhaldavin watched Glar cross the camp with an armload of branches. "I think they may know more about draak than most men."

"And?" Theon prompted as he freed Bhaldavin's arm.

"And they seem to live by a clan code that closes its ranks for protection when threatened. It is a good trait."

"Admiration for the enemy, Bhaldavin?" Theon said softly, smiling.

When Bhaldavin failed to respond, Theon chuckled and ran the back of his hand gently down Bhaldavin's cheek.

Bhaldavin drew away from the man's caress, causing Theon's smile to broaden.

"We are all your enemies, aren't we, Little Fish? Gringers thinks to tame you to harness as his uncle has tamed the other draak singers, but I think he will fail because there's too much anger in you. It shows in your eyes, in the set of your mouth. You want your freedom. I can understand that. But life is full of strange twists, and we don't always get what we want. In the game of life we are no more than what Garv called you—little fish, always swimming against the current."

The next few days passed peacefully. Glar and Ysal divided camp duties and left Theon to keep an eye on Bhaldavin. With so much free time, Theon took Bhaldavin on walks around the small island. The draakhide hobbles that Ysal had fashioned and tied at Bhaldavin's ankles ensured that if Bhaldavin tried to run away, he could be easily overtaken.

It was midday when Theon and Bhaldavin left the pines and walked down to the rock where Ysal sat watching the river.

"No sign of the boats yet?" Theon asked.

"Do you see any?" The contempt in Ysal's voice matched the look on his face.

Neither Ysal nor Glar had been friendly since their arrival on the island. Obviously both men had heard something of Theon's reputation and looked down upon him as an undesirable.

Theon's lips tightened in anger. "You're a haughty bastard, Ysal. One of these days someone is going to have to teach you some better manners."

Ysal sneered. "Not you, *little* man."

Theon moved so fast he caught Ysal by surprise. He grabbed the man's pant leg and pulled him off-balance, so that Ysal fell, striking his head against the rock.

Theon stepped back, fists clenched and ready to fight; but Ysal lay where he had fallen, his eyes closed.

Theon swore softly and went to a knee beside the still form. He checked for a pulse at the side of Ysal's throat, then pulled back one of Ysal's eyelids.

Bhaldavin felt a flutter under his rib cage, wondering if Theon had killed the man.

"He'll live," Theon growled, standing. He grabbed Bhaldavin's arm and steered him away from the fallen man. "Come on, let's go for a walk."

Bhaldavin glanced back.

"Never mind him!" Theon said, jerking Bhaldavin's arm. "He'll wake up in a little while, and maybe next time he'll think twice before he opens his big mouth."

Theon turned Bhaldavin down the beach, and within minutes they were out of sight. They continued on in silence; the pace Theon set made it difficult for Bhaldavin to keep up. Finally he tripped and fell, pulling Theon up short.

Theon helped him up. "Sorry, Little Fish. I forgot your hobbles." He pointed to a good-sized tree standing nearby. "There's a place to sit over there. Let's give Ysal a chance to calm down before we go back."

"What if he doesn't calm down?" Bhaldavin asked, curious about what the small man would do. "What if he wants to fight you?"

Theon shrugged. "If he wants a fight, we'll fight."

"You aren't afraid of him?"

"Because he's bigger?"

Bhaldavin nodded.

"I've been fighting bigger people all my life, Little Fish, and, believe me, bigger is not always better or faster." Theon went on to tell Bhaldavin of some of the better fights he'd been in.

Bhaldavin listened, but felt sure that Theon exaggerated the number of his victories, making his conquests seem much greater than they were; but even if half of what he said was true, Theon was indeed a great fighter.

While he talked, Theon's hand slipped to the back of Bhaldavin's neck, and he began to massage Bhaldavin gently.

Bhaldavin shrugged out from under that touch and stood up, taking a half step away.

Theon pushed to his feet a moment later. "Afraid of me, Little Fish?"

Bhaldavin thought about that for a moment, then shook his head. It was true, he wasn't afraid—not of *this* Theon, with his strange, sad smile. It was the angry, hard-eyed Theon that he feared.

Theon caught Bhaldavin's arm. "You know, I think it's time you and I became friends, Little Fish."

Bhaldavin frowned. Could a Ni and a man be friends?

Theon's eyebrows raised in question. "Well, Little Fish? What do you think?"

Bhaldavin pulled his arm away and shook his head. "I think no. And my name is *not* Little Fish!" he said firmly.

Theon raised his hands in a gesture of peace. "I know! I know! It's Bhaldavin. I'll try to remember." He grinned as they started back along the beach. "I don't give up easily, you know. I think that you and I are going to be friends one day—perhaps more than friends, who knows."

"What do you mean?" Bhaldavin asked.

"Never mind. Come on, let's head back to camp and see if Ysal has stirred."

Ysal and Glar were on the beach when Theon and Bhaldavin rounded the point. They were waiting for the boats that were coming up the channel.

"About time they got here," Theon said, hurrying Bhaldavin along.

Theon pointedly ignored Ysal and Glar and waded out into the water to help with the boats as they approached the shore.

Bhaldavin counted twelve boats, their slim lines cutting the water so smoothly that they created only mild ripples on the calm surface. He saw Seevan in the lead boat; Gringers manned the stern paddle.

Theon and Bhaldavin stood by as the men splashed ashore, bringing the boats high up onto the beach.

"We'll camp here tonight," Seevan said, his voice carrying above the others. "Gringers, you and your friend gather wood for a watchfire tonight. I don't want to have to unload all these boats unnecessarily. Ysal, you and Glar and Beric start something cooking. We haven't eaten since breakfast."

While Seevan continued giving orders to the other men, Gringers walked over to Theon and Bhaldavin. "Everything all right here?" he asked.

Theon nodded.

"And you, Bhaldavin?" Worry shadowed Gringers's eyes.

Bhaldavin hesitated, startled by the man's show of concern. "I'm fine." Why shouldn't I be? he wondered.

Gringers glanced down to the hobbles on Bhaldavin's feet. "Where did they come from?" he snapped at Theon.

"Don't blame me," Theon answered. "They're Ysal's idea."

Gringers drew his knife, knelt, and quickly sliced through the draakhide. He tossed the hobbles aside as he stood up. "I don't want it to be this way between us, Bhaldavin. I've been thinking about this all the way from Natrob. We're going to need your help to—"

Seevan approached. "Gringers, I thought I told you to gather wood for a watchfire!"

"It's early yet," Gringers said. "Theon and I have time to gather enough wood for two fires!"

"An excellent idea!" Seevan motioned with his head. "Go on, get started."

Gringers stared at his uncle, his angry glance more eloquent than words. "Is that the way it is to be?"

Seevan nodded. "For now."

"All right, Seevan," he said, keeping his voice even. "Wood for two fires. Come, Bhaldavin, you can help us."

Seevan took hold of Bhaldavin's arm. "No. He's going with me. I've some things I want to ask him."

"He doesn't belong to you, Seevan," Gringers said darkly.

"Nor to you or your thief-friend."

Seevan glanced meaningfully at Theon, then back to his nephew. "I am leader of the Ardenol clan, Gringers, though you seem to keep forgetting that. And though you are my nephew, you are not above taking orders. You would do well to remember that, or you will find yourself in deep trouble. You would not be the first man to be named renegade."

Gringers's indrawn hiss of anger was like the cry of a young draak. "You wouldn't dare!"

"Because you are my sister's son? That won't stop me, Gringers. If you think so, just test my patience one more time."

Seevan turned his back on Gringers and pulled Bhaldavin's arm. "Come, Green One, it's time for you and I to talk."

Bhaldavin heard Theon speak to Gringers, fast and low; then he was out of earshot, being pushed ahead of Seevan down the narrow path between the pine trees. When they reached the campsite, Seevan led Bhaldavin toward a place a short distance from where Ysal and Glar were preparing food for supper.

Seevan sat down on a tree stump and pulled Bhaldavin down to kneel in front of him. Seevan reached out and lifted Bhaldavin's chin, forcing the Ni to look at him. "Gringers has told me a little bit about you, Bhaldavin, but I would like to know more: where you come from and how you ended up in Fisherman's Landing. I also want to know about Gringers's plans for you. I know you must have heard him talking to his friend. But first, tell me about yourself. Where were you born?"

"In the Deep, north of Annaroth."

"You're far from your homeland. Tell me, how did you get here?"

"I don't know."

Seevan's glance fastened on Bhaldavin's empty sleeve. "How did you lose your arm?"

"I don't remember."

"Gringers told me that you belonged to Theon's brother. True?"

Bhaldavin's head lifted. Seevan had touched upon a raw nerve. "The Ni belong to no one but themselves!"

Seevan's eyebrows raised in mock surprise. "Some would argue with that, I think." He glanced around camp. No one was within earshot at the moment. "We can talk about your people another time. Right now I want to know what Gringers is up to. Is it Barl-gan again?"

Bhaldavin didn't answer. He felt no loyalty toward Gringers or Theon, but neither did he see any reason to betray them to Seevan.

Seevan's hand shot out, striking him across the mouth. Bhaldavin's head rocked with the blow. Flushed with anger, he ran his tongue across his lower lip and tasted blood.

"I'm waiting for an answer, Green One."

Bhaldavin met Seevan's glance defiantly. Gringers and the other raftmen might bend to Seevan's will, he thought, but I will not! The use of pain and force to gain an objective was alien to him and filled him with obstinacy.

Seevan raised his hand again, but this time Bhaldavin ducked and threw himself sideways, rolling into a tuck that brought him to his feet a second later. He glanced around and dove for the nearest path leading out of the pine-tree enclosure.

Two men suddenly appeared before him. Startled by his abrupt appearance, they almost didn't act quickly enough.

"Grab him!" Seevan roared.

Bhaldavin avoided one pair of hands and ran full tilt into the second man in line. He staggered and almost fell, but caught his balance and darted for the opening in between the trees. The second man grabbed the back of his tunic and swung him around, straight into Seevan.

Bhaldavin's lack of combat training didn't stop him from fighting. His doubled-up fist connected with Seevan's nose in an overhand blow that brought a groan from the big man. Encouraged, Bhaldavin struck again, but his arm was knocked aside. There followed an explosion of pain that traveled from the point of his chin to the top of his head. Darkness fell upon him before he touched the ground.

Bhaldavin woke with the taste of blood in his mouth. He opened his eyes and found his head propped against someone's leg. The sky was growing dark; the glare of campfire light came from the left.

He groaned as he sat up. His head and jaw ached, and the new hobbles about his ankles were uncomfortably tight.

Hands caught him as he swayed forward. "Easy, Bhaldavin."

Bhaldavin nodded and wiped at his mouth. "I'm all right. May I have some water?"

Gringers handed him a hide flagon. Bhaldavin took a mouthful of water, swished it around to cleanse his mouth, and spat it out; then he drank the second mouthful.

"Why didn't you answer Seevan's questions?" Gringers asked.

"I didn't want to."

"Brave words. But if you weren't a draak singer, I think you might be dead by now. To strike a clan leader is to challenge his authority to rule. Such a challenge usually ends in death for one man or the other."

Bhaldavin took another drink and handed back the flagon. "I am not a *man*!" The last word rang with abhorrence.

"No, you are not," Gringers said calmly. "You are Ni and a draak singer, and you should be proud of it."

Bhaldavin looked more closely at the man's face, trying to read behind his shadowed features. What was Gringers trying to say?

"I know you hate us, Bhaldavin, and considering all that's happened to you, I think you have that right; but hate and stubbornness won't get you what you want, which is your freedom. Man and Ni, we're two different races, yet before the Sarissan War, we got along well together, at least here in the swamps of Amla-Bagor. But now all that is changed because there are so few of you left, and those we have, we dare not lose for our own safety's sake. I want you to understand that, to know that what we've done to your people wasn't done in hate or greed, but for survival."

"Those you have?" It suddenly dawned on Bhaldavin that Gringers had spoken about other Ni among the rafters. "How many of my people are with the rafters?"

"We have four in the Ardenol clan, there are three with the Draper clan, and two each with the Freeborn and Windover clans. There are other smaller clans with no draak singers in residence. They usually form an alliance with one of the larger clans when spidermoss is ready to be gathered."

Bhaldavin was silent for a little while, lost in his own thoughts. When he looked up, Gringers was watching him. "What is going to happen to me?"

"Seevan means to see you properly trained; then he will either keep you for himself or trade you to one of the smaller clans. You would bring a good price."

"And what of you—and your dream?"

"That will have to wait for now."

"Seevan asked me what you and Theon planned for the future. He mentioned Barl-gan." Bhaldavin wasn't sure why he felt compelled to offer the information.

"What did you tell him?" Gringers asked guardedly.

"Nothing."

Suddenly Theon appeared, crossing the camp toward them.

"How is the watchfire coming?" Gringers asked as Theon squatted down next to him.

"We've wood enough for all night," Theon said. He glanced at Bhaldavin. "How long has he been awake?"

"Just a little while. We've been talking."

"About?"

"Rafters and draak singers."

"Any thoughts yet on how we're going to pry him free of your uncle?"

Gringers looked at the campfire, his glance falling on Seevan, who was busily talking to Ysal. "What we've stolen once," he said softly, "we can steal again—when the time is right."

Chapter 8 ✍

THOUGH THE PAIN IN HIS JAW MADE CHEWING DIFFI-cult, Bhaldavin was hungry and managed to eat everything Theon brought him for supper, and he was licking at greasy fingers, half-listening to Theon tell Gringers about his fight with Ysal, when suddenly Gringers caught him by the arm.

"Up!" Gringers whispered urgently.

Bhaldavin was startled by the command and turned just as six or seven of the rafters approached, one of them carrying a torch. His heartbeat quickened. What was happening? Were they there to punish him for striking their leader?

Gringers kept a hold on Bhaldavin's arm as the rafters closed in around them. Bhaldavin took courage from the strength in that hand and the set to Gringers's jaw. The realization that he did not stand entirely alone helped to still the flutter under his rib cage.

He glanced at the faces of the rafters and noticed that two of them were not bearded. A moment later, he realized that those two were not immature males, but rather females; the differences in form and line were unmistakable.

He looked at the female standing before him, his glance darting from breast to face. Her smile surprised him, for it held no anger or sign of distaste; it was a smile that told him that she knew where his thoughts had been the past few moments, but didn't mind.

"My name is Markasa," she said, introducing herself. "This is my husband, Rafer."

The tall brown-haired man to her left nodded, his eyes bold and direct. "Welcome to the Ardenol clan, Green One."

"His name is Bhaldavin," Gringers said firmly.

Markasa's glance snapped to Gringers. She nodded, accepting the correction, then turned to the woman beside her. "This is Vila, Bhaldavin. She is sister to Isten, over there."

Brother and sister were blonds and very nearly of a height. Isten stepped forward. "We regret what happened earlier, Bhaldavin. Seevan has a quick temper and a heavy hand at times. Still, he is a good leader. Judge us not by his actions today."

"What my brother's trying to say," Vila laughed, "is that you won't be ill used by the Ardenol clan, and it's our hope that, in time, you'll be happy among us."

Bhaldavin thought of the draakhide hobbles at his ankles, but swallowed words of anger.

Markasa went on to introduce the others. The names were strange to Bhaldavin's ears, and he found it difficult to remember them. "And last but never least," Markasa said, pulling someone out from behind Rafer, "this is Lil-el."

The name struck a chord in Bhaldavin's mind. He watched as the small female placed her hands together and bowed to him formally. She was standing in Rafer's shadow, so he couldn't see her clearly.

"Avto, Bhaldavin." The voice was soft and clear; the

greeting was in Ni. "My full name is Lilyana-elsvar, Wind-song at Morning. It is my hope we shall be friends."

Bhaldavin caught his breath as the female's head lifted and the light fell on her face. She's Ni! he thought. He blinked, waiting for the vision to disappear.

Slowly he moved forward, closing the distance between himself and the beautiful Ni female. She wore her dark green hair in twin braids wound about her head like a crown. Her features were delicate, her lips finely drawn, and her winged eyebrows accented crystal-gray eyes that suddenly reminded him of his mother.

He reached out and touched her hand. "You're real," he said softly in Ni.

Lil-el smiled. "Would you like to talk awhile? We can sit over there, out of the way."

Bhaldavin remembered Gringers and turned, seeking his permission.

Lil-el tugged on his hand. "It's all right. You will be with me. Come. No one will stop you."

"It won't cause you trouble?" he asked, unsure of Lil-el's position among the rafters.

"No one gives me trouble, friend Bhaldavin. Nor will they you, in time."

Bhaldavin allowed himself to be led away. Lil-el carefully matched his shortened steps.

"What did they say to each other?" Vila asked as the two moved off.

"You'll never know unless you learn to speak their language," Gringers answered.

Markasa laughed. "You don't need to speak their language to know what was said. One look at Bhaldavin's face tells it all. They should make a good pair."

Warmth flooded Bhaldavin's face as he sat down where Lil-el indicated. Had she heard? Surely she didn't think that he would...they had only just met...such a thing as pairing had not even entered his mind.

Lil-el sat facing the campfire light, as if she sensed his

need to see her face. She still held his hand. "Don't let their words bother you, Bhaldavin. Markasa is only teasing. It's her way. Those who came to greet you are my good friends."

"Friends?"

Lil-el saw the doubt on Bhaldavin's face and nodded.

"And the others? Like Seevan?" he asked.

"He is not a friend, but neither is he an enemy. He is clan leader, and for that I respect him."

"And Ysal?"

"Ysal is . . . Ysal. He will not change. One must accept him as he is. He's a good fisherman."

Bhaldavin looked closely at Lil-el. "What about Gringers?"

"He is a friend, one to be trusted. He may seem hard and aloof at times, but there is an awareness about him that is seldom seen among men. My father says he is deldar, one who sees."

After a moment's hesitation, Bhaldavin asked, "Do you stay with the rafters of your own free will?"

"Yes and no. I could leave, but all that I hold dear, I would have to leave also. My mother and father ride Seevan's raft; my brother, Tesh, rides with Isten. My place is with Rafer and Markasa. If one or two of us go out with the boats to fish or hunt, the others stay with the rafts to protect those who are left behind."

Lil-el looked down at her hands, then her gaze returned to Bhaldavin. "Such a division of labor ensures that the ones who go out *will* return of their own free will. The love bonds that hold us are invisible, yet are as strong as the hobbles you wear this moment."

Bhaldavin glanced around, making sure no rafters were within hearing distance. "If you could leave together? What then?"

Lil-el smiled sadly. "It is impossible."

"Why impossible? If you all got together and planned an escape, wouldn't you be able to . . ."

"The rafters make sure such a thing never happens. We are allowed to visit each other, but are seldom left alone for very long. It's difficult to make plans with someone always listening to your every word."

"Do all the rafters speak Ni?"

"A majority of them do. But enough of the rafters. Tell me about yourself, if you will."

Bhaldavin found that he could not refuse Lil-el. Her voice stirred memories of another time, of days when the only language he had heard was Ni; now its soft lilting cadences brought back loved voices and scenes from his childhood in the Deep.

As he spoke about his homeland, Bhaldavin drank in the beauty of Lilyana-elsvar. How many times in the past few weeks had he despaired of ever again seeing one of his own race? How long had it been since he had been able to speak Ni fluently and be understood?

"The Deep sounds much like certain places in Amla-Bagor," Lil-el said when Bhaldavin paused. "It's a tragic shame that the Sarissa couldn't live in peace with the People. Did any of your family besides you survive the war?"

Bhaldavin looked into Lil-el's eyes and suddenly saw his mother. Memories came tumbling back: memories of burning homes, of people running, his father's hand clasped tight in his as they fled the destruction of their village. Then they were at the river, and he was crouched beside his father. The Sarissa were coming at them. Ni scattered. Bhaldavin ran beside his father; his mother was right ahead of them. More men appeared. Bhaldavin stumbled and almost went down; he caught his balance and tried to catch up with his father. Kion pushed young Dhalvad into his arms and slapped him on the shoulder.

"Follow your mother!" he cried.

"Bhaldavin," Lil-el said softly, "you don't have to talk about it. It doesn't matter. Bhaldavin? Can you hear me?"

Bhaldavin saw his mother holding Telia in her arms. She was running smoothly, not looking back. Just seeing her gave him courage; he lengthened his stride, trying to catch up.

Moments later he reached the shelter of some trees and glanced back, thinking that his father was right behind him. But Kion was back in the center of the glade fighting against four men. The branch and knife he wielded were little protection against the men's swords.

Suddenly the scene wavered.

"Bhaldavin? Bhaldavin, are you ill?"

He heard Lil-el's voice as if from a long way off. He tried to answer, but couldn't seem to push the darkness back. He felt himself falling. Hands caught him, easing him to the ground.

"Gringers!" Lil-el called urgently. "Please come here, quickly!"

"What's wrong?" Gringers asked sharply, concerned.

"We were just talking," Lil-el explained, "and suddenly he just closed his eyes and keeled over."

Others arrived, demanding to know what was happening.

"Back off!" Gringers yelled. "Give us some room!"

Bhaldavin tried to speak, but his mind was sluggish. He felt strong hands lifting him.

"What goes on here?" Seevan growled, pushing through the crowd that had quickly gathered.

"You hit him too damn hard," Gringers spat angrily. "If you've done him permanent damage, I'll—"

"He looked all right a little while ago."

"Well, he is *not* all right now. Get out of my way!"

Bhaldavin's slide into darkness was slow; his last awareness was of Lil-el's voice urging Gringers to try to keep him awake.

Bhaldavin woke to the sound of Lil-el's voice. He opened his eyes and saw her sitting nearby. She was speaking to Gringers, who was rolling up his blankets.

"Lil-el."

She turned so quickly she almost spilled the cup of tea in her hand. "Bhaldavin! Welcome back. You had us frightened."

Gringers stepped over Bhaldavin's legs and squatted next to him, a worried frown on his face. "How are you feeling?"

"I'm fine." He looked at Lil-el. "What happened last night?"

"You passed out."

"I blame Seevan for what happened," Gringers said. "You took quite a wallop from him."

"It might not have had anything to do with that," Lil-el said. "We were talking about Bhaldavin's homeland last night, when suddenly he just collapsed. It could be that he has certain memories just too painful to remember."

"It's possible, I suppose," Gringers conceded.

Lil-el gently brushed Bhaldavin's hand. "I think that it might be best if we spoke no more about the past, not if it causes you so much pain."

After breakfast, Bhaldavin was taken to Gringers's boat. Seevan came to make sure that Bhaldavin was secured so that he couldn't heave himself out of the boat or tip it over, and before he left he gave Gringers orders to make sure such precautions were taken every day.

Gringers nodded, but glowered at his uncle's back as the man went to his own boat.

Theon turned in his seat. "How much longer are we going to put up with that overbearing son of a draak?"

Gringers shoved off. "There's nothing we can do at the moment. Until Bhaldavin has learned to sing draak, we have no choice but to obey Seevan as clan leader."

"How long will the training take?" Theon asked, guiding the boat past several others.

"That will depend upon Bhaldavin."

Theon turned around and glanced at Bhaldavin. "Then learn quickly, Little Fish, because if I have to spend much more time among Gringers's kin, I might well be forced to commit murder, perhaps more than one. That Ysal is a—"

"You'll keep that temper of yours on a tight rein, my friend," Gringers warned, "or it is me you'll be fighting. I won't let you or anyone else disrupt my plans. Not now! I've promised Diak that we'll go to the Draak's Teeth this next harvest, and I don't mean to disappoint him. Have I made myself clear?"

Theon shook his head in disgust. "Sometimes you sound just like your uncle."

"Your word, Theon. I want no fighting."

Theon rubbed at the stubble on his chin. "All right, you have my word. But if Ysal starts something—"

"There'll be little chance of your running into Ysal once we reach Lake Arden because my raft isn't tied to the Homeraft any longer."

"It's not? But you're not far away." Theon sounded worried.

"We're close enough to claim protection if need be, but Diak prefers peace and quiet, and that you can't find on the Homeraft. Hallon's staying with him now."

"Who's Hallon?"

"My second cousin. He's going along with us."

"You trust him?"

"He's never given me cause not to."

Theon shrugged and started to turn around. Bhaldavin's smile stopped him. "What are you grinning about?"

"Seevan's nose!" Bhaldavin said proudly.

Theon smiled. "It did seem twice its normal size, didn't it? I think you really surprised him. The Ni aren't known to be so aggressive."

Bhaldavin's smile disappeared. "Perhaps it is time that we changed our image," he said firmly.

"Perhaps it is," Theon agreed.

Chapter 9

BHALDAVIN LEANED FORWARD, TRYING TO ADJUST HIS position. Six days of being trussed up, hand and foot, had tested him both physically and mentally. Submerging pain and frustration in plans for escape, he watched the riverbanks and studied the undergrowth that promised safety if he could somehow break free.

The Brayen Channel had grown narrow, the water deeper, and the open marshlands had given way to mounds of land upon which pepperbole and pine flourished.

Night was approaching. The large pepperbole trees were heavy with vell vine, creating tunnels of darkness where their branches overhung the water.

Bhaldavin watched a water snake leave the marsh grass at the left bank of the river and swim toward the boat; then, as if deciding such action unwise, it turned downstream and swam back toward the bank. He had seen the raftmen scoop such snakes out of the water with their bare hands. The snakes were venomous, but when cooked properly were both tender and delicious; the rafters made great sport of catching them.

Word passed back from boat to boat that there was a campsite ahead. Bhaldavin sighed in relief, looking forward to the chance to stand up and stretch his muscles.

Theon changed his paddle from his right side to his left. Gringers automatically did the opposite without missing a stroke, keeping the boat on a straight course.

Suddenly a warning cry echoed across the water. "Draak ahead!"

Bhaldavin sat a bit straighter and tried to look around Theon, who had stopped paddling. Their boat was second to the last in line, and a bend in the river prevented them from seeing any more than three boats ahead.

"Keep paddling, Theon," Gringers urged. "Close up!"

"What about the draak?" Theon asked nervously.

"Don't worry about it. Listen!"

A high-pitched fluting sound drifted back toward them; Bhaldavin realized that Lil-el was singing the draak. He strained to hear each note and trill as memories of lessons that years before he had just begun to learn flitted through his mind. Though some of the song was unfamiliar to him, its warbling notes filled him with a strange urgency to be a part of whatever was happening.

"Hurry!" he cried.

Theon glanced over his shoulder. "Hurry? Listen to him, will you?"

Gringers's face was lighted with excitement. "He's a draak singer, Theon. Like calls to like. Come on, paddle!"

Their boat had passed two in line by the time they reached the bend in the river. The scene that greeted them was one Bhaldavin would never forget.

Lil-el sat in the middle of Seevan's boat. Seevan was in the stern, Ysal in the bow. The two men sat calmly, their paddles at rest across the gunwhales, their attention on the large water draak that was head and shoulders out of the water just to the right of their boat. Thankfully it was not one of the Vel-nara, but rather a gray fisher; still, the draak was large enough to upset every boat on the river if angry, its flippered feet and long tail able to create instant waves that would swamp the laden boats in an instant.

Bhaldavin was mesmerized by Lil-el's voice, as was the gray fisher, whose only movement was the serpentine swaying of its neck and head.

Gringers stopped paddling as they came abreast of Seevan's boat. Theon looked back and saw Gringers make a sign to stop. He shook his head in obvious disagreement and continued to paddle, almost sending the boat smashing into Seevan's. Gringers quickly compensated by using his paddle as a rudder. His frown of annoyance was lost on Theon, who kept his face forward and continued to paddle, anxious to get out from under the shadow of the draak.

Bhaldavin had eyes for no one but Lil-el. His lips moved soundlessly to her song; his need to be a part of the taming was an ache that gripped his throat and made his heart pound.

He twisted around and leaned over the side as their boat drew away, following the other boats to safety upriver. He saw Lil-el lift a hand, signaling Seevan and Ysal, who carefully put their paddles back into the water.

Lil-el continued to sing as they moved away from the draak. When they were a good twenty boat lengths beyond the large reptile, she stopped singing and for a few moments all that could be heard was the soft splash of paddles dipping in and out of the water.

Finally the draak shook its head. Released from the mesmerizing music, it turned to look at the departing boats, its red eyes following their progress; then with a loud snuffle, it slipped under the water and resumed its fishing, forgetting the strange logs that had floated by.

The rafters shortly found a good place to camp. The boats were drawn up out of the water, and soon watchfires blossomed in the semidarkness. While supper was being prepared, Gringers and Lil-el took Bhaldavin for a walk.

Bhaldavin wanted to talk to Lil-el about singing the draak, but he didn't know how to start. The flood of excitement that had filled him only a short time ago had begun to ebb, but he could still feel lingering tendrils of the desire that had intoxicated him.

"Your song was beautiful," he said in Ni.

"Lil-el is one of the best, Bhaldavin," Gringers said. "If I ask him, perhaps Seevan will let her be your teacher. That is, if you still think you would like to learn to sing draak."

Bhaldavin saw Gringers's grin and knew the man was baiting him, but for some strange reason, the teasing didn't bother him now. He turned to Lil-el, whose attention seemed to be on the narrow trail they were walking.

"Would you teach me?" he asked shyly.

She glanced at him. "Surely, but I can't tell what kind of a draak singer you'll be until I hear your voice. Do you know any of the draak songs?"

"I recognized parts of the one you sang today. My father had just begun to teach me to sing when the war came. I never had a chance to sing a draak until the day Theon and Garv were caught on the trail. I—I wasn't very successful."

"Theon told me you sang it to a standstill," Gringers said.

"But I couldn't hold him."

"What song did you use?" Lil-el asked.

"My father called it 'Nar-donva.'"

Lil-el nodded. "It's the first song a draak singer learns. Its notes are sung to capture the draak's attention, but once you have the draak's ears, you must hold him, and for that we use 'Vol-nada.' There are only seven draak songs, but each has many variations. Much depends upon the type of draak you're singing and what you want him"—she smiled—"or her to do."

"How long would it take you to teach him, Lil-el?" Gringers asked politely.

Lil-el smiled at Bhaldavin. "Not long, I think, if we can share both our days and evenings together."

Bhaldavin felt warmth rush to his face and was glad for the dark shadows.

"You surprise me, Lil-el!" Gringers laughed.

Lil-el's laughter was carefree and held no hint of embarrassment. "You misunderstand me, Gringers—but then you are a man. I am sure Bhaldavin understands what I meant."

Bhaldavin peered at Lil-el's face, trying to read behind her smile.

"Understands what, Lil-el?" Gringers asked.

"One must go out and practice both day and night if one wants to learn to sing draak, because not all draak are day hunters."

"You're right, and I'm a fool for having forgotten," Gringers said. "It's been so long since anyone has even thought about training a new singer that—"

Bhaldavin was so intent upon the conversation that he forgot his hobbles and took too long a step. The ground was soft with years of leaves to act as a cushion, so nothing but his pride was injured in the fall.

Gringers helped him up.

"Are those hobbles really necessary, Gringers?" Lil-el asked coolly.

"Seevan seems to think so. I could take them off. I did once before. But Seevan would just have them put back on again when we returned to camp."

Gringers tugged on Bhaldavin's arm. "Come. Let's go back. Supper should be ready soon, and I'm hungry."

The walk back to camp was silent. Bhaldavin was so lost in the gloom of his own thoughts that he failed to see the look of pity on Lil-el's face.

As they reached the edge of camp, Gringers stopped

Lil-el. "If I *can* get Seevan's permission, *would* you help with Bhaldavin's training?"

Bhaldavin looked at Lil-el.

"It would be my pleasure," she answered, smiling.

Angry thoughts forgotten, Bhaldavin's heartbeat fluttered as Lil-el stepped close and whispered softly to him in Ni.

"The game of life can be cruel, but only if you let it be. Accept what is and learn to use it to your advantage. Bravery is not always bold and fearless; often it is that inner courage that makes one keep living in the face of disaster. Be brave, my friend, for you are not alone—not now. I'm here, and soon you'll meet others who will greet you as a lost brother."

She leaned forward and kissed him. He stood entranced as she turned and walked away, heading for Rafer's cooking fire.

Gringers squeezed his arm. "What did she say to you?"

"She called me brother."

"Brother?" Gringers laughed. "Judging from the kiss she gave you, I think she may see you as more than a brother."

"Perhaps," Bhaldavin agreed.

Gringers shook his head. "You take your conquests lightly, my friend. Come, it's time to eat. Then you and I have some things to discuss, like how we are going to convince Seevan to let Lil-el be your teacher."

Chapter 10

BHALDAVIN WATCHED AS THE LAND CHANGED AGAIN. The mounds of bushes and trees that had dotted the river like small islands had disappeared as the Brayen Channel opened out into a watery swampland. The pine and pepperbole trees gave way to huge lingerry trees, their massive gray branches overhung with vine and an endless variety of air plants. Some he recognized, some he didn't.

Bhaldavin was curious at first to know how the rafters knew where they were going, for the main channel was no longer visible and the large lingerry trees that stood out of the water made one place look much like another. Then Gringers pointed out a series of marks on the trunks of some of the trees. Once Bhaldavin knew what to look for, he too could pick out the watery route they followed.

Lil-el used her singing skills many times during the next five days, making it safe for the rafters to paddle through the slow-moving swamp waters. Finally they reached a place where the trees began to thin out.

"We're nearing Lake Arden and home," Gringers announced.

Theon turned. "News like that deserves celebrating. My arms are numb and my back feels as if I'd slept on a bed of rocks last night. If I had to paddle this damned boat one more day, I swear, I'd mutiny!"

"That sounds like the Theon I used to know," Gringers said. "You've been so quiet these last few days that I was beginning to wonder if you were ill."

"If by ill you mean sick of snakes, bugs, and wet-everywhere-you-look, the answer is *yes!*"

"You'll feel differently once you're on the raft."

"I doubt it." Theon looked at the line of boats ahead of them. "But I guess I don't have much choice, do I?"

"Not if you want to help me find Barl-gan. Of course, you could always turn back. I'm sure Laran would greet you with open arms."

"Not funny, Gringers. It would mean my death to return to Fisherman's Landing."

"There are other places, such as Port Cestar."

Theon turned and glared at Gringers. "Are you trying to get rid of me?"

"Why would I do that?" Gringers asked innocently.

"So you could keep all the treasure for yourself, you big lump of..." Theon's words trailed off as the smile on Gringers's face grew broader. "Fool," he muttered, as he turned around. "That's all I'm ever stuck with—fools and idiots!"

It took several hours to cross the lake where the rafters made their home. There was a small bay on the west side of the lake that was protected by a combination of lingerry trees and manmade mounds of brush and fill.

As they approached what Gringers referred to as the Homeraft, Bhaldavin's eyes grew wide in wonder, for never had he seen such a form of community living.

The rafts were long and tapered at both ends much like boats and were linked so closely together that they formed a continuous wooden platform over the water. Each raft comprised two layers of logs, and wedged in between the upper layer were bundles of reeds that formed a solid footing for the decks. The wooden structures that sat on top of each raft served as family living quarters.

As the boats drew alongside the Homeraft, the returning rafters were greeting enthusiastically by their families, who had watched them approaching. The swirl of gaily laughing women and children who ran from raft to raft over narrow plank bridges quickly unloaded the bundles of trade goods Seevan had brought; then the boats were commandeered by youngsters, who took them off to be safely secured.

Bhaldavin lost sight of Lil-el as Gringers untied him and helped him up onto the nearest raft. Several young boys took over the mooring lines as Theon climbed up onto the raft looking anything but happy.

"I thought we were going to your raft," he growled, eyeing the busy scene with distaste.

"Later," Gringers said. "I want to talk to my uncle Khalil, and I have to introduce Bhaldavin to Nara and Di-nel—and if we stay around long enough, we can share a homecoming supper. You haven't eaten until you've tasted Aunt Reena's baked eel."

Theon grimaced. "I hate eel!"

"You say that and you a fisherman." Gringers slapped Theon's shoulder and pushed him aside, drawing Bhaldavin past several curious children who had closed in around them, their large dark eyes taking in every detail of the new Green One in their midst. "I don't know how you have survived this long in Fisherman's Landing."

"One can get other things to eat," Theon said, "if one knows where to look. I had a meat supplier who came downriver twice each month. Lord Gabrion has a herd of domestic bomal he's been raising for a number of years, and my friend has certain contacts that help him procure a few head every once in a while. He has quite a herd of his own now and does a good business up and down the river."

"Does Lord Gabrion know where your friend got his start?"

Theon grinned. "Knowing is not proving."

"Such meat must cost dearly."

"It does, so I usually make do with nida or forest hen and occasionally a draak steak. The only time I ever ate fish was when I went to see—Garv."

Gringers glanced at Theon and quickly changed the subject. "You've never met Lil-el's parents, have you?"

"No."

"Would you like to?"

Theon shrugged. "Sure."

Gringers led Bhaldavin and Theon across several planks linking raft to raft. One of the children who had followed them skipped past Theon and jumped from the plank to the next raft, landing beside Bhaldavin.

The child pointed to the hobbles at Bhaldavin's ankles. "Why are you wearing those?" he demanded.

"You must ask your father that question, Samsel," Gringers answered. "It's he who ordered them put on Bhaldavin."

Samsel looked up at Bhaldavin. "Is that your name?"

The boy was young, but already the ring of authority was evident in his voice. Bhaldavin remembered his father telling him that the children of men matured early. "It's because their life span is so short, only fifty to sixty years at best," Kion had explained.

The boy looked at Gringers. "Can't he talk?"

"Yes, he can talk," Gringers replied, "but one can't expect answers to questions if they are asked impolitely."

Admonished, Samsel's head dropped perceptibly. When he looked up at Bhaldavin again, the boldness was gone from his eyes. "Forgive me, Green One. I didn't mean to be impolite." He hesitated, then asked again. "Is your name Bhaldavin?"

"It is," Bhaldavin answered.

"Have you come to sing draak for us?"

"He has come to *learn* to sing," Gringers explained. "Go about your business now—all of you," he said, waving away the children who had gathered. "Bhaldavin will be with us for some time, so you can all get to know him later."

The children scattered as Gringers, Theon, and Bhaldavin continued on toward the raft in the center of the floating village. When they reached Seevan's raft, Gringers led the way to the small addition that had been built onto Seevan's cabin. There was a guard at the door.

"What have you got there?" the guard asked, eyes eagerly assessing Bhaldavin. "He's new, isn't he?"

Gringers nodded. "His name is Bhaldavin. I'm taking him to meet Nara and Di-nel."

As Gringers reached for the door, the guard caught him by the arm. "I didn't know any of the Ni were up for sale anywhere. Where did you find him?"

"Later, Jon. It's a long story."

Gringers knocked on the door twice, then opened it, ushering Bhaldavin inside. Theon followed and closed the door behind him.

The interior of the room was lighted by six small windows. Lil-el, who had arrived ahead of them, made the introductions. Gringers was welcomed back by a pat on the shoulder from Di-nel, Theon received a nod of acceptance; but for Bhaldavin the greeting was more formal. Nara and Di-nel put their hands palm to palm, placed their fingertips to their lips, then extended their hands to Bhaldavin.

Bhaldavin's thoughts whirled back to the days of his childhood, and he remembered the correct response. He placed his hand within Nara's cupped hands first, then he did the same to Di-nel.

The ritual of friendship and hospitality offered and accepted, Nara drew Bhaldavin into the room, inviting him to sit on one of the woven grass mats that circled a small low table in the center of the room.

"Will you join us?" Di-nel asked Theon and Gringers.

Gringers shook his head. "We can't stay, Di-nel. Theon and I have some things to talk over with Uncle Khalil." He lowered his voice. "It concerns Bhaldavin. Has Lil-el told you anything about him?"

"She started to. Don't worry, Gringers, he'll be fine here with us. Go and greet your family."

Though aware of the conversation going on at the door, Bhaldavin's attention was upon Nara, whose crystal-gray eyes were warm with welcome. He could see the daughter in the mother, and there was a sense of serenity about the older female that made him suddenly feel at peace, as if he had come home after long years of wandering.

Di-nel closed the door behind Gringers and Theon and came to join his wife and daughter and their new guest. He brought with him a hide flagon and four wooden bowls.

He smiled at Bhaldavin as he poured a dark red liquid into each bowl and passed them around. "Have you ever had ingler wine, Bhaldavin?"

Bhaldavin sniffed the contents of the bowl. "No," he said. He was unable to place the fragrance in the wine.

"You are in for a treat then." Di-nel raised his bowl and touched it to Bhaldavin's bowl. "Welcome to our home, Bhaldavin. May your stay with us be a pleasant one."

Nara duplicated the gesture of touching bowls. "May you find happiness here, Bhaldavin."

Lil-el reached across the table and knocked her bowl gently against his. "And a new life," she finished.

Bhaldavin looked from face to face, and for one brief moment he saw his own family surrounding him. The lump in his throat prevented him from speaking, so he nodded and put the bowl to his lips. The wine was smooth and berry-flavored, and it sent shivers of pleasure flowing through him. Within seconds there was a warmth in his stomach that seemed to invade his entire system.

"Do you like it?" Lil-el asked impishly.

"Yes, very much."

Bhaldavin took another sip of wine and let his glance wander the confines of the sparsely furnished room. Grass mats covered most of the floor, and there were several large kists against one wall. Wooden pegs and shelves were on every wall. The clothes that hung on the pegs were much like those Nara and Di-nel were wearing: plain leather breeches and cloth tunics.

Di-nel poured Bhaldavin another cup of wine. "Would you like to tell us about yourself, Bhaldavin?"

Bhaldavin's hand tightened around his bowl. He wanted to answer Di-nel, but couldn't. The empty pocket of darkness that encompassed his past was like an open pit into which he would fall if he tried to remember. The pit frightened him.

Lil-el caught her father's eye and shook her head. She put her hand on Bhaldavin's arm. "Would you like to ask us any question about the rafters—or draak singing? I told Father that you were interested in becoming a draak singer."

Di-nel realized that something was amiss and followed Lil-el's lead. "We can always use another singer, Bhaldavin. Have you had any training?"

Bhaldavin's eyes lifted, relieved by the change of subject. "A little, but after hearing Lil-el, I realize I have much to learn."

They went on to talk about the kinds of draak that were common to the marshlands of Amla-Bagor and how the rafters, with Ni help, had managed to live and flourish in the dangerous wetlands. Gradually the conversation worked its way around to the rafters' trading trip to Natrob and Bhaldavin's unexpected appearance. Before he realized it, Bhaldavin was telling them all that had happened to him in Fisherman's Landing and how he had come to be with Theon and Gringers.

When he had finished speaking, Nara spoke. "You have traveled far these past few weeks, Bhaldavin. I think you could do with a good night's rest." She pointed to a sleeping mat next to one wall. "Why don't you go over there and lie down awhile. Sleep if you can. I promise to wake you for supper."

Bhaldavin looked at the grass mat. Suddenly the thought of sleep seemed very good to him. It's the wine, he thought absently as Di-nel helped him up.

Nara brought him a blanket and covered him. Eyes heavy with sleep, he turned on his side, facing the wall. It was in his mind to thank his hosts for their hospitality, but he couldn't seem to get the words to his lips. He heard someone talking, but it was impossible to concentrate on the words.

". . . so don't ask him about his past, Father. He simply blanks out."

"The war must have been terrible for him. He couldn't have been very old."

"Do you think he'll be happy here, Mother?"

Nara glanced at the blanketed form. "Only time will answer that, Lil-el. Only time and his own ability to forgive those who have wronged him."

Chapter 11

*B*HALDAVIN LISTENED TO LIL-EL CAREFULLY, THEN IMI-
tated the trilling sound that had captured a very young
water draak. The draak's red eyes moved from Lil-el and
fixed upon him, then with a soft plopping noise, it disappeared beneath the surface of the water. The evening
light showed small ripples arcing out away from the spot
where it had disappeared.

"Almost, Bhaldavin," Lil-el said softly. "You had him
for a moment. Listen." She repeated the trilling call, and
again the small draak appeared, this time on the other
side of the boat.

At Lil-el's signal, he took a deep breath and repeated
the call. This time he did it right, and the draak remained
motionless.

Lil-el switched to another song they had practiced for
several days and nodded to indicate that he should join
her.

The young draak swam toward them, the underwater

movement of its legs and tail causing only a slight ripple
on the surface.

Lil-el stopped and let him continue alone. The draak's
blunt nose bumped against the boat. Its eyes remained
closed as Bhaldavin's slowly reached over the side of the
boat and gently rubbed a finger along the hard crest between the draak's eyes. Then he withdrew his hand and
let the song fade away. The draak opened its eyes and, a
second later, disappeared beneath the boat.

"Very well done, Bhaldavin," Gringers said softly.

Startled, Bhaldavin turned. Immersed in the song, he
had forgotten that he and Lil-el were not alone; for a little
while, he had forgotten that he was still a prisoner at the
mercy of men who saw him not as a person but as a useful
tool.

Seeing Bhaldavin's lips tighten in anger, Gringers drew
in a deep breath and released it slowly. Making friends
with the Green One was proving very difficult. He leaned
over and drew his paddle from the bottom of the boat. "I
think it's time to go back now. I'm hungry."

"I am too," Lil-el said, picking up the other paddle.

"We can come back after dark if you like," Gringers
offered.

"No. I think not," Lil-el replied, glancing at Bhaldavin.
"We've been out long enough for one day." She started
paddling. "There's no sense in his trying to learn it all in
a few days. We've lots of time."

Bhaldavin's glance met hers, then slid away. Time, he
thought; it was easy to forget the passage of time while
he was with Lil-el. Not only did he enjoy his lessons, he
liked being near her, watching her smile, hearing her laugh,
sitting quietly beside her at night listening to her tell stories about the men and Ni who lived in the swamps. He
wasn't sure that all of the stories she told were true, but
he enjoyed them all the same. As they glided in and out
of the tree shadows, he suddenly realized that Lil-el was

coming to mean much more to him than just teacher and friend.

Behind him, Gringers hummed softly to himself as he guided the boat around a partially submerged tree root. He turned and caught Gringers's eye.

And that is precisely what you want. If I come to love Lil-el, I too will become a victim of love bonds, physically free to run, but emotionally tied to the rafters through my love for Lil-el. His hand tightened on the gunwhale. He couldn't let that happen! He had to be free to run when the chance presented itself. Time was passing, both for himself and his family—if any of them were still alive.

"Something wrong, Bhaldavin?" Gringers asked.

"No. Just thinking."

"About?"

About what you're trying to do to me!

"Bhaldavin?"

Pressed for an answer, Bhaldavin changed the subject. "How much time do I have—to learn to sing draak?"

"Time?" Gringers frowned. "As much as you need. Why?"

"If I'm to go with you and Theon to—"

A warning hand closed on the back of his neck. "What Theon and I are planning has nothing to do with you, Bhaldavin," Gringers said, trying to sound calm. "All you have to concentrate on are the songs Lil-el is teaching you."

"But I thought—"

Gringers leaned close. "Not now!" he hissed softly.

Lil-el glanced back just as Gringers returned to his paddling. She hadn't heard his whispered words. "Don't worry, Bhaldavin. You have a good ear. I promise, you'll be a full-fledged draak singer by harvest time."

Gringers's raft was sheltered under the overhanging branches of a large lingerry tree and hidden so well that only the glow of light coming from the windows revealed its location.

Theon met them at the edge of the raft. It was plain from the frown on his face that he'd been watching for their return.

"Anything wrong?" Gringers asked as he tied the boat to the raft.

"If I have to spend another day mucking around knee-deep in mud and slime, I'm leaving," Theon snarled.

Gringers knew what the problem was without asking. "Someone has to plant elvar roots if we're to have anything to eat in the spring," he said calmly.

"Well, let someone else do it! I didn't come here to become a swamp farmer."

"No, you came to escape Laran's justice," Gringers reminded him, "and if you don't work, you don't eat." He unlocked the light chain that had replaced the constricting draakhide fetters at Bhaldavin's ankles, but kept hold of the end of the chain.

"Is Diak here?" Gringers asked.

"He got back about an hour ago."

"Have you eaten?" Lil-el asked, moving past Theon.

"No. We waited for you. Diak thought you would be right along."

"What are we having?" Gringers asked, steering Bhaldavin toward the small cabin in the middle of the raft.

"Meatless stew, what else?" Theon grumbled.

They were too many to eat at the small table inside the cabin, so Theon, Lil-el, and Bhaldavin took their plates outside. While they ate, Theon asked about Bhaldavin's progress.

"I'm learning," Bhaldavin replied shortly, intent upon the food before him.

Theon chewed on a mouthful of half-cooked vegetables and studied Bhaldavin closely. The Ni was sitting in the light of the open door, as close to the edge of the raft as his chain would allow him to go. The other end of the chain was attached to a metal ring driven inside the doorway.

Theon shook his head. Garv's Little Fish had changed drastically. His voice was firm, his glance direct; he had gained weight and filled out and no longer wore his long green hair loose. Every morning Lil-el combed and braided it for him, sometimes decorating it with a finely woven strip of cloth.

"Theon," Lil-el said softly, making sure her voice didn't carry back into the cabin. "Has Gringers said anything to you about trying to climb the Draak's Teeth?"

Theon looked up, smelling trouble. "No. Why?"

Lil-el shrugged. "I just wondered."

Lil-el finished her bowl of stew and rose. "Theon, I'm going to take the boat to visit my parents. Tell Gringers I'll be back early tomorrow."

"Shall I call Hallon to go with you?" Theon offered.

Lil-el went to the boat and untied the mooring rope. "No," she said, stepping down into the stern. "I'll be fine. It isn't far, and what draak would bother me?"

Bhaldavin and Theon watched Lil-el push off. The evening was growing darker by the moment, and she was quickly lost beyond the tree limbs overhanging the water.

Bhaldavin felt something brush the top of his head. Startled, he looked up and found Gringers standing beside him.

"Where's she going?" he asked.

Theon picked up Lil-el's bowl. "She went to see her parents. Said she'd be back early tomorrow. Are you finished with that, Bhaldavin?" he asked, holding out his hand.

Bhaldavin ducked beneath Gringers's hand and passed his bowl to Theon. Then he swished his hand in the water and dried it on his pant leg.

"Did you say anything to Lil-el about the Draak's Teeth, Gringers?" Theon asked.

"No. Why?"

"She was asking about us climbing the mountains. I thought maybe you'd said something to her."

"No. Nothing."

Theon shrugged and went into the cabin. Bhaldavin looked out at the lights coming from the other rafts just beyond the point. He was very much aware of Gringers standing behind him.

"Bhaldavin," Gringers said, "you are *not* to say anything to Lil-el about us climbing the Draak's Teeth. One wrong word to the wrong person and Seevan would be down on us like a male draak in rut. It would mean the end of our venture and, very possibly, the end of any chance you might have of earning your freedom." Gringers paused. "You do understand what I'm saying, don't you?"

Bhaldavin was irritated by the warning tone in Gringers's voice. He wasn't stupid. He knew his best chance for escape and freedom lay with Gringers. Should Seevan learn of his nephew's plans, he would probably take Bhaldavin away from Gringers and have someone else see to his training. But he did not consider Lil-el a "wrong person." She wouldn't say anything to Seevan if he asked her not to. He was sure of that!

Again Gringers's hand touched the top of his head.

"It wasn't easy to convince Seevan to let me have you to train," Gringers said. "He wanted to give you to Ysal for training. If not for Uncle Khalil siding with me, I wouldn't have you now, so it's imperative that we give Seevan no cause for suspicion. Understood?"

Bhaldavin reached up and knocked Gringers's hand away. "I hear you."

Gringers held his position and said nothing. Moments passed.

Uneasy, Bhaldavin looked up, wondering if he had overstepped that invisible barrier that had, up until that moment, protected him from Gringers's anger. The light coming from the open cabin doorway cast a golden glow around Gringers. There was a pensive look on his face,

overlaid by a sadness that made it difficult for Bhaldavin
to meet his glance.

"Do you hate me so much, Bhaldavin?" The words
came softly.

Hate? Bhaldavin thought about that a moment. Hate
was a strong word and not exactly the one he would have
used to express his feelings toward the man; but if not
hate, what then did he feel? Certainly not love or friendship. Still, there was a sense of safety when in Gringers's
presence; and though he couldn't explain it, he realized
that he trusted Gringers to be fair and reasonably honest.

Theon suddenly appeared in the doorway, squinting
into the darkness. "Gringers, Diak says he's ready with
the box if you want to begin."

Gringers ignored Theon and continued to look down
at Bhaldavin. "I'm sorry, Bhaldavin. I had hoped we could
be friends."

"Is something wrong, Gringers?" Theon asked as Gringers turned and started for the doorway.

"No."

"Will Little Fish be all right out here alone?"

"Where would he go?"

"Nowhere. I just thought you might want to have him
come inside."

"It isn't necessary. I think he would like to be alone a
little while. Come in and close the door behind you."

Bhaldavin sat quietly staring out into the darkness after
Theon and Gringers left. He tried to get his mind off
Gringers by concentrating on the night sounds around the
lake, the chirring of insects, the splash of a fish or frog
leaping out of the water, the deep cough of a draak as it
cleared its mouth and throat of water after a dive.

A moment or two passed, and he heard the song of
"Vol-nada" floating over the water. The voice was Di-
nel's, and it came from the Homeraft.

Bhaldavin sighed deeply, wishing he could slip free of
his ankle chain and go and find Lil-el. He wanted to talk

to someone, and she was the only one who seemed to understand him.

A small shaft of light suddenly fell across his shoulder. He turned and saw that the cabin door had opened a crack. He could hear the men inside talking, but the words were indistinct. He remembered Theon speaking earlier about a magic box. What, he wondered, was a magic box, and what were the men doing with it? Curiosity finally drove him to investigate. He carefully caught up his chain and approached the door.

". . . have been here for a week and still haven't seen how this wondrous find of yours works!"

Bhaldavin recognized Theon's voice and gently pushed against the door, opening the crack wide enough so he could see inside.

Theon moved around behind Gringers and took a seat opposite Hallon, who sat facing the door. Hallon had straight brown hair, a long narrow nose, brown eyes, and heavy eyebrows that met over his nose when he frowned, which he was doing at that precise moment.

"Before I go gallivanting over some unclimbable chain of mountains," Theon said, "I want to have some assurance that what we're looking for does exist."

"It exists," Hallon said, glaring at the small man. "The box proves it."

"Show me!"

Diak drew a box from his lap and set it in the middle of the table. Diak was shriveled and wizened by age; his white hair was tied in a club at the back of his neck; his dark blue eyes were sunken in a skull-like face. But his voice was firm as he answered Theon's challenge.

"You look upon a mystery, Theon," Diak said, smiling. His teeth, what few he had left, were yellow and crooked. "A mystery that comes down to us from the First Men, the Ral-jennob. Only a few have seen the magic box work, and no one, myself included, understands how it works. When you see the wonders that lie within the box, you *will* believe in our search for Barl-gan; unless, like others, you choose to see only evil in that which you don't understand."

Theon looked from the box to the old man, his dark brown eyes snapping. "You don't frighten me, old man."

Diak reached for the box. It was approximately two hand lengths long and a hand length wide. It was decorated by intricate carving and showed evidence of having been painted at one time. He released the leather thong over the wood toggle on the front of the box, then carefully lifted the lid. Leather hinges prevented the lid from dropping back too far.

"Our legends have it that man came from another world," Diak began, "dropping from the sky in a great metal ship that carried perhaps as many as a thousand people. Judging from what I have learned from this device, I believe it was chance that brought our ancestors here and accident that kept them here."

Theon leaned over, trying to peer into the box that Diak covered with his hands. "Well?" he prompted, looking up with impatience. "Get on with it!"

Diak reached into the box and drew out a small, mirrored octagonal container and set it gently in the middle of the table.

"What is it?" Theon asked.

Diak smiled indulgently. "It seems to be a device that produces mental images—or records lifelike images that may be retrieved upon command. A life recorder. In a way it's very much like the journal I have here."

Diak reached into the box again, to take out a leather-bound book. "This journal was written seven to eight hundred years ago, I believe. I bought it from a man who claimed that it had been in his family for generations."

Diak laid a bony hand on top of the journal. "In this book are written many historic truths. Most people think of them now as only legends. The stories don't go back to the First Men, but they do go back as far as the beginning of the Sarissan empire—over a thousand years ago. Much of our earlier history was passed down in spoken form, as it still is today." Diak's hand moved from the journal to the metal container. "But once there was another way."

Diak looked at Theon. "I can't explain how this device works. For all of my tinkering with it, it still remains a mystery. But it does work. Gringers, Hallon, and I have all experienced its magic."

Theon frowned. "Magic?"

"Just a term, young fellow," Diak smiled. "Nothing to be afraid of."

Theon glared at the old man. "I'm not afraid!"

"Good. Then let's get started."

Bhaldavin pulled the door back further, enabling him to get a better look at the tabletop. He wasn't familiar with the term *magic*, but one good look at the strange metal box sitting between the old man's hands and the terrible scowl on Theon's face told him that whatever *magic* was, it walked side by side with fear—all the more alarming since Theon wasn't the kind of man to openly display such an emotion if he could help it.

Bhaldavin almost turned away, not wanting to become involved with man's *magic*, but something held him there, some intangible need to understand his enemies, especially the man Gringers, who professed to want Bhaldavin's friendship, yet would not release him from his chain.

Theon eyed the metal container with distrust. "What do we do?"

Diak's white bushy eyebrows raised. "We do nothing but watch."

"Watch what?"

"You'll see." Diak reached into the wooden box once more and drew out a small white piece of cloth. He unwrapped the cloth and exposed a luminescent green crystal which he set on the tabletop. He then pried off the top of the metal box.

Theon started to reach for the crystal, but Gringers caught his hand in midreach. "Not wise, friend. I tried that once and got such a jolt that I was out for fifteen minutes."

"What is it? I don't think I've ever seen such a stone."

"I'm sure it has a proper name," Diak said, carefully picking the crystal up with the cloth, "but I don't know what it is. I only know that when I put it in here"—Diak dropped the crystal into a small depression within the metal container—"and place a finger on one of the five dark-colored panels on the side of the box, things begin to happen."

Bhaldavin felt his heartbeat quicken. Cautiously he opened the door and stepped into the room. Diak had one of the power crystals known as fire stones, the precious crystals often found in Ni jewelry and used by the Ni Seekers.

Bhaldavin was moving toward the table when suddenly the room dissolved around him and he found himself standing on a beach staring in open-mouthed wonder at a huge grayish sphere sitting like a small island in a body of water. Smoke poured from one of three dark openings in the sphere, and where the sphere touched the water, ribbons of steam rose to create a cloud overhead. There were several fat, buoyant boats in the water, and people were swimming hand over hand away from the sphere.

Bhaldavin turned and found himself among strangers, most of them wet and clutching bundles made of a strange silver material.

One of the odd boats approached the beach. Quickly people and supplies were unloaded. The first tide of swimmers reached the shore and straggled up onto the beach. Suddenly someone screamed and there was pandemonium in the water.

Bhaldavin looked out over the heads of the swimmers and saw a large water draak rising out of the water, the body of one of the swimmers caught between its jaws.

Arms and legs flailing wildly, the man was screaming for help; then his cries ceased abruptly as the draak sank back under the water.

Words and song came to Bhaldavin's mind as he waited for another draak to appear, for where there was one there would likely be others. Forgotten in that moment was the fact that these people were not Ni and had no claim upon him.

Another draak appeared, but before Bhaldavin could sing even one note, a shaft of eye-blinding light shot across the water, catching the draak in the snout. The draak shook its head, roaring in pain. Another shaft of light struck the draak as it threw itself backward into the water. The splash of its tail sent water spraying high into the air.

Out of the corner of his eye, Bhaldavin saw three men kneeling at the edge of the water, their arms held out straight before them. Each held something in his hands, but he couldn't be sure what it was.

There was a swirl of motion in the water. One of the kneeling men pointed at it, and a flash of light leapt from his hands. The water hissed and steamed where the light touched it.

Bhaldavin was so lost in the wonder of the strange weapons the men were wielding that he felt a slight disorientation as the scene abruptly changed. Now he was watching people build something on a hill overlooking the water. The gray sphere in the water was still visible, but seemed to be sinking.

He listened to the men and women as they worked around him; they were speaking a form of trader, which, if he listened closely, he could just make out, though many words eluded him.

Again there was a shift in scene, and he was among a group of men walking along a narrow stone path with a wall of rock to the right and open space to the left. He looked down over the ledge of the trail and felt his stomach muscles tighten, for they were far above the valley floor.

The man in front of Bhaldavin turned and spoke to him. "Do you think we'll be any safer up here?"

Bhaldavin didn't know what to say. Where was up here? Suddenly he noticed that the man wasn't looking *at* him, but rather through him, as if he wasn't there. In that moment, he finally understood that what he was seeing wasn't real, at least not for him; and in that same moment he also remembered the metal box in Diak's hands and the stone that had activated the device Diak had called a life recorder.

He blinked and rubbed at his eyes with his hand. The scenes continued; he couldn't push them aside, though he knew they were not in his own reality. Slowly he reached out, his hand searching for what he knew had to be there. His fingers brushed a shoulder; then he found the tabletop.

Gringers's voice came out of the void. "Diak! Turn it off!"

Bhaldavin gasped in pain as hands twisted his arm behind his back, forcing him to his knees. A second later the scene around him disappeared and he was back on the raft, kneeling between Gringers's legs.

"What happened?" Diak demanded, looking from Gringers to Bhaldavin.

Gringers let Bhaldavin get to his feet, but caught his wrist so that he couldn't move away. "I felt someone touch me. I thought—I thought it was someone else. Seevan. I forgot about Bhaldavin."

Diak glanced at Bhaldavin. "No harm done." He turned to Theon. "Well, what do you think about what you saw?"

"I've never seen anything like it. You say you've shown these—these pictures to other people, and they weren't interested?"

"More afraid than interested," Diak answered.

Theon looked at Gringers. "You told me that Seevan saw this magic box work."

Gringers nodded. "He called it evil and named Diak a drogo, witch-man."

"I am outcast among many of the Lake Arden rafters because of Seevan's big mouth." Diak looked at Gringers. "By offering me shelter and a home, Gringers has also become somewhat of an outcast, tainted by association, as it were."

"Don't forget me," Hallon spoke up.

Diak smiled at the solemn young man. "Yes, you too I have touched with my *evil* plans, and it irritates Seevan to no end, I am sure. He would get rid of me if he could find a way to do it quietly."

Theon shook his head. "I don't understand. If Seevan doesn't believe in Barl-gan, why should he care what you are doing?"

"He wouldn't care, except that I have drawn Gringers and Hallon into my plans."

Gringers spoke. "Hallon and I are cousins, Seevan's sisters' sons, almost as close a tie to Seevan as a true son. Seevan sees Diak as one who has usurped the love of two he considered his own. We've both denied any lessening in our love and respect for him, but he won't listen, not as long as we stand with Diak."

Hallon stared down at his hands, folded before him on the table. "If we would renounce Diak and forget all of our plans to go searching for Barl-gan, Seevan would take us back with open arms." Hallon's head lifted. "But that we won't do. No matter how he pressures us. I want to learn more about the First Men, because I believe the visions I see in the recorder. Just think! If man once knew how to create such things as this"—he touched the recorder—"what other marvelous things have we forgotten?"

It was a long speech for so reticent a man. Theon was suitably impressed. "I hear what you're saying, Hallon, and after seeing the box work, I know what you're feeling.

Still, a lot of time has passed. A lot! There may not be anything left to find."

"It's a chance we'll have to take," Diak said, reaching for the box. "This lasted. Why not other things?"

Bhaldavin stood quietly listening to the conversation between the men, his eyes on the glowing crystal resting inside the open container. The crystal should not have been in the possession of men. It didn't belong to them. Such stones were meant to be in the keeping of the Nilach.

Gringers's grip on his arm had loosened. Bhaldavin glanced behind him to the open doorway. He knew he had no time to take the stone and hide it, but he could take it and throw it away, out into the water where the task of retrieving it would be difficult, if not impossible.

Without the fire stone, the men couldn't work their strange box, and without the box, Gringers and the others would have no guide to Barl-gan and therefore would not need him to sing draak for them. That would mean he could stay at Lake Arden with Lil-el until he found a way to gain his freedom. Perhaps he could even persuade Lil-el to leave her family and go with him, back to the Deep or to some other place where they could live freely, as Ni were meant to do.

Better for all concerned if the fire stone was lost to the mud below, he thought. He pulled away from Gringers and snatched up the green stone.

"Stop him!" Diak yelled.

Bhaldavin moved so fast that he was almost to the door before any of the men could react. Theon darted around the end of the table; Gringers overturned his chair as he lunged for the doorway. Hallon leaped over the fallen chair and was only a step behind Gringers as Bhaldavin passed through the doorway.

Bhaldavin felt a hand snag the back of his tunic; but he was hardly aware of it, for suddenly he was awash in a whirlwind of colored lights and sounds. Then a strange warmth flooded him, shutting off the world around him. He never felt the jerk on his leg chain, or the impact of his body against the raft as Gringers bore him down.

"Get the crystal!" Diak cried from the doorway. "Don't let him drop it!"

Theon threw his weight into the tangle of arms and legs. In the darkness, it was difficult to tell one person from another. "Have you got him?" he yelled.

"Yes, damn it," Gringers snapped. "Get off me! I've got his hand. You get the crystal!"

Theon followed Gringers's arm down to Bhaldavin's fist. He worked at Bhaldavin's fingers, but couldn't pry them apart.

Diak appeared carrying a lantern. "Do you have it?" he asked anxiously, peering over Hallon's shoulder.

"I can't get his fingers open," Theon growled.

Hallon went to a knee beside him. "Here, let me try." Moments later he sat back. "I don't believe it! His fist is like a rock."

Sitting on Bhaldavin's stomach, Gringers glanced at Hallon and Theon, then tried his own strength against the long, slender fingers that seemed to have turned to stone. Like the others, he failed.

"What do we do now?" Hallon asked.

"The only way you're going to get it is to break his fingers," Theon said.

"Diak, bring that light closer." Gringers rolled Bhaldavin's head up and held it up to the light. He slapped Bhaldavin lightly across the mouth. "Bhaldavin. Open your hand. Let me have the crystal."

"Look at his eyes move," Theon said. "What's wrong with him?"

"Bhaldavin!" Gringers said louder. "Bhaldavin, look at me!"

Theon shook his head. "I don't think he's hearing you."

"It's the crystal," Diak muttered. "He shouldn't have touched it with his bare hand. We have to get it away

from him. There's no telling what harm it might do to him
if he holds it for very long."

Bhaldavin was unaware of the men hovering over him.
The fire stone he held drew him into another world, and
he was falling, tumbling over and over into darkness.

Chapter 12

*B*HALDAVIN WAS RUNNING. THE SARISSA WERE CLOSE behind. His mother ran before him, carrying baby Telia. Kion pushed young Dhalvad into his arms and slapped him on the shoulder.

"Follow your mother!"

Bhaldavin clutched Dhalvad tightly and ran after his mother, fear giving him strength. Moments later he reached the shelter of some trees and looked back, sure that his father was right behind him; but Kion wasn't there. He was back in the open fighting four men, using a branch and his knife to keep the men at bay. Then suddenly Kion was down, his branch knocked aside.

A man lunged forward, driving his sword into Kion's chest. The other men closed in, their swords flashing in the morning sun. Again and again they struck Kion, hacking at his body until he stilled.

Bhaldavin backed away, his inarticulate cry of grief causing Dhalvad to whimper in fright.

One of the men looked up from the bloody corpse at his feet and pointed toward the youth.

Bhaldavin turned as the men started toward him; he ran panic-blind for a few moments, ducking branches and taking the path of least resistance. Sanity returned when he heard a man shouting somewhere ahead of him.

He veered to the left, searching wildly for a place to hide, but he could hear the snap of branches behind him and he dared not stop, fearing the enemy would blunder into him.

Dhalvad was getting heavy in his arms. He shifted the child to his left hip and continued on, more slowly now, eyes alert for any movement in the dense bushes around him. Somehow he pushed his father's death aside. His only thought now was to find his mother.

Minutes passed. Suddenly a scream rent the air. A new fear sent him into another panic. He wanted to call out, but knew it would be death to do so. He hurried his pace; he had to find his mother; they must not be separated!

As if sensing their danger, young Dhalvad rode silently in his brother's arms, his crystal eyes round with fear.

Bhaldavin paused as he reached a small opening in the trees. He looked left and right, then made a wild dash over the open ground. He was halfway across the small meadow when something caught his eye: a body, lying facedown in a patch of trampled grass.

His steps faltered and he stopped. Slowly he approached the body, forgetting the danger found in the open. Dark green hair blended with the grass; the body was in a strange, twisted position, and the brown tunic and leggings were slashed and stained with blood.

Bhaldavin's heart thundered loudly in his ears as he set Dhalvad down and knelt by the body. Slowly he turned it over. Through tear-blurred eyes he saw his mother's face, her eyes open, a river of blood glistening in her hair. Baby Telia, also dead, lay beneath his mother's body.

Rage and grief carried Bhaldavin away from the scene,

Dhalvad once again in his arms. There was a time of hiding. Then came Haradan, a tall, dark-haired man who carried no sword; who led them safely through the woods; who took them across the river farther into the Deep where no one would follow.

Days passed. The man stayed with them, built a tree home for them, and promised his friendship—but Bhaldavin dared not trust.

One night Bhaldavin came and knelt beside the sleeping Haradan, a knife clutched tightly in both hands. One quick downward thrust and the man would cease to be a problem, he thought, but if he failed to kill quickly and cleanly, he would never get another chance. Haradan was too strong a man and would be too formidable an enemy.

He listened to Haradan breathe, and suddenly the thought of struggling in the darkness against such an opponent sapped his will. Slowly he sat back on his heels, trying to calm the wild beating of his heart.

Minutes passed as he tried to recapture the sense of urgency that had driven him to attempt murder. It had begun with the discovery of a dead campfire and a series of twigs set upright in the ground—a Ni trail marker.

Haradan rolled over in his sleep. Bhaldavin froze, hardly daring to breathe. In that moment he knew that killing Haradan was not the answer to his problem.

Since seeing that marker, he had decided to go in search of the Ni who had passed their way. But he would have to leave Dhalvad behind. He had no doubt that he could take care of Dhalvad by himself, but there would be danger on the trail, from draak, gensvolf, and man; and the thought of trying to evade such dangers while burdened with his young brother made him acknowledge the fact that he needed Haradan a while longer.

Slowly, cautiously, he backed away from the man and made his way to his brother's pallet. He kissed the top of Dhalvad's head and carefully placed a leather thong around the child's neck. Hanging from the thong was his father's fire stone ring, a promise to Dhalvad that he would be back as soon as possible. Moments later he was out the cabin door and descending the tree.

At first light he located the markers he had discovered the day before and started out, his heart light with the hope that by the end of the day or early the next, he would catch up with the unknown Ni who had left the trail.

The Deep was alive with birds, the bushes and grass wet with morning dew. The different shades of green and brown that bedecked the swamplands were enhanced by the contrast of white-and-yellow flowers growing on the fringe of small bogs and along the streams leading to the main river.

Once or twice that morning, he slowed his ground-eating pace and stopped to study his surroundings. He wasn't familiar with the lands north of the Gobar River, but he knew that men had begun to settle there.

Dusk entered the Deep. He located a protected place between the exposed roots of an old tree and sat down to eat. A handful of hait nuts and several dried bora roots were washed down with water; then he climbed the tree and settled down for the night.

Late in the afternoon of his third day on the trail, he had the distinct feeling of being watched. Eyes and ears alert for sounds or movement, he stepped up his pace. He jumped a small rivulet and found the Ni trail markers once again, this time indicating the left fork in the forest trail ahead.

Again and again he turned to look behind him, but saw no one. Soon the back of his legs began to ache and his breathing became labored.

Suddenly some inner warning made him turn and look back just as three dark shadows loped into view.

Gensvolf! Their dark-furred bodies flashing in and out of the dappled sunlight, the four-legged carnivores ran silently, yellow eyes gleaming with the sight of their prey.

Bhaldavin turned and bolted down the trail, feet flying over fallen branches and uneven ground. He searched frantically for a climbable tree, but those that offered any safety also had branches too high to reach. The thought of sharp teeth ripping at his throat lent him new strength and he redoubled his efforts.

The path ended abruptly at the edge of a river. Bhaldavin never hesitated, but threw himself into the water headfirst, abandoning his small pack. He surfaced and stroked for the opposite shore. He heard two splashes behind him, then a third.

When he reached the opposite shore, he looked back to see the tenacious beasts paddling after him, heads and shoulders high out of the water as they swam.

Bhaldavin ran on, taking the narrow path that led away from the river. The gensvolf lunged out of the water and took up the chase only moments behind him. He slipped and almost fell, and suddenly one of the gensvolf was at his heels, snapping at his legs.

Terrified, Bhaldavin broke out into the open and dashed past two startled men who were cutting and stacking long grain, the waist-high grass that men called wheat.

One of them shouted when he saw Bhaldavin; then both were diving out of the path of the gensvolf, scrambling for their weapons.

Bhaldavin ran straight for the wagon in the center of the field. The three men working near the wagon saw the danger approaching and quickly dropped their loads of wheat, turning to snatch up swords or bows.

A heavy weight hit Bhaldavin from behind. He heard the click of teeth as the ground came up at him. Quickly he rolled into a ball, trying to protect his neck and throat from the ravaging teeth. Suddenly something clamped on to his left arm above the elbow.

A man's yell drowned out Bhaldavin's cry as a sword flashed downward. The gensvolf released Bhaldavin's arm and leaped away, then fell, its almost-severed leg dragging it down. Snarling defiance, the beast got up.

Bhaldavin rolled to one side and looked up just as the wounded beast leaped for the man's throat. The solid thunk of an arrow striking its target was clearly audible. The gensvolf yelped and dropped back, then flopped around on the ground a moment or two before it stilled.

Bhaldavin lay where he had fallen, trembling with exhaustion. The two men who had been at the edge of the field ran up to join their friends. The other two gensvolf had disappeared, retreating back into the forest to find easier prey.

One of the men knelt beside Bhaldavin. "Are you all right, boy?"

Bhaldavin flinched as the man pulled at his tunic, exposing the torn skin on his arm.

The man who had cut the gensvolf with his sword cleaned his blade in the dirt, then came and stood nearby. "Another minute and the gensvolf would have had him."

"He's bleeding, Lanier," the other man said, "but I think he's more frightened than hurt. Boy, what are you doing out here alone? What village are you from?"

Suddenly Lanier leaned down and grabbed a handful of Bhaldavin's wet hair. After a close look at the hair, he forced Bhaldavin's head back, exposing his face.

Bhaldavin tried to shield his eyes with his hand, but it was knocked away.

Lanier dragged Bhaldavin to his feet. "Draak scales, Kelsa! It's one of the Green Ones!"

"Easy, Lanier," Kelsa admonished. "He's hurt."

The two men who had been looking over the gensvolf joined their friends, closing in a circle around Bhaldavin.

"Look what we caught," Lanier said, thrusting Bhaldavin forward, yet keeping a tight grip on the back of his neck.

One of the men, older than the others, looked into

Bhaldavin's eyes and frowned. "Are you alone, Green One?"

When Bhaldavin failed to respond, Lanier tightened his hold. "Answer him!"

"Yes," Bhaldavin answered in trader.

The older man looked at Lanier. "Let him go."

"No! He's worth money. The Sarissa are paying twenty-five marks a head for them, even the young ones."

Gradually the strength was returning to Bhaldavin's legs. He glanced around at the other men as his breathing steadied.

"It's blood money, Lanier," the old man said. "I say let him go. The Green Ones have never done anything to us."

Lanier pulled Bhaldavin back against him. "If you don't want a share, Vaan, we won't make you take it, will we, Kelsa?"

"We can argue about this later," Kelsa said. "Right now we have the rest of the field to clear. Come on, let's get back to work. I want to be back inside the stockade before dark."

"Kelsa's right," one of the others said. "Lanier, why not tie him up near the wagon for now. We can take him back with us and decide what to do with him later. You'd also better tie up that wound."

Vaan and Lanier finally agreed, and as Lanier led Bhaldavin toward the wagon, the other men returned to work.

Bhaldavin waited for the right moment, and as Lanier set his sword on the wagon seat and bent over to search for a rope, Bhaldavin leaned over and bit Lanier's hand.

Lanier gasped and swore as Bhaldavin tore from his grasp; then he started yelling at the top of his lungs.

Bhaldavin sprinted across the cut field toward the trees. He glanced over his shoulder and saw Lanier, Kelsa, and another man coming after him. He reached the shelter of the trees moments ahead of them and ran on, leaving the open trail and weaving in and around bushes that would slow down the larger men. He heard them pushing through the underbrush behind him; they were swearing and yelling at each other. For the first time in days, Bhaldavin smiled.

Once well away from the men who had thought to sell him to the Sarissa, he spent several hours searching for Ni trail markers, but all he found was a path that led to the outskirts of a man village situated on the south bank of a river. He retreated to the forest. Some time later he found a good place to swim the river. He moved cautiously from that point on, wary now of stumbling upon other man settlements.

Darkness found Bhaldavin perched high in the branches of an aban tree. He was tired and hungry, and his wounded arm was a fiery torment. He tried to find a more comfortable position and eased his back against the trunk of the tree. The compress of wet lonary leaves he had put on his arm had long since dried, but he was too tired to climb back down the tree to rewet them.

As the last rays of light faded from the sky, he thought about his brother and the man Haradan, and for a little while he wished himself back with them, safe and well fed. But then he remembered Lanier and Kelsa and what they had wanted to do with him. How long before Haradan succumbs to the same greed? he wondered.

He pictured his young brother in his mind, and silently vowed to return to him as soon as possible.

Bhaldavin woke from restless sleep to hear a gensvolf snuffling at the base of the tree. He remained motionless and listened as it circled the tree several times and moved off.

Later that morning, just as Ra-shun's light touched the sky, a large draak appeared out of the mist, its green scales glistening with dew. Its long reptilian neck wound back and forth as it searched the tall meadow grass south of Bhaldavin's tree. It moved with surprising stealth.

Suddenly something moved in the grass. The draak lunged forward, its jaws snapping up a young bomal on its second bound. The death cry of the usually silent bomal made Bhaldavin shiver. The draak moved off a short distance and proceeded to devour its kill.

Watching the draak eat made Bhaldavin feel ill. He raised a hand and wiped a sheen of perspiration from his forehead, then laid his head down on his good arm and breathed deeply, trying to quell the churning in his stomach.

After the draak had moved off, he climbed down the tree and made his way across the meadow to a small stream he had passed the day before. He scanned the nearby trees looking for potential danger, then sat down at the edge of the water and drank greedily. He wasn't sure if the poison in his system had come from the gensvolf's bite or from the river water he had used to soak the lonary leaves, but whatever the source of the poison, what mattered now was finding the right type of herb poultice to draw it out.

Hours passed. He continued walking, and renewed the poultice several times, shuddering with relief as the burning heat gradually lost its bite.

Later in the day his sight blurred. He stumbled and fell several times, and found it harder and harder to get up again. The sharp cry of a neeva bird brought him out of his stupor, and he pushed to his feet again, taking the path that seemed to open before him.

Suddenly he smelled smoke; it had a strange, unpleasant smell and came drifting to him from the east. He could just see wisps of it pass through the trees ahead. He took the pathway to his right and a few minutes later came to a row of upright stakes, sharp points slanted outward. He had seen such stakes before, around a large Ni holding at the edge of the Enzaar Sea only two days from his old home.

He hurried forward and stepped through the narrow

gateway. The first thing he saw was the smoldering ruins of what had once been a house and, beyond that, more houses, their rambling structures and open design identifying them as Ni. He held his breath as he walked past the first building. The stench of charred flesh was strong now, and he needed no closer look to know that one or more Ni had died in the fires. He continued walking, his hopes dying.

He moved toward the front door of one of the homes and peered inside. An ominous growling erupted from one corner of the first room. The shadows were deep, but in the gloom he saw the glimmer of amber-colored eyes.

The gensvolf stood up, snarling. Bhaldavin took one glance at the gaping hole in the body on which the gensvolf was feeding and backed away, sickness welling up inside.

He stumbled past another house, then fell to his hands and knees as his stomach gave up its contents. Minutes later he sat braced by his good arm, trembling and weak. He knew he should get up, but his legs didn't want to cooperate. He crawled to a nearby tree and slumped down.

Night shadows deepened under the trees, and still he didn't move. He saw the gensvolf finally slink out of the house, its stomach bulging. It stopped and looked at him, then moved on, disappearing into the surrounding night.

The Ni holding was dead, and though he hadn't seen the men come, he knew they had been there, for the People would never leave one of their own to be food for carrion eaters. How many others lay dead in their homes? he wondered. How many had escaped?

I'll look for their trail come morning, he thought.

You will be dead in the morning if you don't move, a small inner voice warned.

Bhaldavin's eyes grew heavy. "No. I'll stay here. I'm not afraid."

The gensvolf will come.

"Let them."

The small voice continued to whisper warnings, but he was past hearing them.

"Is he alive?"

Bhaldavin felt hands on his face. He tried to open his eyes, but couldn't.

Another voice came out of the void. "He's breathing and his heart is beating strong, but he's burning with fever. One arm has been chewed badly. Judging from the marks, I'd say he's fought with a gensvolf."

"We must have missed him in our first gather. It's lucky we found him before the gensvolf returned to make a meal out of him."

Bhaldavin's next awareness was of something wet at his lips. He drank as someone held him up. A few minutes later he opened his eyes. He blinked several times, and gradually his sight cleared. A man knelt beside him and gently laid a cool cloth on his forehead.

Another man stepped into view. He had a bushy gray beard and hard blue eyes. "How is he?"

Bhaldavin was sure he had never seen either man before. He was vaguely aware of other voices nearby, but any fear he might have felt was so overlaid with pain that there was no room to give it notice.

"His arm is bad, Wils. It's poisoned his entire system."

"Will he live, Bran?"

"I don't know."

"Gavin means to sell the old and wounded and keep the young healthy ones."

"He probably won't have to worry about this one. He'll be lucky to live out the week."

Days passed. Sometimes Bhaldavin was aware of those around him; at other times he was lost in a dreamworld where he was being chased by gensvolf or men brandishing swords.

One morning the man called Wils reappeared. "Any change in him?"

Bran looked up. He had just finished draining off some of the pus from Bhaldavin's wound. "He drinks, but can't keep any food down, and he runs a fever most of the time. As you can see, the arm is getting worse."

Bhaldavin lay shivering in bed, eyes wide in pain. Bran released the ropes that held Bhaldavin during the painful process of cleansing the wound.

Wils motioned to Bran, and together the two men moved to the other side of the room where they talked quietly for a few minutes.

Wils left. Bran returned and gave Bhaldavin a drink of kansa juice laced with verron sap, a bitter-tasting brew that was often used as a painkiller. Bran forced Bhaldavin to drink deeply, then sat beside him until he was sure the drug was taking effect.

A strange fuzziness crept over Bhaldavin's mind, and he lost track of the movements in and out of the hut. Once he opened his eyes and saw Bran sorting through a number of knives lying on a benchlike table on the other side of the room.

Wils appeared in the doorway carrying a large pan of steaming water. "Are you going to need any help, Bran?"

"I have Nathan, but could always use another pair of hands," Bran replied. "If you have the stomach for it."

Wils nodded grimly. "Whenever you're ready."

"I'm ready. Help Nathan move him over here."

Bhaldavin moaned as the two men moved him to another bed. Wils tied him down again; then with quick, deft movements, he tied a piece of cord around Bhaldavin's upper arm.

Bhaldavin cried out as the cord bit into tender swollen flesh. Pain-sharpened awareness gave him strength, and he began to struggle.

"Hold him, Wils!" Braun ordered. "Nathan, over here on my other side. You'll have to keep him still."

Bhaldavin turned his head and saw the knife in Bran's hand; then suddenly Bran was Bran no longer. Kion stood there, frowning down at him.

The last thing Bhaldavin heard was his own scream as a grim-faced Kion stepped close and began cutting away at the rotten flesh that had once been Bhaldavin's arm.

Chapter 13 🖎

"NE! NE, ADDA! NO, FATHER!" BHALDAVIN SCREAMED.
Theon, Gringers, and Hallon threw themselves
on top of Bhaldavin as he began to thrash around, his
anguished cries filling the night air.

Suddenly he arched his back and let loose with a blood-
curdling cry that reverberated in the skulls of the men
who held him down. There was agony, terror, and rage
in the cry, and it filled them all with dread.

Once, twice, three times that agonized scream was
repeated and out from the depths of the lake it was answered. Within seconds the air was filled with the roaring
of angry draak. They hissed and flailed with their heads
and tails, churning through the water in their confusion,
challenging anything that got in their way.

Then the high-pitched trilling notes of a draak singer
rose over the din. First one voice was heard, then another
as the draak singers joined forces to try to calm the great
water creatures.

Hallon stood up when he saw a flash of light from the

Ardenol Homeraft. An answering flash of light came from the Draper Homeraft on the other side of the inlet.

"Seevan is asking what happened," he reported to the others. "Draper answers he doesn't know. I think we are in for some trouble."

Theon, who had scrambled to his feet at Bhaldavin's first scream, stood beside Diak swearing softly to himself. Gringers was still on top of Bhaldavin, but all the fight seemed to have gone out of the Ni, who lay quietly, eyes welling tears.

Gringers sat up and saw a strange greenish glow out of the corner of one eye. "Diak!" he hissed, pointing to the crystal cradled in Bhaldavin's hand.

Diak knelt and used a fold of his tunic to pluck the crystal from its resting place. "Bring the lantern," he said to Theon as he headed for the cabin door. "We've got to make this and the box disappear."

The return of pain-filled memories released a floodgate of tears that Bhaldavin couldn't control; soon his body shook with his weeping. Gringers reached out and drew Bhaldavin close. This time the Ni didn't flinch away.

"Everything will be all right, Bhaldavin," Gringers said softly. "It's just the crystal that made you feel this way. It affects everyone differently. I passed out completely. It put Hallon into a trance. Come on, it's all over with now. I just wish you hadn't touched it. What were you going to do with it, huh?"

Bhaldavin heard Gringers and tried to stop crying, but the tears, bottled up in him so long, would not be denied.

Diak and Theon returned. "He'll make himself sick doing that," Theon said. "Can't you make him stop?"

"And how do I do that?" Gringers asked darkly. "Twist his arm maybe?"

Minutes passed. The voices of the draak singers could be heard across the water even though the draak had all disappeared.

Hallon stood watching the lights along the inlet. He stiffened. "Company coming!"

Three boats bumped the raft a few minutes later. Seevan, along with several other men, climbed aboard. The scowl on his face made Theon finger the knife at his belt.

"What in the name of Brogan's draak is going on over here?" Seevan yelled, advancing on Gringers, who still sat cradling Bhaldavin in his arms.

Lil-el appeared from one of the other boats and came to kneel beside Gringers. "Bhaldavin? Bhaldavin, where are you hurt?"

"What did you do to him?" Seevan demanded.

"We did nothing to him!" Gringers answered defiantly. He glanced at Lil-el. "On my word, Lil-el, not one of us touched him."

Lil-el stared at Gringers, the set of her lips saying that she didn't believe him. "Let me have him!" she commanded.

Gringers frowned, but moved aside as Lil-el's arms closed protectively around Bhaldavin. He stood and faced his uncle. "I swear! We did nothing to him!"

"Then what happened?" Seevan growled fiercely.

Gringers licked dry lips. "We were—were showing Theon the picture box. We thought Bhaldavin was outside. He wasn't. He came to the door and—"

"And went mad when he saw those damned visions," Seevan finished for him. "That's what happened, isn't it?"

Gringers cast a quick glance at Theon, then turned back to his uncle. "Well, yes, I guess so."

Seevan held out his hand. "I want it. *Now!*"

Gringers frowned. "Want what?"

"You know damned well what. Go get me that box— and Diak! He and his plaything have caused all the trouble they are going to."

"You have no right to—"

"Right?" Seevan's voice rose. "I have every right after what happened just a short time ago. I'm responsible for our clan and for all its people, including such spine-heads as you. The other clans won't stand idly by while you create havoc among the lake draak. If the draak singers had been a little slower to respond, there would have been great damage among the rafts, and all because you and that doddering old fool won't let the past die! Now get him out here!"

"No."

Seevan signaled to two of his men. Gringers stepped in front of one, but the other man slid by and headed for the cabin door. Theon took a step in the direction of the cabin, then stopped when he felt the prick of something sharp in the middle of his back.

"Stand quietly, fisherman," Ysal crooned softly.

Seevan's man went into the cabin and returned a few moments later. "No one in there, Seevan."

Seevan glared at Gringers. "Where is he?"

"I don't know," Gringers replied evenly.

"Oh, you know. But I would have Brogan's own time getting you to tell me, wouldn't I?" Seevan snapped his fingers and pointed to two of his men. "Pick up the Ni and put him in my boat."

"What? Where are you taking him?" Gringers cried.

"To the Homeraft! It's plain that you can't be trusted with him. His kind are too valuable to throw away on such as you. If I left him here another day, you would ruin him for any kind of work."

"He belongs here!"

"He belongs where I say he belongs!"

"You have no rightful claim to him!"

"No more do you!"

Gringers looked at the men standing by his uncle and realized the stupidity of physical violence. Throwing the men off the raft would prove nothing. He faced Seevan as Ysal and another man loaded Bhaldavin into a boat. Lil-el went into the boat after Bhaldavin. She spared Gringers one venomous look, then turned to her charge.

Bhaldavin was aware of those around him, but still his tears flowed, and though he tried to be quiet, small hurting animal sounds continued to escape his lips.

Seevan signaled his men back into their boats, then turned and stepped down into his own boat. As he took his place in the stern, he left Gringers one last piece of advice.

"Get rid of Diak, Gringers; then come back to the Homeraft. This is the last time I'll ask."

"And if I don't?"

Seevan pushed the boat away from the raft and pointed it down the tunnellike exit made by the overhanging tree limbs. "Then you will be free to form your own clan, Nephew, but don't look for help from any of the Arden Lake clans."

Bhaldavin saw Theon and Gringers through tear-blurred eyes. They stood side by side as the boats slipped past. He tried to sit up, but hands caught his shoulders and pressed him back down.

"Relax, Bhaldavin," Lil-el said softly. "Everything is going to be all right. You are safe now."

Exhausted by the emotional upheaval caused by his contact with the fire stone, Bhaldavin had no strength to resist Lil-el's voice and calming touch. He felt himself slide into darkness. His last awareness was of something soft brushing his forehead.

Bhaldavin woke to voices. He opened his eyes and saw Lil-el standing in the doorway confronting Gringers. Her arm barred his passage.

One quick glance around the room told him that he was in Nara and Di-nel's cabin. Neither of them were present.

"... is the third time I've come. Isn't he awake yet?"

"No. He isn't," Lil-el responded firmly.

"I must see him, Lil-el. I must!"

"Has Seevan given his permission?"

"Would I be here if he hadn't?"

"Knowing you, yes."

Gringers glanced away, then looked back at Lil-el. "Please, let me come in," he pleaded softly.

Curious, Bhaldavin rolled to his side and leaned over, looking past Lil-el. He saw one of Seevan's men standing guard at the door, which explained why Gringers didn't try to force his way into the room.

Lil-el studied Gringers a moment, then relented. "Wait here. I'll see if he's awake yet." She closed the door and crossed to Bhaldavin's pallet. She smiled when she saw that his eyes were open.

"Welcome back," she said. "You have a visitor. It's Gringers, but you don't have to see him if you don't want to. I can send him away."

Bhaldavin needed a moment to think it over. "How long have I been here?"

"Two days. You've been sleeping most of the time. How are you feeling?"

Bhaldavin leaned back against his pillow. "Empty," he said, and it was true. He felt nothing inside, not fear, not anger, not loss. He just felt empty. The fire stone had not only taken his memories, it had purged him of all emotion.

"Shall I let Gringers in?" she asked, concern in her eyes. "He says he must talk to you."

He nodded, not caring. "I'll talk with him."

"Are you sure?"

"Yes. Let him in."

Lil-el went to the door and ushered Gringers inside, then moved to the other side of the room and began preparing a small fire in the brazier. A clay hood over the brazier carried the smoke upward through a hole in the roof.

Gringers sat down next to Bhaldavin's pallet and laid a hand on his arm. "I came to tell you that I'm sorry, Bhaldavin, for what happened the other night." He shrugged. "I'm not exactly sure what *did* happen, but I would never knowingly cause you such pain."

Bhaldavin met Gringers's glance and tried to revive the inner anger he had always felt when Theon, Gringers, or any man touched him, but that too was gone.

Numbed physically and emotionally, he forced his thoughts to center on the cause of his strange lethargy. "What happened to the crystal? Did I—throw it away?"

"Is that what you were trying to do?"

"Yes."

"Why?"

"The fire stones belong to the Ni. Men should not have them."

"Fire stone," Gringers repeated. "Is that the name of the green crystal in Diak's box?"

"Yes."

Gringers frowned. "Why should Ni have them and not men?"

"Their power can be dangerous in the wrong hands. My father once told me that one must be atuned to the fire stones in order to handle them safely."

The frown lines on Gringers's face softened. "It's too bad you didn't think about that the other night."

"I was sure it wouldn't hurt me. I've held one in my hands before. It was in a ring that belonged to my father. But this stone was different. It—hungered. It seemed to absorb my every thought and memory as if it couldn't help itself. The pain didn't come from touching the crystal—it came from remembering."

He looked into Gringers's eyes. "I didn't throw the crystal away, then?"

"No. Diak has it. He slipped off the raft before anyone could stop him. He'll hide out for a few days, then come back."

"And you? I heard Seevan ask you to return to the Homeraft."

Gringers shook his head. "I can't. Diak and Theon

could never make it alone in the swamps, and I doubt any of the other Homerafts would have them, because Theon isn't a rafter and Diak has been named renegade."

"And Hallon?"

Gringers hesitated. "He's decided to accept Seevan's offer and return to the Homeraft. It's probably for the best."

Lil-el approached carrying a tray with cups of hot tea. Gringers helped Bhaldavin sit up and asked Lil-el to join them.

"Thank you, I think I will," she said.

Gringers waited until she had made herself comfortable, then caught her glance. "Has Bhaldavin told you what happened the other night?"

Lil-el shook her head. "I told you before, he's slept most of the last two days, but perhaps you didn't believe me."

Gringers looked down at the cup in his hands. "Don't be angry with me, Lil-el," he said contritely. "I believe you—and what happened the other night was unforeseen." He looked up, his dark eyes expressive. "You know that I wouldn't do anything to harm Bhaldavin."

"I'll believe you, *if* you will tell me what happened." She glanced at Bhaldavin. "Unless you would like to tell it?"

Bhaldavin's hand was unsteady as he raised his cup to his lips. How could he explain, he thought, when he himself wasn't sure what happened? From the moment he had touched the crystal, the present world had dissolved into a maelstrom of long-forgotten memories, and after he had disgorged all the pain he had suffered, the crystal had released him and he had cried all the tears that had been so long denied him.

"Bhaldavin?"

Lil-el's voice brought him back to the present. He looked at Gringers. "You tell it," he said softly.

Gringers nodded and told the story, not once straying

from the truth, up to and including Bhaldavin's theft of the crystal. He then looked at Bhaldavin. "The rest of the story is yours because, in all honesty, I don't know why you screamed."

"It was the crystal. It made me remember things from my past. I remembered my parents' deaths; I remembered how I lost my arm. I even remembered some of the time I spent with Garv. The crystal woke those memories and fed upon them. It hungered for knowledge and for contact with life."

"Hungered?" Gringers frowned. "Are you saying the crystal is somehow *alive*?"

"Yes, in its own way, and it craves learning and knowledge that it can't get while you hold it prisoner in Diak's box. Please, give it to Di-nel or Nara, or anyone of the Ni among the rafters. They'll know what to do with it. It isn't meant for men, Gringers. Only the Ni can be atuned to the lifeforce within the fire stones."

Gringers traced the top of his empty cup with a finger. "We may not be atuned to it, Bhaldavin, but we have found a use for it. Without the crystal, Diak's box won't work."

"To use it so is wrong. You value the crystal only as a tool. We value it for its spiritual essence and its ability to Gift the Tamorlee, parent crystal to all fire stones."

Lil-el's face was lighted with excitement. "You're talking about one of the Seeker stones, aren't you?"

Bhaldavin nodded.

"Where is it now?"

"Diak has it—and he's gone," Gringers answered.

"Oh." There was disappointment on Lil-el's face. "I've heard my father speak about the Seeker stones, but I've never seen one. When will Diak return?"

"I don't know." Gringers abruptly changed the subject, as if uncomfortable with the direction of the conversation. "I understand that Di-nel is to take over Bhaldavin's training."

Lil-el nodded. "So I have been told."

"Why not let you continue?"

"My father is the best draak singer on Lake Arden. He should've taught Bhaldavin from the beginning."

"You don't feel slighted?"

"No."

Gringers studied Lil-el's face a moment. "Now I think it's you who are lying," he said, smiling faintly. "You liked teaching Bhaldavin, and you would like to continue."

Lil-el stood up. "I think it's time you go now, before Seevan returns. You've had your visit."

Gringers stood and handed her his cup. "Thank you for your hospitality. Bhaldavin, my best to you. May I come again?" he asked as he followed Lil-el to the door.

"That will depend upon Bhaldavin," Lil-el replied primly.

"One more thing before I go. I would like to ask you not to say anything to Seevan about the fire stone. You may tell your parents if you like, but not Seevan. If he realized the value of the crystal Diak holds, he would think it his duty to appropriate it for the good of the clan." Gringers's eyebrows raised in question. "Will you keep it our secret?"

Lil-el considered it a moment, then nodded. "Yes, if I can tell my parents about it, and if someday I can see this picture box for myself."

Gringers tipped his head. "Agreed."

Chapter 14

THE RAFTS LEFT LAKE ARDEN AND MOVED UPRIVER, stringing out in a ribbonlike formation that wound around small islands of trees and upthrusting patches of waist-high grass that signaled water levels too shallow for the large rafts to pass over. Everyone old enough to use a pole helped move the rafts along. When the water became too deep for poling, boats were brought into position and the rafts were towed along until poles could be used again.

The cold passage was long over, and it was time to begin the summer harvesting of spidermoss, a gauzelike fiber that when woven made a durable fabric that was much in demand throughout the Enzaar Sea territories.

It had been two years since the Arden Lake clans had harvested a good crop of spidermoss, but all the weather signs had been excellent that spring. Everyone was sure that this year's harvest would be one of the best, provided they reached the Moss Islands first and staked out their territorial claims before any of the other rafter clans to the south arrived.

Bhaldavin watched the rafters from a position atop Seevan's cabin. He was a full-fledged draak singer now, and it was his responsibility to protect all the rafts and boats within his sphere of vision. Di-nel was somewhere up ahead on another raft; Lil-el somewhere behind; and farther back still was Lil-el's brother, Tesh.

Bhaldavin had been with the rafters only four months, but already it seemed that he had always lived among them. He knew that part of that feeling was due to the fact that Lil-el and her parents had treated him as one of the family, filling the emptiness that the return of his memory had brought him. Also, Di-nel had gifted him with all the love and knowledge that was rightly due a son. His long conversations with the older Ni had helped to put many things into perspective, chief among them a partial understanding of the men known as rafters.

Di-nel's voice sounded from ahead, his trilling yodel unmistakable. Bhaldavin stood up, feet braced wide.

Seevan passed by the cabin walking a pole. "See anything?"

"Not yet," Bhaldavin answered, scanning the riverbanks.

Several minutes passed before he saw the draak. It was a small brown fisher, a scavenger by nature. It wasn't as much of a threat to the rafts as it was to those who manned the smaller boats that escorted the rafts.

Bhaldavin took up Di-nel's song as they approached the draak. It stood up on its hind legs, its forelegs hanging in a relaxed position, its spine-covered head almost level with the top of the cabin.

"Sing it off," Seevan ordered. "No sense in taking chances."

Bhaldavin nodded agreement, his glance never leaving the draak. He used one of the songs Di-nel had taught him, imitating one of the draak's own danger signals. As

it turned and splashed off along the riverbank, he realized
that Di-nel could have sent the draak away but had held
it purposely to give Bhaldavin a chance to practice his
singing.

Seevan slapped Bhaldavin's foot as he poled toward
the back of the raft. "Well done!"

Though Bhaldavin hadn't come to like the Ardenol clan
leader as he had some of the other rafters, he did respect
Seevan's authority and felt a small glow of pride in the
man's praise.

He sat down again and continued his surveillance of
the river. It was strange, he thought, but in singing draak
for the rafters he had found a sense of purpose, something
he had never felt before. If not for the ankle chain, he
thought he would actually be happy. The rafters were not
unlike his own people in their calm acceptance of nature's
patterns, their humor, and their zest for living that mani-
fested itself in their games and stories. The stories he
liked best.

At night, after the rafters had secured their boats and
rafts and had set up watches, they would gather in groups
to tell stories or sing. Several men were so highly respected for their talents in these crafts that they were
called bards. Such men were often called in as arbitrators
among the clans when there was a question about or dis-
pute over territorial rights or trade agreements.

The word bard translated into the Ni language was
synonymous with the word *elan-oden*, or wise one. Bhaldavin remembered one of the elan-oden who had graced
their small holding for more than a year and who had told
stories about the Tamorlee, the One Who Never Forgets.
The Tamorlee, having been in the Ni's keeping for over
seven thousand years, was the ultimate historian, the one
to whom the elan-oden went for verification of a teaching.

Thoughts of the Tamorlee brought to mind the green
crystal in Diak's care. How men had come to be in possession of such a large fire stone was something of a

mystery, for the Ni had always jealously guarded those special pieces of crystal that glowed with the inner energy known as *polu*.

Nara and Di-nel had been greatly disturbed when they learned that Diak was in possession of a fire stone and that he was using it as a source of energy to make his magic box work. But there was little they could do about it. Apparently, Diak had never returned to Gringers's raft.

Bhaldavin could still see the fire stone as it lay in Diak's box. He was very much aware of the fact that touching the crystal had somehow changed him. Not only had it released the block on his memory, it had left him with a strange urgency to hold the crystal again. Remembering what had happened to him before, he knew he might well be in danger if he touched the fire stone again, but the threat of danger was far outweighed by an irresistible compulsion to become linked with the lifeforce within the crystal.

Bhaldavin saw a small whirlpool near one of the boats to his left. Thoughts of the fire stone vanished as he scrambled to his feet. He recognized one of the boys in the boat heading straight for the whirlpool.

"Samsel! Turn away!" he yelled. "Draak!"

His warning came too late. A good-sized gray fisher rose out of the water, its right shoulder bumping the boat and tipping it over. While in the boat, the boys were in little danger of attack from a fisher draak, as fishers were not as aggressive as their larger cousins the blues, but once into the water, the boys became fair game. Their splashing strokes as they swam for the safety of the raft attracted the fisher's attention.

The excited shouts of the men and women on the raft drowned out Bhaldavin's first few notes of song. The fisher lunged for Samsel, its pointed mouth open, its sharp teeth visible.

The instinct for survival, coupled with the endless swimming games the rafter children played, saved Samsel's life. A quick tuck at the waist and he dove downward, then darted to the left underwater, the maneuver bringing him out from under the fisher as it dove to follow him.

Bhaldavin raised his voice in a high-pitched warble that overtopped the anxious cries of those aboard the raft. The other boy was now close enough to be pulled to safety, but Samsel was still in danger.

Bhaldavin's song caught the gray fisher just as it surfaced and sighted the boy a second time. The draak stopped almost as if it had run into a solid wall. It shook its head, trying to rid itself of the enticing sounds it heard; then slowly it subsided, sinking down into the water until nothing but its head was visible.

Bhaldavin continued to sing as Seevan dragged his son out of the water, hugging him fiercely. Moments later the draak was gone, its small brain filled with thoughts of a large fish hiding beneath a log along the riverbank.

As Seevan gave orders to several of the men to retrieve the overturned boat, Bhaldavin sent a warning call back to Lil-el to keep watch for the fisher. When he turned back around, he saw Samsel climbing the ladder to the roof of the cabin. The boy's hair was plastered to his head; his clothes were dripping.

"Thank you, Bhaldavin," he said, his face pale.

Bhaldavin nodded and dropped his hand to Samsel's shoulder. "Perhaps you should stay a little closer to the raft," he suggested.

Before Samsel could reply, Seevan called to him. "Come, son. Your boat is ready."

Samsel stiffened and glanced down at the river.

Seevan approached the cabin and held up his arms. "Come, Samsel, Kaffy is waiting for you."

Bhaldavin squeezed Samsel's shoulder and let him go. Samsel's lips tightened with determination as he went to the edge of the roof and fearlessly dropped to his father's hands. Seevan swung him down, then turned and walked him to the waiting boat. As he helped Samsel into the boat, his hand lingered for a moment on top of the boy's head. Samsel looked up with a forced smile.

Bhaldavin watched the two boys paddle out until they were several boat-lengths to the side of the raft. *Fear is something to be met and conquered, never run away from!* That axiom had helped the rafters survive and grow strong. Bhaldavin turned his attention back to the river, musing over the rafters' strength of spirit. Di-nel's words echoed in his mind: "These are a good people, Bhaldavin. I like them."

"Even though they hold you and your family prisoner?" he had asked.

Di-nel had smiled. "The rafters have a very strict code of right and wrong. In their hearts they know what they do to us is wrong, but they are afraid right now. When their fears have lessened, I have no doubt but that our freedom will be returned to us."

"How long before that happens?"

"Soon, I hope, but I can be patient."

But I can't, Bhaldavin thought. I want my freedom now.

Day followed day, and slowly the rafters wound their way westward through the swampland waterways. Some days Bhaldavin used his voice so often that by nightfall he could barely speak. On those occasions, Nara would dose him with a concoction of lemel juice and lingerry syrup, a soothing drink that restored his voice within hours.

Negotiating the waterways of Amla-Bagor took strength, determination, and luck. Every once in a while Bhaldavin saw the ruins of rafts along the riverbanks, their partially submerged hulks splintered and rotting. Each time he saw such a derelict, he couldn't help but wonder to whom the raft had belonged and how many had lost their lives defending it.

The dark chain of mountains called the Draak's Teeth became more and more pronounced as the days passed.

What had started out as a narrow strip of gray across the western horizon had grown into jagged peaks that stretched from south to north in what appeared to be an impregnable wall.

Bhaldavin had glimpsed the mountains through breaks in the trees, but not until the rafts were poled out into the open at the edge of Lake Waunau did he begin to realize the magnitude of the barrier Gringers intended to climb. Did the man truly believe he could scale such forbidding heights?

According to Hallon the answer was yes. Gringers still meant to climb the Draak's Teeth, and he meant for Bhaldavin to go with him. Though Hallon had swallowed his pride and returned to Seevan, he had kept in touch with Gringers through Lil-el, who said that Gringers and Theon were with the Draper rafts. There was no report of Diak, but Hallon was sure the old man had to be somewhere among the Lake Arden rafters.

Bhaldavin watched the raftmen maneuver their floating homes out of the river channel and onto the open waters of the largest freshwater lake in Amla-Bagor. All boats were tied to the rafts, and large sails were quickly put in place.

It took the rafters three days to sail across the lake. On their fourth morning, they reached the borders of the Moss Forests. The forests were situated on a string of small islands that lay at the foot of the Draak's Teeth. On these islands grew the famous clendarri trees, home for the sarian spiders that produced a spinning fiber unparalleled for strength and softness.

First to reach the Moss Forests, the Lake Arden clans were free to choose the largest islands for harvesting—and there was an abundance of spidermoss that year. Clan boundaries were set and marked off by pieces of colored cloth. The following day there was a celebration on the Ardenol Homeraft.

The celebration was in full swing by late afternoon.

The Homeraft rested only a few lengths off one of the islands, so the overflow of visitors soon ended up on the island, where there was singing and dancing taking place. Earlier in the day, the island had been used for games between the clans.

When not on duty, Bhaldavin watched the celebration from his place in front of Di-nel's cabin. His ankle chain was locked into a ring on the outside wall. He did his best to ignore the chain by dividing his attention between the arrival of visitors from the other clans and the food and drink brought to him by Samsel and several other youngsters. After weeks on the river, he knew many of the rafters by sight. Those he didn't know were introduced to him by Nara, who had chosen to keep him company.

Suddenly Gringers appeared. He walked up the raft gangplank and smiled at Nara as he approached. "Hello, Nara, Lil-el asked me to ask you if you would spell her a little while. I don't think she's eaten yet."

Nara's lips pursed in indecision, then she nodded and stood up. She touched the top of Bhaldavin's head. "Would you like me to send Lil-el to sit with you awhile?"

Bhaldavin knew Nara would not accept no for an answer. "If she would like, but tell her to eat first."

Nara gave Gringers a look that said she was none too pleased to see him there. "Does Seevan know you're here?"

Gringers nodded. "We've called a truce," he explained, "until the harvest is over. Every pair of hands means more moss for trade. I've promised Seevan half of whatever Theon and I gather in exchange for clan rights this season."

Nara's eyebrows raised in surprise, and her voice softened. "Can I believe what I'm hearing?"

Gringers smiled. "I'm not always the spine-head Seevan names me, Nara, though I do, upon occasion, give people cause to think so. I know when it's wisest to compromise."

Nara took a step closer to Gringers and looked up into his face, her crystal eyes intent. "And what about your wild scheme to climb the Draak's Teeth?"

Gringers shrugged. "Just a dream, Nara. One that will probably never come true."

"Sometimes dreams are better left alone, Gringers. You are wise to stay with Seevan. He means only good for you." She nodded to Bhaldavin and started for the ramp. "I'll send Lil-el along as soon as she's eaten."

Gringers waited until Nara was gone, then sat down next to Bhaldavin just within the doorway of the cabin, from where he could see anyone approaching.

"She's a gentle soul," Gringers said, "but she doesn't fool easily. Do you think she believed me about the Draak's Teeth?"

Bhaldavin kept his eyes directed at the dancers on the island. He knew why Gringers was there, but he didn't know how he was going to answer him. He wanted his freedom, but was not sure he was willing to pay the price Gringers would ask of him.

Minutes dragged by as Gringers joined Bhaldavin in watching the festivities.

"It's been a long time since I've seen you," Gringers said finally. "How has it been with you?"

Bhaldavin looked Gringers in the eye. "I fare well enough."

"I see you still wear Seevan's chain. I had hoped you would be rid of it by now. I guess I'll have to do something about it. You certainly can't climb the Draak's Teeth dragging it."

Bhaldavin glanced up at the towering ridge that blocked out most of the western sky. "Do you really think you can climb over those mountains?"

"It was done once; it can be done again."

"You're sure your ancestors came over the mountains?"

Gringers nodded. "There's a song the bards sing about

a man named Nathan Ardenol. It is sung that he braved the heights of the Draak's Teeth in order to lead his people to a new land where they could live in peace and thrive. The rafters of Amla-Bagor are said to be the descendants of Nathan Ardenol and those people he brought with him.

"The song goes on to tell of Nathan's first meeting with your people and how friendship developed between man and Ni. It also tells about certain powers that Nathan's people possessed: powers over illness, the ability to communicate over long distances, and the weaponry to kill draak."

Gringers looked at Bhaldavin and shrugged. "I know, it doesn't sound possible. I wouldn't have believed it years ago. But now that I've seen the pictures in the recorder, Nathan Ardenol's story rings true."

"Are all men descended from Nathan's people?" Bhaldavin asked, dropping his pose of indifference.

"No. The Sarissa, who are light-skinned, and the Utura, who are dark, both claim that their ancestors came to the Enzaar Sea through the Straits of Annarothal by boat. The Sarissa claim that they are the direct descendants of the First Men, but it's a known fact that raftmen plied the waters of Amla-Bagor long before the Sarissa laid claim to the Escarpment as their home. I don't know that it matters who came first, not now. All that really matters is finding Barl-gan and reclaiming the knowledge and powers of the First Men."

"When are you going?"

"After the harvest. I've promised Seevan half of what Theon and I gather. The other half I'll leave in trade for the clothes and supplies we'll take."

Steal, you mean, Bhaldavin thought as he turned to face Gringers again. "I haven't seen Diak. Is he with you?"

"No. Seevan wouldn't have him back. He's with some friends. He'll be safe as long as he stays out of sight."

Gringers started to say something else, but stopped as

someone ascended the ramp. Theon had changed little in the weeks since Bhaldavin had seen him. He had let his hair grow long, and he wore a headband similar to those worn by the rafters, but still he was clean-shaven and fastidious in his dress. His bouncy walk, darting glances, and sly grin reminded Bhaldavin of the first time he had seen Theon in Garv's cabin. He wondered if Theon ever thought about Garv.

Theon smiled as he greeted him. "Hello, Little Fish. Ready to do some mountain climbing?"

Bhaldavin shook his head.

Theon glanced at Gringers, a frown replacing his smile. "What's wrong? I thought you were going to talk to him."

"I *was* talking to him," Gringers said sharply. "Sit down and let me handle this."

Theon muttered something under his breath, but did as Gringers ordered.

Gringers pulled at Bhaldavin's ankle chain. "Do you love your chain so much, Bhaldavin? I was told that you wouldn't give Seevan your word not to run away. Does that mean you've come to accept your slavery? That you don't want your freedom any longer?"

Bhaldavin kept his eyes focused on the island dancers. Yes, he wanted his freedom, but the size of the mountains frightened him, and the thought of leaving Lil-el stirred memories of an emptiness within that he didn't want to experience ever again.

"Well?" Gringers pressed. "Do you want to live the rest of your life as a slave?"

Bhaldavin turned to face Gringers. "No. I want my freedom. Tell me what I must do to earn it."

"Just come with us and protect us from any draak we meet. It's all we ask of you."

"How long must I stay with you?"

Gringers glanced at Theon, then back to Bhaldavin. "Until we find what we're looking for."

"Barl-gan?"

Gringers nodded.

"And then I'll be free to leave you."

"Yes, if you want to."

"Have you made any plans for returning to Amla-Bagor?"

"We've discussed it," Gringers answered evasively, "but due to the time we'll be crossing the Draak's Teeth, we'll probably have to spend the cold passage on the other side of the mountains, unless we can find Barl-gan quickly and can return over the mountains before the weather prevents us."

"Well, Little Fish, do you join us on our quest?" Theon asked. "If we find what we hope to find, we'll see that you are handsomely rewarded."

At Theon's mention of a reward, Bhaldavin's thoughts centered on Diak's crystal. He remembered the touch of the fire stone, and suddenly he ached to hold it again, to delve into those hidden passages he had glimpsed while one with the crystal, to touch again that awareness that had greeted him as a long-lost child, that promised him a kind of friendship that none but a few ever experienced.

He turned to Gringers. "I accept your offer of freedom as *partial* payment for my services as a draak singer."

Gringers frowned. "What else do you want?"

"The crystal in Diak's box."

Gringers shook his head. "It's not mine to give."

"If you want my help," Bhaldavin said firmly, "you'll convince Diak to relinquish the crystal."

Theon released a deep sigh. "Gringers, I'm afraid that Garv's Little Fish is growing up. If we aren't careful, he's going to end up owning us!"

Chapter 15 🌿

*B*HALDAVIN KNEW NOTHING ABOUT SPIDERMOSS AND WAS startled the first time he saw the huge sarian spider; its body alone was the size of his fist. Theon was no less startled, but managed to hide it behind a scowl as Samsel caught one of the large arachnids and brought it close for their inspection.

"Are you sure it's nonpoisonous?" Theon asked, keeping a wary eye on the spider.

"I'm sure," Samsel said, holding the spider up by one furry leg. "It depends upon the tree thorns to protect it from its enemies, which are mostly birds and lizards."

Samsel pushed the spider close to Bhaldavin's ear. "Listen," he laughed. "Hear it sound? All hiss and no strike."

Bhaldavin leaned away from the faceted green eyes, which seemed to be glaring at him, and wished the boy would stop playing with the ugly creature.

The spider finally twisted free and dropped to the ground.

"Get that out of here," Theon yelled as it started to crawl toward his legs.

Samsel grinned as he retrieved the spider. "It won't hurt you."

"I don't care if it will or not. Just get it out of here!"

Ysal, who was in the branches of a nearby tree, dropped another clump of moss. "Let it go, Samsel, and get back to work."

Samsel made a face at Ysal, but did as he was told, placing the spider on the trunk of a tree that had already been stripped of its moss. Relieved, Bhaldavin and Theon watched the furry spider scramble up out of sight, then returned to work.

Before spidermoss could be laid out and rolled, it had to be cleaned of all the leaves and insects caught inside the tangled threads. It was painstaking work, but it had to be done. No one was exempt from the work up to and including Seevan, though most of the men spent a good part of their working hours high in the branches of the trees where their experienced hands were required to extract the silver-gray moss from the thorny branches without tearing it to pieces.

Those not directly involved with collecting spidermoss spent their time either cleaning the moss or fishing and gathering mollusks from the shallows to help supplement their meals. The preparation of food also became a joint effort, and the cooking fires moved from island to island following the pickers.

Samsel picked up the clump of moss Ysal had dropped and gave it to Bhaldavin, then went in search for more. Bhaldavin was able to work one-handed by holding the clump on his lap, part of it caught between his knees.

Bhaldavin heard Theon swear under his breath. He looked up to see the small man sucking a finger.

"Damn thorns!" Theon muttered. "You know, Little Fish, there are moments when I wonder if I haven't lost my mind. How I ever let Gringers talk me into going on some crazy hunt for a lost city, I'll never know. Right now I'm thinking about Fisherman's Landing, and what I'd be doing if I was there. It's strange, but sometimes I even think that if I went back, I'd find Garv alive. Sometimes I think—maybe he didn't die that night. Maybe Gringers made a mistake, and somehow Garv is still alive." He looked out through the trees to the lake. "When I get to thinking like that, I want to jump into the nearest boat and start paddling." He paused. "Of course, I'd never make it back alone."

Bhaldavin felt sorry for Theon, who had yet to find acceptance among the rafters. The man was tolerated because of Gringers, but he was not really welcome—and he knew it.

"Have you thought what you'll do if and when Gringers finds Barl-gan?" he asked, trying to get Theon's mind off Fisherman's Landing.

"I've thought about it, but can't get past the fact that once over the mountains, we'll have to find a way back." He looked up at the craggy peaks. "And I don't relish the thought of climbing those mountains twice."

"Perhaps there is a way around them?"

"It's possible, I suppose. I just hope that when we find Barl-gan, we find someone still living there. I'm tired of swamps, rivers, and wilderness. Personally, I'd like to see a little civilization again!"

Bhaldavin looked up at the mountains, a new thought stirring. "Theon, do you think there's a chance some of *my* people might live on the other side of the mountains?"

"I don't know why not. Gives us both something to think about, doesn't it?"

It was long after the supper hour. The last of the gather of spidermoss had been rolled and put away. The walls of every cabin were lined with upright bundles of moss lashed in place. Weeks had passed since their arrival on the Moss Islands, and Seevan was pleased that the harvesting had gone so smoothly. Soon it would be time to begin the trek back to Lake Arden where the moss would be spun and repacked for shipment to Natrob.

Bhaldavin sat quietly looking out over the water. It was dark, but the western skyline was still visible. The air off the water was cool and fresh, and after a long day of working under the twin suns, it felt good just to sit and relax. Most of the rafters were already abed.

He shifted around and heard the clink of his chain. The thought of escape, uppermost in his mind for so long, was countered by the knowledge that he was far from his homeland. Months of travel separated him from Fisherman's Landing, and to get from there to the Deep, he would have to cross the Enzaar Sea. He brushed the stump of his arm and felt despair eat into his heart. How far could he paddle with only one arm? Not far, and surely not fast enough to outrun the boats Seevan and Gringers would send after him.

He looked again to the horizon and realized that he would never be able to make it back to the Deep alone. He had come too far, and so much time had passed. Was it possible that his brother, Dhalvad, had survived? He shook his head, worried that he might never know the answer to that question.

Someone approached from behind. "Bhaldavin? May I join you?"

Thoughts of his brother faded as he turned and held out his hand. "Please, Lil-el, I would like that."

She sat down close to him. "Tired?" she asked softly.

"Yes. It was a long day."

"Seevan sets a steady pace. Another three or four days and we should be done with the harvesting."

He glanced at the mountains behind Lil-el. Yes, he thought, the harvesting will be done, and you will go one way, I another, and only the wind knows if we'll ever meet again.

"I love you, Bhaldavin."

The softly spoken words sent shivers down Bhalda-vin's spine. An aching sense of loss brought tears to his eyes, and he couldn't speak. Part of him wanted to reach out and hold Lil-el, to tell her that he returned her love, that he wanted to spend the rest of his life with her; but another part of him longed for the peace of mind that for him would come only with freedom.

He hated the thought of leaving her behind, but couldn't see himself staying with the rafters for the rest of his life. If I do stay, he thought, some day I'll blame her for my loss of freedom, and that I don't want.

Bhaldavin could feel Lil-el's glance and was glad of the darkness. He didn't realize that his tears reflected the lantern light, giving him away.

"When do you and Gringers leave us, my love?" Lil-el asked, surprising him.

"You know?" he cried softly. "How?"

"Gringers."

Bhaldavin was shocked. "He told you his plans?"

"He didn't have to. I've been watching him closely for several weeks, ever since I saw him pilfering from the food stores. Just last week I found him cutting boot patterns out of an old pair of draakhide pants. Judging from the three-layer soles he was sewing together, it looked like he was planning to do some rigorous climbing. When I told him that, he said no and claimed that he was just geting tired of going barefoot. One look at the size of the boot, and I knew he wasn't making them for himself. They were far too small for him—more your size, I think."

"Does he know you know about his plans?"

"I'm sure he suspects."

"And he trusts you not to say anything to anyone?"

"Gringers and I have been friends a long time, Bhal-davin. We played together as children. He *knows* I wouldn't betray him."

She hesitated, then continued. "Gringers is a very spe-cial kind of man, Bhaldavin. If he had been born a Ni, I believe he would have been a Seeker, for there is an inner strength in him, a power that draws people to trust him. Seevan sensed Gringers's special quality years ago, and for some reason he saw it as a threat to his own standing among the rafters. I think he may have feared that Gringers would oust him from his position before he was ready to give up his leadership.

"To this day I don't think Gringers understands exactly what happened between himself and his uncle. Until the age of fifteen, Seevan loved Gringers as a son, then suddenly nothing Gringers did was right. He tried his best to please Seevan, but it only made things worse. Seevan started to call him names and belittle him in every way possible; then Gringers would get mad and do something foolish, giving Seevan cause to punish him. It was no wonder that Gringers finally turned to someone else for understanding."

"Diak?"

"Yes. The old man offered Gringers a place where he could be himself, where no one would holler at him or punish him without just cause. The two soon became inseparable, and in time, Diak discovered that he had found a kindred spirit when it came to dreaming big dreams. I can still remember the first time Gringers told me about Barl-gan. He was not yet a man, but already he was making plans to go adventuring with Diak."

She glanced up at the mountains and released a deep sigh. "They've been dreaming of climbing the Draak's Teeth for years. I think the time for them has come. They'll do it—or die trying." She turned back to him. "My only regret is that they are going to drag you along with them."

"I must go, Lil-el. I have no choice."

"I know what they look for beyond the mountains, Bhaldavin, but what is it you hope to find there?"

"Freedom," he said, careful that his voice not carry to the guard atop the nearby cabin roof.

"I thought as much. And is that all they offered you?"

"Theon spoke about a reward when they reached Barl-gan, but I haven't any faith in his promises. I told Gringers that I would go with him for my freedom *and* the fire stone Diak carries."

"What did Gringers say?"

"At first he said no, then he said he'd think about it. Two days ago he said he had talked with Diak and the old man had agreed to give me the crystal when we reached Barl-gan." He hesitated. "Do you think they will?"

Lil-el thought a moment. "Gringers will keep his word. The other two, I'm not so sure. A lot might depend upon what you find in Barl-gan—if you find it at all."

Someone approached. The creaking of the wooden ramps that led from raft to raft seemed loud in the still night air.

"Lil-el, your turn for watch."

Lil-el turned at the sound of her father's voice. "Coming."

"Bhaldavin?" Di-nel said, pausing at the cabin door.

"Yes."

"Best get some sleep. You're on watch after Lil-el."

"Yes, sir."

"Who is supposed to walk your rounds with you tonight?"

"Rafer."

The guard stationed atop Di-nel's cabin wished him a good night. Di-nel thanked him and went inside.

Bhaldavin caught Lil-el's hand as she started to rise. "I'm sorry," he said softly. "I wish there was some way I could stay here with you. If things were different, I—"

She leaned down and kissed him, her lips shutting off his words. When she stood up, she squeezed his hand. "Bhaldavin, do you love me?"

"More than I have ever loved anyone, but—"

"No buts, Bhaldavin. It's enough that I know. You haven't said when you're leaving. Do you know when?"

"No."

"Well, good night then. I'll see you in the morning."

He watched Lil-el disappear into the darkness, sick with the knowledge that his last word to her had been a lie.

It was the first hour of morning. All was quiet. The darkness was broken only by the four watch lanterns placed at each corner of the interlocked rafts.

Bhaldavin quietly followed Gringers over the narrow board bridges linking raft to raft and stopped in the shadow of the last cabin on the north side of the Homeraft. There were three boats moored alongside the raft.

Gringers had freed Bhaldavin from his leg chain after quietly disposing of the guard atop Di-nel's cabin. The guard would have a terrible headache come morning.

Gringers thrust a bundle at Bhaldavin and told him to follow. When they reached the boats, Gringers quickly loaded the bundles in the middle boat and directed Bhaldavin to get in. "Hurry," he whispered. "Lil-el will be headed back this way soon."

"Where's Theon?" Bhaldavin asked, taking his place.

Gringers pushed off. "He's with Hallon and Diak and the rest of our supplies. There was no way we could do it in one trip."

Bhaldavin looked back as the boat slid quietly away from the Ardenol Homeraft. As the darkness swallowed them, a solitary figure passed the northern watch lantern and paused at the place where, only moments ago, their boat had been moored. The figure gazed down at the water, then looked out into the darkness beyond the raft.

Bhaldavin realized that Lil-el was too keen-eyed to miss the telltale ripples on the water. If she thinks the ripples were caused by a draak, she'll start singing, he thought.

Seconds passed. Gringers's paddle dipped soundlessly in and out of the water carrying them farther and farther away from the raft. Lil-el stood quietly, listening.

She knows, Bhaldavin thought. She knows. He looked at Gringers, his heart thundering in his ears. *Stop! Go back! She knows we've gone!* The words formed in his mind, but never reached his lips; then it was too late. Lil-el was moving again, continuing her rounds.

Bhaldavin's hand tightened on the gunwhale as she disappeared beyond a cabin wall, for in that moment he realized how much he loved her. I could still go back. All I have to do is stand up, dive over the side, and swim. Gringers couldn't stop me, not without turning back himself, and how would he explain his nightly excursion and the absence of Theon and Hallon?

"Safe away! I don't think Lil-el saw us," Gringers whispered. "Well, Bhaldavin, we're finally on our way. How does it feel to be free?"

Bhaldavin turned and faced forward. I'm free, free as long as I don't return to the rafters. But Lil-el is there and I love her.

"Bhaldavin? Everything all right?"

"Yes. Fine."

Gringers was quiet for a moment. "You love her, don't you?" he said finally.

"Yes."

"I'm sorry."

It took Gringers over an hour to find the place where he had left Hallon, Diak, and Theon. The small campfire Hallon tended guided the boat to the rocky shore. Theon and Hallon met them at the water's edge and helped bring the boat up out of the water.

"Any trouble?" Hallon asked as they started toward the campfire.

"No," Gringers responded. "Everything went fine. Have you got everything packed and ready to go?"

"Almost. Diak has some tea brewing. Want a cup?"

"Sure. Why don't you and Theon see to hiding the boat. Diak and I can finish with the packs. I want to get as far up into the mountains as we can by daylight. If and when Seevan finds our camp, we should be out of reach. I doubt he'll waste much time trying to come after us. He's known me too long not to know where we're headed."

"I hope you're right," Hallon said. "I don't relish the thought of Seevan catching up with us and dragging us back like errant children."

"Don't worry. All he'll be thinking is good riddance."

Bhaldavin was offered a cup of tea and several fire-warmed rolls filled with thick drenberry jam. He ate what was given him, suspecting that he would need every bit of strength at his command. He had never climbed a mountain before, and the Draak's Teeth were not what he would have chosen for a first experience. As he ate, he listened to Diak's stories of his earlier climbs into the mountains, which described the kinds of obstacles they would face, such as rock slides; sheer cliffs of rock, snow, and ice; thin air; and very cold temperatures.

Theon and Hallon returned just as Diak drew a crude map from his pack.

"I made this years ago," Diak began, "following several unsuccessful trips into the mountains. I've charted the way up to here, near the timberline." Diak's forefinger rested on the map three-quarters of the way up the mountain. "From this point on, I tried going north to what appeared to be a wedge, a place where the ridges overlapped, but I couldn't find a break in the mountains. I was sure that the best way to cross the mountains would be here"—his fingers moved farther north—"or here. But I was wrong."

Diak pulled out the worn diary. "According to Freeman's diary, his ancestors came over the mountains through a pass farther south. At the foot of the pass, there's a place where hot springs send steam shooting into the air. Beyond the springs lies a valley where rock cliffs shelter a river of ice that leads up over the mountains."

Theon frowned at the old man. "What if the diary is wrong, and this pass doesn't go anywhere? What then?"

"There has to be a way through the mountains. The journal says so."

"How long has it been since the last time you were up in these mountains, old man?" Theon demanded.

Diak's eyes stayed on the map. "Fifteen or sixteen years."

"Sixteen years! But I thought that—"

"Theon." Gringers's voice held a warning note.

Theon glared at his friend. "I don't like this, Gringers. You made me believe that this old man knew where he was going."

"I made you believe nothing. You're here because you are a greedy devil, and you hope to be in on a rich find. Well, no one's going to force you to climb these mountains. Go! Take one of the boats and go back to the Homeraft if you want to. Finish out the season with Seevan, and return to Fisherman's Landing. Go on! No one here will try to stop you."

Theon made a face. "I've nothing back there, and you know it."

"Then stay! But stop complaining. If we're going to get over these damn mountains, we're going to have to work together."

Theon looked at Diak, then turned back to Gringers. "All right. Together."

"No more complaints?"

Theon shook his head. "No more complaints."

"Good. Then finish up. It's time we got started."

Chapter 16 🖎

THREE DAYS OF STEADY WALKING BROUGHT GRINGERS and his small party up out of the foothills. From that point on, the slopes grew steeper and aban and lingerry trees gave way to gian and rilror pine. Narrow, sheltered valleys provided refuge each night, and Bhaldavin easily sang away the three immature draak they encountered. There were no signs of gensvolf in the area.

On their fourth night out, Gringers chose a stand of gian pine for their campsite. Here the trees grew so close together that none but the very smallest of draak would venture in.

Camp was quickly set up. Diak and Bhaldavin, who had succumbed to the fast-moving water and slippery rocks of the river they had crossed that day, stripped and hung their wet clothing on branches near the fire. Gringers and Theon helped sort through their packs while Hallon tended the fire.

Bhaldavin was tired, and a quick glance at Diak told him that he wasn't the only one to feel the weight of his pack and the strain in his back and legs. Just thinking about the climb still ahead of them made him wonder if the old man was going to make it—if any of them would.

Supper was dried kansa, a handful of hait nuts, several strips of smoked nida, and a hot cup of rayil tea laced with a few drops of luclatch, a potent brew distilled in the Reaches.

Bhaldavin looked up at the darkening sky and sipped at the last of his tea. The warm passage was nearing its end, and the daylight hours were growing shorter. Already there was snow on the high peaks, and Diak's claim that they wouldn't be able to cross the mountains without running into some snow made Bhaldavin nervous. He had never before seen snow or ice, and Diak's description of his own venture into the heights made him shiver and edge a little closer to the fire, pulling his blanket tight around his shoulders.

Theon sat down beside Bhaldavin. His hand casually dropped onto Bhaldavin's bare thigh. "Warm enough, Little Fish?"

Bhaldavin nodded. The fire's warmth and the density of the pines helped negate the coolness of the wind that had suddenly sprung up.

"Your clothes should be dry soon," Theon continued. "How is your foot?"

"Tender." He lifted his left foot and inspected the cut on the outside of his ankle. The rocks in the stream had been sharp as well as slippery, and he had sliced his foot when he lost his balance. The ankle was sore to the touch, but the bleeding had been minimal.

Gringers approached carrying something. He frowned as his glance touched Theon.

Theon grinned and removed his hand from Bhaldavin's leg.

Gringers shook his head. "You never stop trying, do you?"

"Just trying to make you jealous, my friend."

"You're a lost cause, Theon."

Theon shrugged. "Perhaps."

"Here, Bhaldavin," Gringers said, handing Bhaldavin a pair of boots. "Try these on."

Bhaldavin cradled the boots with his legs and looked them over, fingering the three-layered soles and the overlap below the knee where the boots were tied.

"We'll all be wearing them from this point on," Gringers said. "The climbing will get rougher as we go higher. They'll help protect your feet."

Bhaldavin had never worn any kind of foot covering; it was hardly necessary in the Deep, where the forest floor was soft with layers and layers of old leaves.

"Try them on," Gringers urged. "I want to see if they fit."

Bhaldavin put the boots on and wiggled his toes as Gringers leaned forward and tied the laces for him. The boots felt strange, confining.

Gringers caught the look on Bhaldavin's face and lightly slapped his legs. "You'll get used to them. Give them time. Believe me, you'll be glad of them before long."

Gringers looked at Theon. "What about you?"

"I'll wear my sandals awhile longer. They're comfortable."

"It would lighten your pack if you'd wear your boots."

"Not that much."

"Theon, I don't want to argue with you. I want you—"

"Gringers!"

The urgent tone in Hallon's voice brought Gringers to his feet. "What is it?" he demanded.

Hallon stood facing the trees on the downward slope. "I heard something."

"Draak?"

"I don't know. It was a snapping sound."

Gringers crossed to where Diak sat and retrieved his bow from the ground. "Diak, put more wood on the fire.

Theon, stand ready. Bhaldavin, get over here. If it's a draak, you'll have to..."

Gringers's words trailed off as someone stepped out from behind the trees.

"Not a draak, Gringers," Lil-el said calmly. "Just me."

Bhaldavin was past Gringers and Hallon in several quick strides. "Lil-el!"

She opened her arms to him, ignoring his nakedness as his blanket slipped from his shoulders. They held each other a moment or two, then Gringers was there, pulling them apart.

"What in the name of Brogan's draak are you doing here?" he demanded angrily.

Lil-el faced him squarely. "I am where I want to be: with Bhaldavin."

"What about the rafts? And Seevan? When he finds you gone, he'll spit blood!"

"Let him."

"But—but you don't understand," he yelled. "He might've overlooked our taking Bhaldavin, but if he thinks we took you too, he'll—he'll—"

"He will what? Follow you into the mountains? I doubt that. He might spend a few days looking for me, but he has others to think about and he still has three draak singers, enough to see him and the rest of the clan safely back to Lake Arden."

"That's not the point. He'll think I took you!"

"But you didn't, and I'll tell him so when I see him again, *if* I ever see him again."

Gringers took hold of her arms. "You can't come. You must go back."

Lil-el tried to remain calm, but her voice rose. "I won't! You can't make me. I've chosen Bhaldavin for my life mate and I go where he goes."

"Why you—"

Bhaldavin saw Lil-el wince and quickly pushed himself

in between them. "Let her go, Gringers! Let her go, or I'll *never* sing for you again!"

Startled by the vehemence in Bhaldavin's tone, Gringers released Lil-el and stepped back, glaring at the two Ni. He pointed a finger at Lil-el. "You are not going to stay."

"I am."

Suddenly Theon stepped in. "Gringers, enough! She's here; she'll have to stay. Not unless you want to escort her back—straight into Seevan's waiting arms. He'd like that."

Gringers turned on the small man. "Be still!"

"Go ahead, yell," Theon taunted, ignoring the baleful look on Gringers's face. "Get it out of your system. Then after you've calmed down, you'll realize that Lil-el's being here might mean all the difference in our making it to Barl-gan. Just think, now we've got two draak singers to protect us. Two! And an extra pair of hands if we need them."

"Damn it! You don't understand."

"Oh, I think I do. It's Seevan, isn't it? And what he thinks about you. Damn it, why do you care anymore? He's called you thief, spine-head, and a dozen other names I could mention. Gringers, grow up! Live for yourself! Not for that self-righteous bastard who just happens to be your uncle. I begin to think that this whole thing about finding Barl-gan is just a way for you to get Seevan to notice you. That's it, isn't it? That's what climbing this damn mountain is all about."

Gringers lashed out, moving so fast that Theon was caught off guard. Reeling from the blow to his nose, Theon fell backward into Hallon, who caught him and lowered him to the ground.

Hallon quickly stepped away as Gringers came to stand over Theon.

"Barl-gan is for *me* and for *Diak*!" Gringers snarled. "Seevan has nothing to do with it, is that clear?"

Theon nodded and slowly sat up, blood trickling from his nose.

Gringers turned and glared at Bhaldavin and Lil-el. Both took involuntary steps backward. Neither had ever seen him so angry.

He bent, snatched up Bhaldavin's blanket, and threw it at him. "Cover up or get dressed! You'll be no good to us if you catch cold. Hallon, keep watch until I get back."

"Where're you going?" Hallon asked quickly.

"Not far."

They watched until he was out of sight, then Bhaldavin went to Theon and gave him a hand up.

"Are you all right?" Lil-el asked Theon.

"I'll live," he answered. He crossed to the fire and sat down next to Diak. Lil-el joined them while Bhaldavin checked on his still-damp clothes.

Hallon looked at the opening in the trees where Gringers had disappeared. He was a quiet man by nature, a follower, and he had chosen Gringers as his leader. "Should I go after him, Diak?"

The old man shook his head. "Leave him alone a little while. He needs to think."

"About my staying?" Lil-el asked.

"Yes. And about what Theon said."

Theon picked up his cup and took a drink of lukewarm tea. "I was close to the truth, wasn't I?"

Diak nodded. "Too close. It's something he'll have to acknowledge eventually—only then can he put it behind him."

Bhaldavin came to the fire and sat down beside Lil-el. "Was it true," he asked softly, eagerly. "What you said about choosing me for your life mate?"

"Yes."

"What about your parents? Do they know where you went?"

"I told them before I left. They argued a bit, then made

me promise that if I didn't catch up to you within two days, I would return to the rafts."

"How far behind us were you?"

"Only a few hours, my love. I've had my pack ready for weeks, just in case Gringers decided to leave early."

"You meant to come all along?"

She smiled at him. "If you were going, I was going."

"And if we don't come back this way? If you never see your parents again?"

"Will it matter if we're together?"

Bhaldavin shook his head, pulled her close, and kissed her, oblivious to the looks he was getting from Diak and Theon.

Gringers was quiet for three days. He allowed Diak to take the lead and dropped back to act as rear guard. Cautioned by Diak to ignore Gringers's moodiness, Lil-el, Hallon, and Bhaldavin continued on as if nothing was wrong. But Theon couldn't leave Gringers alone; he spent his time vacillating between teasing and trying to placate his friend.

Theon's constant chatter finally got to Gringers. One night as Theon walked by him, gathering branches for their fire, Gringers stuck out his foot. Theon tripped and fell, his armload of branches scattering in all directions. He rolled over and sat up, glaring. His glance fell on Gringers.

"What are you grinning about?" he demanded.

Gringers's smile broadened.

"You tripped me on purpose!" Theon yelled.

"I had to find some way to shut you up," Gringers responded mildly.

"Why you—"

Gringers met Theon's charge with open arms, grasping the smaller man by the shoulders and carrying him over onto his back. Theon cursed and twisted around, kicking and squirming to break free; then the two of them were rolling over and over down the slight incline at the edge of the camp.

Hallon started after the two combatants, but Diak stopped him. "Let them alone. They need this."

Bhaldavin and Lil-el looked at Diak, then at each other, not understanding.

The battle lasted only a few minutes, and it was quickly apparent that neither man was doing the other much harm. It was more a wrestling match than a fight, and it ended with Gringers sitting atop Theon's stomach. Both men were laughing.

Theon tried to free his hands, which were being held securely at either side of his head. "Come on, get off. You're as heavy as a draak!"

"Only if you promise not to say another word tonight," Gringers demanded.

Theon looked pained. "You ask a lot."

Gringers just smiled.

"All right, you win. Let me up."

Gringers stood and gave Theon a hand up. "Remember," he said, dropping an arm over Theon's shoulders as they climbed back up the rise, "no more talking the rest of the night."

"Agreed," Theon said.

"If you two are finished playing," Diak asked caustically, "can we get on with preparing supper?"

Gringers gave Diak a mock bow. "Your wish is our command."

Theon glanced at Diak, who gave him a small nod of approval.

Bhaldavin noted the silent message that passed between the two men and saw the look of satisfaction on Theon's face as he turned to pick up the branches he had dropped. Gringers had won the scuffle, but Theon had won something more important.

In that moment Bhaldavin began to grasp that elusive something that linked the two men in friendship: Theon loved Gringers and would do anything to return their friendship to a solid footing.

Several times in the past few months, Bhaldavin had entertained the thought that Theon was *zelfar*, a free lover. If true, it explained his past behavior on several occasions. The Ni, unlike men, accepted zelfar in their society and did not ask them to be other than they were.

Watching Gringers and Theon work at building the campfire together, he wondered how long it would be before Gringers realized the obvious and what his reaction would be, for according to Di-nel, men did not always respond to love as did the Ni.

Di-nel's words echoed in his mind as he reached for Lil-el's hand. "The body is illusion; the inner being is reality. One may be attracted to the outer form, but until the inner being is recognized and accepted, love will elude the most aggressive of hunters."

Chapter 17

BHALDAVIN LOST TRACK OF THE NUMBER OF DAYS THEY had been on the trail. Lil-el thought it was seventeen; Theon said twenty. They argued good-naturedly about it as they followed Gringers up a narrow rocky ravine. The climbing was steep, and loose shale made the footing treacherous in places. A length of rope linked them one to another in case someone slipped.

Gringers finally reached the top of the ravine and, with a little scrambling, pulled himself up onto level ground. He stood up and looked around, shielding his eyes with his hand as he gazed at the slopes ahead.

Suddenly he gave a delighted cry.

"What is it?" Diak called up from below.

Gringers pointed upward and to the right. "Something over there. It could be the hot springs." .

"Help me up!" Diak demanded excitedly.

Gringers took one last look and bent to give the old man a lift over the edge. One by one the others followed. With only one arm Bhaldavin was at a slight disadvantage,

177

but Hallon steadied him while Theon gave him a hand from above.

"See? Over there!" Gringers pointed as Hallon and Bhaldavin joined him.

Bhaldavin looked but saw nothing until a plume of white shot into the air. "What is it?"

"The hot springs, I hope," Diak said, pushing past Gringers. "Let's go take a look!"

The hot springs were sheltered in a narrow ribbonlike valley hidden by ledges of rock. It took them only a short time to climb up to the valley floor. During their ascent, they saw another explosion of steam and water into the air.

"I've never seen anything like this before," Lil-el said, awed by the height of the plume of water.

Diak shifted his pack to ease tired muscles. "There are hot springs like this in the Reaches. I saw them once when I was much younger. They're in the foothills of the mountains east of Lachchen Holding. Lord Elson discovered them, I believe. The waters from the springs are said to have some medicinal value."

"How hot are the waters?" Bhaldavin asked.

Diak smiled. "Hot enough to boil a draak alive if he chanced to fall in, so I advise everyone to watch where you step."

The valley floor was strewn with large boulders, and winding in and out among the rocks was a shallow river that bubbled and steamed.

"Do we cross or go around?" Hallon wanted to know.

"Safer to go around, I think," Diak answered.

Gringers led out. By late morning they were three-quarters of the way around the main springs. They stopped and ate their midday meal near a large upthrusting cone of rock, one of many they had seen in the valley.

"The water shoots out and leaves a residue each time," Diak explained. He started to say something else, but a strange rumbling in the ground interrupted him.

"Grab your packs!" Gringers yelled.

There was mass confusion for a moment, then everyone was up and running. Diak stumbled and fell to his knees, but he was down only a second or two before Hallon came along and lifted him to his feet.

Bhaldavin felt the tremor in the ground; it was followed by a *whoosh*ing sound of water and steam. He glanced back over his shoulder and almost lost his footing. He caught his balance and slowed, coming to a stop by the others who had turned to watch.

Gallons and gallons of water shot high into the air, forming a mistlike fog that dropped softly over the valley and wet the small band of travelers.

Gringers looked at Theon and laughed. "Interesting."

"To you, maybe," Theon said, "but I'm not ready for another bath. Let's get out of here."

Night found the travelers high above the hot springs, tucked away in the shelter of a small stand of gian pine; a bright fire chased back the evening shadows. Armloads of branches were gathered and piled near the fire.

"We'll use that tonight and gather fresh in the morning," Diak said. "We're nearing the timberline, and from this point on, if we want a fire, we'll have to carry our wood with us and we'll have to use it sparingly."

Hallon added a few branches to the fire. "Are there many draak this high up in the mountains?"

"They don't care much for cold weather, and they really aren't built for mountain climbing," Diak answered. "Still, we'll keep watches just the same."

The next morning Gringers led his small band up the narrow river valley that overlooked the hot springs. The climbing wasn't too difficult at first, then the valley floor sloped upward sharply, and Gringers was forced to stop every few hours to let Diak rest. Hallon finally took Diak's pack; the wood both men carried was distributed among the others.

Everyone was exhausted by the end of the day, and the chilly wet air that swept down from the peaks seemed twice as cold after the suns went down. Rather than expend their wood for a fire, Gringers ordered everyone to undress and put on the spidermoss vests and pants they had carried with them. The pants and vests would act as insulation under their regular clothes, the gossamerlike fabric holding in warmth while allowing the body to breathe normally.

"Here, Lil-el," Gringers said, tossing a tightly wrapped bundle to her, "you wear mine. The cold doesn't bother me much, and I—"

"Thank you, Gringers," she said, tossing it back. "But I have my own."

"You do?"

She smiled. "Don't look so startled."

"Where did you get them?"

"The same place you got yours," she answered impudently.

Gringers's eyebrows raised in mock disbelief. "You—a thief?"

Lil-el stood up, her chin raised in pretended disdain. "I do not think of it as theft. I prefer to look upon it as a reward for long years of service. Now if you'll excuse me for a few minutes, I'd like a little privacy."

Gringers smiled as he watched Lil-el out of sight. As he began to undress, his glanced touched Bhaldavin. "She's one in a thousand, Bhaldavin. I've never seen her equal."

Bhaldavin saw something in Gringers's face that made him uncomfortable. "Gringers." He hesitated; then because he had to know, he asked, "Do you love her?"

Gringers's eyes were hooded as he bent to untie his boots. He didn't respond for a moment; then he looked up. "Yes, Bhaldavin," he said softly. "I love her. I have loved her since we were children. I will always love her, but perhaps not in the same way you do. Does that make sense to you?"

Bhaldavin thought about it for a few seconds, then nodded, remembering Lil-el's own words about the bond she shared with Gringers. He felt a flicker of jealousy, which he quickly buried.

Finished dressing, Gringers offered to assist Bhaldavin in pulling on the spidermoss vest. Bhaldavin had done fairly well learning how to dress himself with only one hand, but the tight-fitting vest eluded him, and, in disgust, he finally allowed Gringers to help him with it.

Following supper, Diak brought out the magic box, and for the first time, Lil-el experienced its magic. The pictures within the imager were unlike anything she had ever seen before, but once she got past the feeling of disorientation when the scenes changed and the queasiness in her stomach settled down, she lost all fear of the magical device and became immersed in the glimpses of Barl-gan and the Ral-jennob. She found them very much like the men and women she had known all her life, yet there was an alienness about them that showed in their dress, their tools, their very speech. She recognized the trader tongue, though at times the accents were so strange to her ears that she missed what was being said; then too, there were some words she simply didn't recognize at all.

Diak tried to explain some of those words after he turned off the imager, but even he didn't understand all the words.

"Is that all there is?" Lil-el asked, as Diak prepared to put the box away.

"No. There is more," Diak said, "but it is best if taken in small doses. Each night, if we stop soon enough, we'll use the life recorder to learn more about Barl-gan. I think it would be wise for us all to refresh our memories and try to imprint some of the scenes we'll be seeing on our minds so as to be able to recognize landmarks if and when we see them."

"A good idea," Gringers agreed.

Bhaldavin's glance fell on the fire stone as Diak took

it from the box. Desire filled him, and he held out his hand. "May I hold the crystal a moment?"

Gringers leaned forward and grabbed Bhaldavin's wrist. "No. Not after what happened to you the last time."

"That won't happen again."

"How can we be sure?"

Bhaldavin looked at Gringers and realized that no amount of pleading would get him what he wanted. Gringers simply couldn't take the chance of having one of them fall ill at that time. He glanced at Diak as Gringers released him.

"The crystal *will* be mine when we reach Barl-gan?"

Diak looked at Gringers and nodded. "That is our agreement."

After the crystal was put away safely, the talk centered on what lay ahead of them. Diak checked back through several pages of Freeman's log, but there was little mention of the trek over the mountains except for a description of the river of ice that should point the way to the summit.

They decided that they would give themselves seven days in which to find the ice river. If by the end of that time they had not found the river, they would consider returning to the Moss Forests. Seevan and the rafters would probably be gone by then, of course, but they had Lil-el's boat and the two they had hidden, and with the few supplies they had, they could return to Lake Arden without too much trouble.

Bhaldavin saw the grim set to Gringers's lips as Diak spoke about going back. He had a feeling that whether it was seven days or seventy, Gringers would not go back without a fight.

The next morning they filled the empty places in their packs with small chunks of wood, then lashed bundles of lighter branches to the tops of their packs. Blankets were rolled and tied into a sling that could be worn over one shoulder along with their bows.

The day was overcast as they started out, but by mid-day Ra-shun had burned through the cloud cover, and the rest of that day, she and her sister watched over their slow progress upward.

Night followed day. Bundled in their hooded coats and spidermoss mittens, the small band huddled together for warmth as they slept, hoarding their supply of firewood for the colder nights ahead.

Four days of steady climbing made it abundantly clear that Diak was weakening. The stops for rest came more often, and the old man couldn't seem to catch his breath. All of them were feeling the effects of the altitude some-what, but for Diak it was much worse. As they climbed higher and higher, his vision began to blur and eating made him queasy.

Late in the morning of their sixth day of climbing, they finally came upon the glacier mentioned in Freeman's diary. The edge of ice rose straight up and stretched across the valley they'd been following. There were large boulders and mounds of smaller rock at the base of the cliff.

"When the ice melts, it must go underground," Diak observed. He was leaning on Hallon's arm, breathing heavily.

Gringers's eyes glittered with excitement. "Well, we've found what we were looking for—now all we have to do is follow the glacier to the summit. The ice is too sheer to climb. We'll have to try the edge of the valley." He pointed to the right. "That side looks easiest to climb."

They reached the side of the valley a short time later and had their midday meal before tackling the rocky slopes. Gringers was the first up. When he reached a level place, he threw down one end of a rope and hauled the packs up one by one. Then the others climbed up. Hallon and Diak went first, the younger man helping the older over the rough spots; then came Lil-el and Bhaldavin. Theon brought up the rear.

Bhaldavin pulled himself up and over the last ledge of

rock and caught his breath as he looked out past Gringers's legs. He got to his feet, awed by the width and depth of the glacier as he traced its winding length up out of sight.

"We follow that?"

"It's a natural roadway, Bhaldavin," Gringers responded. "Take a look at the rocky peaks to either side and tell me you'd rather climb them."

Bhaldavin looked at the snow-capped peaks that towered over them and shook his head. "No, thank you," he said and pointed to the ice. "That way looks easier."

Gringers looked down at the old man. "Diak, how do you feel?"

"Stop worrying about me," Diak grumbled.

"It'll be an upward climb all the way, but the grade doesn't look as steep as what we've climbed so far. You let me know when you're tired and we'll stop, all right?"

Diak nodded and bent to pick up the small bundle that held the diary and the imager. Hallon interceded. "I'll take it, Diak, until you get your strength back."

Diak looked about ready to protest, then clamped his mouth closed. He knew he was slowing everyone down, but there was nothing he could do about it. He could not go back, and they wouldn't leave him.

"I should've done this years ago, when I was younger," he muttered. "I never should've waited."

Gringers dropped a hand to his shoulder. "We'll make it, Diak. We can't be many days from the summit."

"You hope," Theon said, pulling his pack into place. "We have food enough for two weeks if we're careful, but not enough wood for a daily fire. If it gets much colder up there, we're going to be in trouble."

Gringers gave Theon a look that told him to be quiet and went to help Lil-el and Bhaldavin with their packs. A short time later they stepped out onto the ice and started upward once more.

The valley glacier wound in and out among the towering crags, and as the small band pressed forward, they quickly learned that the road they walked was not without its dangers. Not only was there danger from falling rocks, but there were crevasses in the ice. One particularly large crevasse forced them into a detour to the other side of the valley. Linked by rope, they trudged on, stopping at intervals to rest, sleep, or eat.

On their fourth day on the ice, the sky grew dark, and by late afternoon it began to snow. The wonder of seeing the delicate white flakes of crystalized water fall from the sky was soon lost to the bite of the cold damp wind and the loss of visibility.

Gringers cut toward the valley wall to the right, seeking shelter. An hour later he found a partially enclosed spot under a large slab of rock leaning against the cliffside. They used the rock and their packs as a windbreak and huddled over a small fire. Lil-el stewed dried strips of nida together with a handful of sliced dried nabob roots. They washed the stew down with scalding rayil tea, then melted down some snow to fill their water flasks, which they carried inside their coats.

They posted no guard that night, and all slept fitfully, Diak's rasping cough disturbing their slumber.

The following morning they were confronted by a blanket of white that reached to their calves and doubled the danger of falling into unseen crevices. Gringers swore softly to himself as he led out. The others wisely kept silent.

Chapter 18

COLD. ICE.

Bhaldavin shivered uncontrollably. He had never been so cold before. He couldn't feel his toes any longer, and the stump of his arm ached relentlessly.

Days and nights of nothing but freezing temperatures had taken their toll. Everyone was exhausted, and tempers were short, and to add to their misery, there was very little food left and only a few pieces of wood.

He looked out into the growing darkness. The small ice cave where he, Lil-el, Theon, and Diak sheltered was narrow and confining, but it was better than being out in the strong icy winds that swept down from the summit.

Lil-el moved against him. "Asleep?"

"No," he answered. "Afraid to. Theon? Are you awake?"

There was no answer.

Bhaldavin kicked the small man with a foot. "Theon!"

"What?" came a surly growl.

"Stay awake! Gringers said that—"

"I know what he said: Sleep and you won't wake up. Damn it! I just wish he'd hurry up and get back here. How long have they been gone?"

"Seven or eight hours, I would guess. It's hard to tell with the suns down."

"We should've stayed together," Theon complained. "If not for the old man, we could've."

"How is he?" Lil-el asked.

Diak moaned aloud as Theon checked him over. "He's alive, but his breathing is ragged. If we don't get down off these heights soon, he isn't going to make it."

Diak wasn't the only one affected by the terrible heights they had climbed. All of them were having trouble breathing now, and any great expenditure of energy left them weak and trembling.

Hallon and Gringers seemed to be the least affected by the altitude, but even they had found the constant cold debilitating. Their pinched faces and grim looks as they had set out early that afternoon had mirrored their inner struggle and determination to keep going.

Bhaldavin closed his eyes, remembering the sight that had met them that afternoon as they reached the summit. The mint-green sky had been clear; the cliffs of ice to either side of the valley on the other side of the summit had run down in step formation, and beyond . . . beyond that the valley had literally dropped off into the sky.

Everyone had been shocked by the length and depth of the escarpment that fell thousands of feet straight down into cloud-covered valleys below.

Gringers had stood for a long time just staring out into space, a strange, bemused expression on his face. Then he turned and looked at his companions. "The First Men climbed up. We can climb down. There has to be a way!"

Lil-el's voice brought Bhaldavin out of his thoughts. "Do you think we should start a fire to help them find the way back?"

"We haven't enough wood to keep it going for very

long," Bhaldavin said. "I think we should save it until it's darker."

"I agree," Theon said, "though I'd like nothing better than a hot, toasty fire right now. We'll give them a couple more hours, then start a small fire. We'll use half of what we've got and save the rest for tomorrow."

"Anyone hungry?" Lil-el asked. "There's enough for everyone to have a strip of dried nida."

"Damn near broke a tooth chewing that last piece you gave me," Theon muttered. "I'll save mine and heat it in the fire later, if you don't mind."

"Bhaldavin, you?"

"Not hungry." The thought of food suddenly nauseated him.

"Are you all right?" Lil-el asked him.

He heard the worry in her voice and tried to reassure her. "I'm fine. Just too cold to eat."

"Me too," she said and snuggled closer. She was quiet for a little while, then asked, "Do you think they'll find a way down?"

"Lost your faith in Gringers?" he teased, trying to lighten her mood.

"No. If there's a way down, he'll find it. I just wish he had more to go on. Freeman's diary said nothing about what we'd find on this side of the mountains."

"If Freeman wrote his diary when Diak said he did, then the man did not actually cross these mountains. He only wrote down something that he'd heard from someone else, probably a story that had been passed down from generation to generation."

"The diary doesn't matter now," Theon said. "We have Diak's box to help us now. Once we get down off this mountain, we can use the pictures it carries as our guide. All we have to do is match the landmarks we see in the box with where we are."

"Landmarks change, friend Theon," Lil-el said softly,

especially after two thousand years. It's even possible the Barl-gan the box remembers may no longer exist."

"Don't say that," Theon said darkly. "Don't even think it. It has to be there. It has to!"

Bhaldavin was the first to wake the next morning. Nature called, and he could not ignore her summons. He forced stiff cold muscles to work and stood up. He stepped over Lil-el's legs and leaned down to pull their shared blankets up around her chin. She stirred at his touch.

"Time to get up?" she asked sleepily.

He glanced outside. The sky was light to the east. "Might just as well," he said. "Wake the other two. We have an important decision to make."

He stepped over the dead embers of their fire as Lil-el turned and nudged Theon awake. Theon grumbled, and poked Diak.

"Gringers?" Diak asked, his rheumy eyes peering up over the top of the blankets he shared with Theon.

"He's not back yet," Lil-el said.

Theon joined Bhaldavin outside. The dawn air was cold and still. There was a thick blanket of clouds below the escarpment.

"If that gets up here," Theon observed, "we'll be in for some more snow."

Bhaldavin stamped around, trying to jar some feeling back into his toes. "Do you think we should try to follow them?"

Theon was looking for signs of movement down along the edge of the escarpment. "It's either that or sit here and freeze to death. I would just as soon get moving."

"I agree."

Theon slapped Bhaldavin's shoulder. "Then let's get going, Little Fish. I want *down* off this mountain!"

Lil-el and Diak agreed with the decision to try to follow Gringers and Hallon. Breakfast consisted of a handful of nuts that had to be softened in their mouths before they could be chewed and a strip of nida that was so brittle it could be snapped off in bite-sized pieces and sucked on as they walked. Unable for the past three days to keep food down, Diak settled for several mouthfuls of water.

Progress was slow but steady their first few hours out. The downgrade Gringers and Hallon had followed upon leaving the summit led back from the escarpment's edge, then ran parallel to the cliffs for a good distance. The wind had shifted a dusting of fresh snow across the tracks in several places, but the trail was easily discernible. All of them were thankful for the hard crusty snow that held them up.

Diak's legs finally gave out on him early in the afternoon. Coughing and gasping for breath, the old man simply crumpled.

When Lil-el suggested they stop and rest awhile, Theon wouldn't hear of it. "We've half the day ahead of us," he snarled. "We can't stop now."

"What do you suggest?" she demanded angrily. "Just leave him here?" She had been helping Diak along when he collapsed at her feet.

Theon glared down at the old man. "He's not going to make it anyway. Look at him! He's half-dead already."

Bhaldavin knelt beside the old man and put an arm around his shoulders to help him sit up. Diak's face was pinched and mottled with grayish-white patches; there were dark smudges below his eyes and a fleck of red in the spittle at the side of his mouth.

"Go on," he gasped. "Leave me! I—can't make it!"

Bhaldavin had no love for Diak, but he knew he couldn't leave him alone to die. The six of them had shared too much time and pain together; it had forged a bond that would not be easily broken.

He turned and looked up at Theon. "We can leave him," he said meaningfully, "but Gringers won't like it."

"He'll understand," Theon protested.

Bhaldavin stood and faced Theon. "Will he? I wonder. They've been friends a long time."

Theon growled a curse and swung around, looking down toward the broken path in the snow ahead of them. "All right," he said a moment later, turning back around. "All right. We take him with us, but we can't carry him."

"We could pull him as long as it's downhill," Lil-el said. "We could wrap him in one blanket and pull him along on another. Here, let me show you."

Theon and Bhaldavin followed Lil-el's instructions, and soon they had a cloth carrier rigged. Tied at both ends with rope, the blanket formed a cradle of sorts. Theon took the front end, Bhaldavin the back, and Lil-el walked ahead, keeping watch on the trail.

The downward slope was gradual at first, then it grew steeper. Sometimes the trail wound around huge outthrusting boulders; at other times it followed a reasonably straight line. After a while Lil-el relieved Theon in pulling the blanket carrier, then Theon relieved Bhaldavin.

Ra-shun and Ra-gor passed over the peaks, and by late afternoon the weary travelers were in deep shadow.

"Lil-el!" Theon called ahead. "Start looking for a place to stop for the night. We can't go on much longer, and it will be dark soon."

Lil-el waved to indicate that she understood, and kept walking. Then suddenly she stopped, sure that her eyes were playing tricks on her. Something was moving off to their right, farther down the trail.

She stood still, blinking, wanting to believe, but afraid to. Theon and Bhaldavin approached from behind.

"What's wrong, Lil-el?" Bhaldavin called out.

She pointed to the dark spot that was moving toward them.

Theon took one look and let out a whoop that echoed off the cliffs surrounding them.

The small black spot stopped, then began to move again.

"There's one," Theon said, starting past Lil-el, pulling on the blanket with renewed energy. "But where's the other?"

Gringers and Hallon were too much of a size to be distinguishable at a distance, especially when they were bundled in layers of clothing. Theon, Bhaldavin, and Lil-el continued downslope, exhaustion pushed aside in their need to see who had come to meet them and to find out what had happened to the other one.

Theon's stride lengthened as the distance closed between them and the one below. Bhaldavin had all he could do to keep up. Lil-el finally fell behind.

"Gringers?" Theon yelled. "Gringers—that you?" There was an unmistakable tremor of fear in his voice.

Bhaldavin wasn't surprised when Theon dropped his end of the blanket carrier and ran the last few paces toward the man who waited for them at the bottom of the slope. He still couldn't see if it was Hallon or Gringers.

The man opened his arms to Theon and greeted him with a hug.

"Gringers?" Lil-el said, catching up.

"Yes," Bhaldavin said.

She stepped around Diak and picked up the end of the blanket Theon had dropped. "Let's go find out what happened to Hallon."

Gringers greeted them all with a smile and a hug, then eased their fears about Hallon. "He's all right," he said, kneeling beside Diak. "There was no sense in both of us making the climb back up to you. Diak? Diak, wake up!" He slapped the old man's face sharply.

He looked up at Lil-el. "How long has he been like this?"

"He collapsed early this afternoon. We couldn't carry him, and we wouldn't leave him."

The old man's eyelids fluttered. It took him a moment to focus on Gringers. Somehow he found the strength to smile.

Gringers unwrapped the blanket. "Come on, Diak, get up. You'll freeze lying there." He helped the old man to his feet and steadied him as he took a few steps.

"Can't feel my feet," the old man complained.

"Walking should help," Gringers said. "Hallon and I have found a place to stay the night. It's not much, but with a fire you all can thaw a bit."

"We haven't much wood left," Lil-el said.

"We'll have to make do," Gringers replied.

"Have you found a way down?" Theon asked.

"We think so. It's near a ravine that cuts back toward the escarpment. Come on, let's go. When we reach the shelter, we'll build a fire, heat some water, and make a stew. Then, with a good night's rest, we'll start down tomorrow morning."

Theon came up beside Diak and helped Gringers steady the old man as he walked. Gringers looked at Theon and smiled. "I'm damn glad you didn't wait for me to return. You saved me a long climb up."

"We should've gone with you in the first place," Theon said reproachfully. "It would've saved you the trouble of coming back this far."

"What if we hadn't found a way down, and we had to go all the way back to the summit and try the other way?"

Theon looked over Diak's head, straight into Gringers's eyes. "I *don't* like being left behind, even if it is for my own good."

Gringers met Theon's glance. "I'll remember that," he said carefully.

Chapter 19

*B*HALDAVIN SAT ON THE LEDGE WAITING FOR GRINGERS'S signal. He felt a tug on the rope around his chest and turned over onto his stomach, slowly pushing himself off the ledge. Hallon caught his legs from below and guided his feet onto the shelf of rock beside him. Next came Lil-el, Theon, and Diak.

Everyone looked up as Gringers made the drop last. He inched his way off the ledge and hung by his hands, his long arms and greater stature giving him the height he needed to drop free to the ledge below. Hallon was there to steady him just in case he needed it.

Snow and biting winds had plagued them as they began their descent but, linked by rope, they had slipped, slid, and crawled down to a point where they could stand and proceed on foot.

After two days in the ravine, the wedge of sky overhead grew wider and the rocky slopes opened out into a great chasm that brought them out below the escarpment. The climb down from that point on was by no means easy, but as they left the snow and ice behind, their spirits rose considerably.

Diak began to cough. Bhaldavin saw Gringers offer the old man some water. Diak's breathing had improved slightly as they descended the mountains, but he was still a very ill man; weak with altitude sickness and unable to eat, he was simply wasting away.

As Gringers helped Diak to his feet, Bhaldavin realized that without Gringers's and Hallon's strength to call on, Diak never would have made it that far.

"And he isn't the only one," he said softly, unconsciously brushing the empty sleeve of his coat. How many times had the two men reached out to help him over some difficult place?

Lil-el came up beside him. "Did you say something to me, Bhaldavin?"

He shook his head. "Just thinking aloud."

"About what?"

He glanced up at the mountains. "About climbing that mountain again. You and I would never make it back alone."

She followed his gaze and knew what he was thinking. "Then we'll simply have to return another way, won't we?"

Another way. The words echoed in his mind. Why not another way? Suddenly he felt as if a great weight had been lifted from his shoulders. There was no real reason for them to climb back over the Draak's Teeth. Surely there was a way around them. It might take time, but what did time matter?

He turned to find Lil-el smiling at him. He reached out and pulled her close. "Are all females so smart?" he asked softly.

She laughed. "The majority of us are."

"Lil-el? Bhaldavin?" Gringers called. "Are you ready to go?"

They turned and saw that Hallon and Theon had al-

ready started out, working their way over a mound of
rock that led down to the next shelf below. The two Ni
stepped into line, leaving Gringers to follow with Diak.

The clouds overshadowing the lower valleys lifted by
late afternoon, and strong gusts of warmer air funneled
up through the chasm, bringing the smell of pine trees. It
was late afternoon as they approached the timberline.
Hallon was in the lead.

He stopped suddenly, and Bhaldavin walked into him.
"Look at that view!" he exclaimed.

Bhaldavin had to agree that the scene before him was
not only extremely welcome after several weeks of seeing
nothing but snow, rocks, and ice, but also breathtaking.

The forested slopes that ran down from the mountains
were dark blue-green in color and had the appearance of
a hand-woven carpet, and as the eye followed the contours of the lower hills down to the valleys, the colors
faded to warm greens with shades of yellow sprinkled in
mosaiclike patterns.

Hallon pointed to the left. "Look! Water! It's a string
of lakes, and they must be large to be able to see them
from here."

Gringers came up from behind and studied the scene
before them, his glance returning to the lakes. "Some of
the pictures in the life recorder were in and around a large
body of water. Let's plot a course toward the lakes and
see what we can find."

They reached the timberline before dark and celebrated
their arrival with a large fire that helped melt the last of
the ice from their bones.

Later that evening, Bhaldavin sat beside Lil-el soaking
up the fire's heat. The stump of his arm had ceased to
ache, and though he was exhausted by the last push downslope to the trees, he was filled with a sense of peace. He
had climbed over the Draak's Teeth and had lived to tell
about it. Frostbitten fingers and toes would be sensitive
for a long time to come, but he had come through alive,

and now he was free. Gringers had promised. He and Lil-el would stay with Gringers until they found Barl-gan; then they would go their own way.

Theon brought Lil-el and Bhaldavin a bowl of stew made from the last of their food, which meant that they would be foraging from then on.

"Eat up," Theon said. "There's a little more, if you want some."

Lil-el looked across the fire to where Gringers and Hallon sat. Diak lay between them. Gringers had carried the old man on his back the last part of the way.

"How is Diak?" she asked Theon.

"Gringers is trying to get him to eat a little of the broth. Time will tell if he can keep it down."

"It's been a long time since he's eaten," Bhaldavin said. "It's a wonder he's made it this far."

"His not eating doesn't bother me as much as that cough," Lil-el said. "If we could find some gillan root, we might be able to ease his breathing."

"We can look for some tomorrow," Bhaldavin said, tasting the stew. "But I doubt we'll find any growing up this high."

Their progress down the forested slopes to the lower valleys was slow at first because Diak simply wasn't up to a fast pace. Also, to replenish their food supplies, part of each day was spent foraging for edible roots and berries that would sustain them until they could hunt and fish once more.

Little was found their first three days in the forest, and everyone felt the pinch of hunger by the time they stopped each night.

Lil-el brewed a strong tea that she made from the bark of a young sapling, and as she passed cups around, Bhaldavin drew a handful of short stalks from his pocket and offered one to Theon, then to the others.

Theon eyed the stalk, frowning. "What am I supposed to do with this?"

"Cut the round bulge open and eat what's inside. Lil-el, will you cut one for me?"

"What is it?"

Bhaldavin glanced at Theon. "It's a bee in the larva stage. They have a nutty flavor. They won't fill you up, but it's better than an empty stomach."

Theon watched Gringers, Diak, and Hallon each try one of the larvae, his glance darting from face to face to see their reactions.

"Crunchy, but not bad-flavored," Hallon said, holding out his hand. "May I have another, Bhaldavin?"

Theon hesitated a moment, then cut his stalk open and, without looking at the creature inside, popped it into his mouth and chewed quickly.

Gringers watched Theon out of the corner of his eye and hid a grin behind his cup as Theon made a face and swallowed.

Bhaldavin divided the rest of the larvae and passed them around.

Theon looked down at the three stalks in his hand and quickly handed them to Gringers. "Here. I'm not hungry right now," he said, rising.

"Where are you going?" Gringers asked as Theon turned and stepped away from the campfire.

"Ah . . . nature calls," Theon mumbled, moving into the darkness.

Moments later they heard Theon being sick. Gringers caught Bhaldavin's glance and grinned. "He has a delicate stomach."

Bhaldavin returned the smile. "So it would seem."

Gringers cut open another stalk. "Bhaldavin, if you have any other things like this you know about, tell us what to look for, and together maybe we can find enough for a real meal."

Bhaldavin nodded, pleased to be asked.

* * *

The following days passed quickly. Time not spent walking was spent foraging and watching for landmarks that would match up with the pictures inside the imager.

Lil-el found some gillan root and nightly dosed Diak with its pungent fumes, easing the old man's cough. Everyone was very much aware of the frail oldster and did everything they could to try to help him regain his strength; even Theon pitched in, massaging Diak's legs each night and rubbing him down with an ointment Bhaldavin had made from the thick syrup of the allbey runner, commonly known as tangle vine.

"I didn't know you were so well-versed in herb lore," Lil-el said to Bhaldavin one day. "Where did you learn?"

"From my mother," he answered, thinking back on the many days he had spent learning one plant from another. His childhood seemed a lifetime ago.

Lil-el started to say something else, but stopped, her hand clamping around Bhaldavin's arm. "Smell!"

It took only a second to recognize the odor. He turned full circle, closely scanning the nearby trees. He saw nothing.

Hallon and Diak came up to them. Diak leaned heavily on a walking stick Gringers had found for him. "What's wrong?" Hallon asked.

"Draak," Lil-el said shortly. "Bhaldavin, bring them along. I'll run ahead and warn Gringers and Theon. Be careful!"

"And you," he called after her.

The three hurried after Lil-el, ears and eyes alert for signs of draak. Upon entering the lower forests, they had come across several draak runs, but had not as yet encountered any of the large reptiles.

The smell of draak grew strong as they worked their way down between the trees. Hallon kept a hand on Diak's arm to prevent the old man from slipping on the pine-needle carpet beneath their feet.

Lil-el's voice rose through the air, the strains of "Nardonva" filtering up from below. Bhaldavin waved Hallon and Diak forward, urging them on; then he turned and continued downward, slipping and catching at branches to steady his own descent.

He broke out into the open a few moments later and saw Lil-el standing at the brink of a shallow cliff, a brown draak crouched below her, its head weaving back and forth in a snakelike movement. There was a large cave behind the draak and a litter of bones scattered about the floor of the shallow ravine.

He looked around, searching for Gringers and Theon. Lil-el caught his eye and pointed down. He moved closer to the edge of the cliff and saw Theon sprawled facedown halfway down the side of the ravine. He wasn't moving.

Gringers was down there too, working his way carefully across the shale-covered slope toward Theon. He looked up, saw Bhaldavin, and signaled with one hand.

"He wants you to send the draak away," Bhaldavin told Lil-el.

Lil-el glanced up the ravine and nodded, then changed the song she was singing. The draak's head ceased its weaving, and the large creature rose to its feet; its head almost reached the top of the cliff. Lil-el backed off a little and began walking the edge of the ravine, leading the draak away. It hissed softly as it followed her.

Hallon and Diak appeared behind Bhaldavin. "Where's Gringers?" Hallon demanded, his glance following the draak's progress up the ravine.

"Down there with Theon," Bhaldavin answered.

Hallon stepped to the edge and took in the situation with a glance. He quickly slipped off his pack and freed the coil of rope that hung over the horns of his pack.

Bhaldavin looked up the ravine. He could still see the draak, but Lil-el was lost to sight, her voice growing fainter as she led it away. He started after her, but Hallon caught his arm.

"Where're you going?"

"To help Lil-el."

"Better stay here in case there are more draak around. She'll be all right. She knows what she's doing."

Bhaldavin started to object, but Diak's voice cut him off. "Something moving down there just inside the cave. Get ready, Bhaldavin."

It was a baby draak, only a few weeks old, its spiny red headcrest flopping comically as it waddled out into the daylight.

Bhaldavin glanced down at Gringers and Theon. Neither were in danger from such a young draak, but where there was one, there were apt to be others. He decided it was wisest to stay where he was.

Gringers finally reached Theon. He turned the small man over and checked him for injuries, then signaled to Hallon to throw down one end of the rope, which he quickly fastened under Theon's arms.

"Take him up carefully," Gringers ordered.

Theon regained consciousness as he was being drawn back up the cliffside. Pale, his face smeared with blood and dirt, he cursed softly as Hallon and Bhaldavin pulled him to safety.

Hallon turned back to throw the rope down to Gringers—but Gringers was gone. "Where in the hell did he go?" he growled, searching the shale slopes below.

"There!" Diak pointed.

All eyes turned to see Gringers moving in and around the bones and rock near the draak lair. Suddenly the baby draak moved, hissing a challenge at the strange two-legged creature that had dared enter its home territory.

"Get out of there!" Theon yelled, as Gringers danced around the young draak and leaped up onto a large boulder next to the cave entrance.

The young draak stretched its neck and head as high as it could, but it couldn't reach the strange-smelling thing that was so tantalizingly close. Hissing in anger, it backed off a step and shook its head.

Theon tugged on Bhaldavin's pant leg. "Sing, Little Fish! That draak may be small, but it's still got teeth."

The young draak turned and looked up as Bhaldavin began to sing, then it was caught by the intrinsic notes of song its kind could not ignore.

Gringers waved a hand in thanks and slid down off his perch. They all watched from above as he poked about in front of the cave for a few minutes.

"What's he doing?" Hallon asked.

Gringers stooped down and picked something up. He looked it over, then dropped it and continued on, working his way slowly back toward the side of the ravine.

"What happened, Theon? How did you fall?" Diak asked, while they waited for Gringers.

Theon wiped at the trickle of blood oozing from a cut over his eye. "I was standing where you are right now. No draak in sight, then suddenly it appeared, moving out of the cave so fast it startled me. I turned to run, and suddenly the ground gave way. Gringers reached for me, but missed, then I was falling. I must have hit my head, because I don't remember anything after that until Gringers was putting a rope around me."

Bhaldavin stopped singing as soon as Gringers started climbing. The baby draak watched the man scaling the side of the ravine, but made no noise. Gringers caught hold of the rope Hallon tossed down to him and quickly climbed back up to them.

Theon backed out of the way as Hallon drew Gringers over the edge.

"Are you all right, Theon?" Gringers asked when he saw the blood on Theon's forehead.

"I'll live," Theon replied testily. "Now, how about telling us what you were doing down there. Baby draak or no, you were taking a chance."

Gringers stood and brushed himself off. "I was looking for bones."

"For what?" Theon demanded, allowing Hallon to give him a hand up.

"Human bones, proving that we're not alone on this side of the mountains." Gringers shrugged. "But I didn't find any. It was just a chance."

As they moved back away from the edge of the cliff into the protection of the trees, Bhaldavin glanced up the ravine, looking for Lil-el. She had been gone only a little while, but for some reason he suddenly felt uneasy.

He wasn't the only one to notice Lil-el's absence. Gringers's hand dropped onto Bhaldavin's shoulder. "Seems like she should've been back by now, doesn't it? As soon as Hallon tends Theon's cut, we'll go look for her." Seeing Bhaldavin's worried expression, he smiled. "Don't worry, Bhaldavin. She's probably headed back this way right now. No draak could ever harm her."

Chapter 20 ☙

HOURS LATER, BHALDAVIN AND THE OTHERS WERE MANY
miles from the ravine. They had followed Lil-el's trail
to a point where she must have released the draak and
swung around to return to them; then her trail veered off
sharply, running southward along an open stream, following the path of least resistance.

It had taken Hallon and Gringers only a few minutes
to find the reason for Lil-el's flight: a pawprint belonging
to a huge gensvolf.

The small band hurried along Lil-el's trail, fearing the
worst. Bhaldavin was terrified that they would be too late
to help her. He knew how it felt to be alone in the forest,
running, afraid of every tree shadow or unusual noise.
His thoughts ranged back to the day he had run with
gensvolf at his heels, and he relived the terror that had
driven him, blind and gasping for breath, into the arms
of his enemies—man!

But here there were no swamp farmers, no one to
whom Lil-el might turn to for help, unless there were men

living in the area, descendants of the First Men. It was a faint hope, he knew, because during their trek down out of the mountains, they hadn't seen any signs of civilization: no tilled lands, no roads, no buildings.

The path of broken branches stopped, and they burst out into the open, coming to the edge of a narrow but deep river.

"Did she swim it?" Theon asked, looking doubtfully at the rushing water.

"She might have if she thought she could shake the gensvolf," Gringers said. "What I don't understand is why she didn't just climb a tree."

Diak straggled up, breathing heavily. "Find anything?"

Gringers shook his head. "Hallon, look for tracks upstream. I'll go down. The rest of you stay here."

Bhaldavin looked toward the other shore, searching for signs of Lil-el's passage: broken branches, crushed grass, anything that would give him hope she was still alive.

"Hai! Come here," Gringers called. He was kneeling by the water's edge just a short distance away. Bhaldavin was the first to reach his side.

"What is it?"

"Look! Have you ever seen such a track before? And here," he said, pointing, "another, and beside it the pawprint of a gensvolf."

Bhaldavin drew on memories of time spent in the Deep, but he could not remember ever having seen such a track. The back footpad was wide at the front and tapered at the back; the front three pads were spread apart and had the appearance of bird tracks; a pointed indentation in front of each of the foremost pads indicated a claw of some kind. The size of the print implied a large creature.

Hallon came running up. "What've you found?"

Gringers stood away, allowing Hallon to take a closer look at the prints. "I don't know, but whatever it is, I don't like the look of it. It's either running with the gens-volf or following it—I can't tell which."

"What do we do now?" Theon asked.

"It looks like they've all crossed the river. We'll have to follow, but until we know what we're following, every-one be on alert—bows out and swords ready."

The strongest swimmer, Gringers went across first, trailing a length of rope that he tied to a tree on the other side. Then he returned to help with the packs.

The crossing didn't take long, and as Hallon recoiled the rope, the others spread out searching for tracks. Bhal-davin was the first to find something.

"A bootprint!" he yelled. Further search rewarded him with a handprint where Lil-el had slipped and fallen.

Hallon found several sets of the strange three-toed prints only moments later. "We're dealing with more than one creature, whatever they are," he said. "And judging from the way this print is still holding water, we aren't far behind."

"Good," Gringers said, pushing past Theon and Diak. "Come on, let's go."

Ignoring their wet clothes, they took up the trail, grim now and determined to follow it to its end. The courage and strength Lil-el had shown in staying ahead of her hunters gave them hope that somehow she could outwit them.

Gringers took the lead, followed closely by Bhaldavin. The grueling pace he set soon had the others strung out along the almost invisible trail he followed. A cry from Theon finally made Gringers slow his pace. He stopped and turned and saw no one but Bhaldavin behind him.

"Have you lost the trail?" Bhaldavin demanded as he caught up.

Gringers shook his head. He was breathing deeply, but evenly. "We've left the others behind."

Bhaldavin's need to find Lil-el had washed all thought of anyone else from his mind. He turned just as Theon appeared on their trail. By the time he had reached them, Diak and Hallon were in sight. Both slowed to a walk when they saw the others waiting.

"It was stupid to run ahead like that," Theon snapped, trying to catch his breath. "Who knows what kind of monsters breed in these forests. We've got to stay together!"

Gringers surprised Bhaldavin by apologizing. "I'm sorry, friend. You're right. This is no place to get separated." He slapped Theon on the shoulder. "I keep forgetting I've got longer legs than most."

Diak plunked down on the ground as soon as he reached them. "I can't keep up, Gringers," he panted. "You'll have to go on without me. Leave a trail, and I'll follow. If I see any draak or gensvolf, I'll just climb a tree."

Hallon looked at Gringers. "I can stay back with him if you want me to."

"No," Gringers said. "We'll have to stay together."

Bhaldavin moved away as the others talked, his attention on the ground. He found another series of clawed footprints and was about to call everyone's attention to them, when he noticed that the distance between the prints had changed. He stood and paced them off.

Gringers saw what he was doing and came over. "Found something?"

Bhaldavin looked up. "They're not running any longer. I think they've slowed to a walk. Do you think they've lost her trail?" Hope shone in Bhaldavin's eyes.

Gringers began to follow the footprints. "Let's find out."

Hallon helped Diak up, and they all set out again.

Gringers stopped minutes later and pointed to Lil-el's bootprints. "She's still ahead of them, Bhaldavin, but she's slowed down too."

"I've counted four sets of tracks," Hallon said. "One gensvolf and three of the others. Since they outnumber her, why don't they attack?"

"It could be that they're afraid of her," Diak offered.

"Afraid of Lil-el?" Bhaldavin repeated, disbelieving.

Diak nodded. "If they saw her controlling the draak, they might just be a bit reluctant to tangle with her. Gensvolf are cunning, and like most scavengers, they tend to pick on the weak and wounded. As for the other creatures, who knows what they might fear."

"Well, bird or beast, they travel on two legs and have the running stride of a man."

"Or a derkat," Theon chimed in. "Could it be a derkat?"

Gringers shook his head. "The footprint isn't long enough, and the shaping is wrong. Anyway, derkat are four-toed, not three."

"Then what the hell are they?" Theon asked.

"Only one way to find out," Gringers said. "Let's go. Diak, if you get winded, yell, and we'll—"

A gensvolf's howl stopped Gringers in midsentence. He started running. "Hallon, stay with Diak. Don't leave him behind! Theon, Bhaldavin, follow me!"

Gensvolf were usually silent hunters. Only after a kill did they voice their conquest. For Bhaldavin that run downtrail was a nightmare of whipping branches, slippery footing, and dreadful images of Lil-el being torn apart by the most savage of forest hunters.

Gringers's headlong rush stopped at the edge of a small clearing where marsh grasses stood waist-high.

"See anything?" Theon gasped, coming up behind Gringers.

Bhaldavin was only a few steps behind Theon. He too was breathing heavily.

"Nothing," Gringers said. "I think I've lost the trail. Theon, you go that way, I'll go this way. Look for trampled grass, and keep your eyes open for snakes. Bhaldavin, you wait here for the other two."

Minutes passed. Bhaldavin anxiously waited for Theon or Gringers to announce they'd found the trail again. Behind him, he heard Hallon call. He raised his voice and answered, and a few minutes later the two men appeared. Diak was flushed and coughing.

Theon was the first to return. "No sign of anyone passing that way. Let's go and see if Gringers has had any luck."

He led out, not waiting for anyone's approval. He followed Gringers's path through the grass bordering the clearing. The others followed along behind.

Suddenly they came upon a swath of trampled grass. Several clear footprints indicated that they had found Lil-el's trail again, and that of her hunters.

Theon hesitated and looked across the marshland. All was quiet, and no one was in sight. A slight breeze rippled the tops of the grass, making the dry stalks rasp against one another. It was a lonely sound.

Theon raised his voice. "Gringers! Where are you?"

"Here!"

Gringers stepped into view on the other side of the clearing. "No!" he yelled as Theon started across the grassy lea. "Go around the edge. It's safer. It's boggy in the middle."

"Did you find Lil-el's trail?" Bhaldavin called.

"Yes. Come look."

It took them a few minutes to reach the place where Gringers waited. He was sitting on a fallen tree, wiping mud from his boots as they approached. He pointed to a place at the edge of the clearing where the grass was crushed and broken.

"Lil-el's trail leads into the meadow from over there, and straight into the bog." He indicated the spot they had passed just moments ago. "She must have been halfway across before she realized her danger and tried to veer off, but by that time she was up to her knees in mud and water just like I was. I managed to back out, but I don't think she was able to."

Heart thumping wildly, Bhaldavin turned and looked into the swampy meadow. "You mean she—"

"No, Bhaldavin," Gringers said quickly. "She's not in there still. She got out. I'm sure of it."

"How sure?" Bhaldavin demanded.

"Very sure. I went in from this side and saw where she either crawled out or was pulled out."

Bhaldavin suddenly felt sick to his stomach. "You're saying that the things that hunted her have her now?"

"Yes, I'm afraid so."

A pit of darkness opened in front of him. "She's dead then," he said softly.

"No, Bhaldavin, I don't think so."

"She's dead."

Gringers stood quickly and grabbed Bhaldavin by the shoulders. "Bhaldavin. Look at me."

When Bhaldavin failed to respond, Gringers slapped him sharply across the face. "Look at me, Bhaldavin— and listen!"

Pain pushed the darkness back. Bhaldavin looked up at a scowling Gringers.

"Are you listening to me, Bhaldavin? Do you hear me?"

Bhaldavin nodded mutely and fixed his attention on Gringers.

"We don't know that Lil-el is dead. I don't believe she is. If whatever followed her had wanted her dead, she would have died hours ago. Think about it! The gensvolf is somehow being held back. Whatever it is that hunts with them has brains enough not only to control the gens-volf, but to outmaneuver Lil-el whenever she's tried to circle back to us. No, Bhaldavin, she isn't dead. They want her alive—for how long or for what purpose we don't know, but don't mourn for her yet. I swear, we'll keep after them, and we'll get her back!"

* * *

Darkness finally caught up with them. Tired and depressed, Bhaldavin looked out into the night. He had wanted to go on because Lil-el was out there somewhere, but Gringers was right—to search blindly in the dark would accomplish nothing.

He turned around as Gringers passed him, carrying an armload of branches. Theon already had a fire going, and Hallon was cutting up raw nabob and tree ears for a soup.

Bhaldavin glanced once more at the men, then stepped away from the camp into the darkness of the surrounding trees. He lifted his voice and called Lil-el one last time. His fluting warble was filled with longing and his need to know that she was out there alive and listening.

The lonesome cry trembled on the air; then it was gone. He stood for a long time straining to hear an answer to his call, but all he heard was the soft crackle of the fire behind him.

Chapter 21

*B*HALDAVIN WOKE FROM FITFUL SLEEP AND ATE WHAT had been prepared for breakfast: hot mint tea, a handful of wild jinsa beans, and a pot of overripe kansa cooked down to thick stewlike consistency. Even so small a meal was better than nothing.

It was still dark while they ate, but by the time they had their camp things packed and the fire out, the sky was growing light.

Gringers took up the trail of the splayfooted creatures with an urgency they all shared, and they moved as quickly as they could. Before Ra-shun was a finger length into the sky, they discovered the place where their quarry had rested the night. A stand of close-growing pine had offered Lil-el's captors a modicum of safety from night-wandering draak, and the small stream nearby had offered food. Fishbones and empty snail shells testified to the fact that the hunters were not herbivorous.

"No fire," Theon noted. "They like their food raw."

"Either that or they're ignorant of fire," Gringers said.

"Or," Diak added, "they didn't want to chance giving their location away." He started to poke around under the trees. "Look around, everyone. Let's see what other clues they've left behind."

"We haven't time, Diak," Gringers said. "This place isn't an hour away from the place we camped last night, which means that we're close. We've got to keep moving."

"I just thought we might learn something more about them, something that would help us to—"

"Gringers, here," Bhaldavin cried. "I think Lil-el slept here. See! It looks like she tried to write something, but it's not very clear."

Gringers knelt beside Bhaldavin and pushed aside a scattering of pine needles. He studied the marks on the ground, but could only make out one or two letters.

"I can't read it, Bhaldavin, but at least we know she's alive. Come on, let's keep moving."

They had left the deep woods behind by midday. Streams and small ponds abounded in the lower valleys, and the rolling hills were alive with draak walks. They spotted several nida and a variety of eating birds, which reminded them all that it had been a long time since they'd stopped to have a good solid meal.

The steady pace began to tell on Diak, who wheezed and coughed as they walked along. Gringers finally called a halt to allow the old man to catch his breath. While Gringers pointed out Lil-el's bootprint in the mud at the edge of a stream they had yet to cross, Theon ambled along the edge of the stream, his gaze on the mountains visible through the break in the trees.

"How far ahead are they?" Bhaldavin asked Gringers.

"Hard to tell. Maybe a half hour. We'll catch up today." Gringers looked up. "But if we don't, we won't give up, Bhaldavin."

Hallon hunkered down near the stream and cupped a handful of water to his mouth. He wiped the dribble from his chin and glanced at Diak, who was sitting back, braced by his arms. "Do you think they know they're being followed, Diak?"

"It wouldn't surprise me," Diak responded.

"Then why don't they try to cover their trail?"

"Maybe they *want* us to follow," Gringers suggested.

"A trap?"

"It's possible."

Hallon looked skeptical. "If they planned a trap, they would have to—"

Hallon was cut off by a shout coming from downstream. Everyone turned and saw Theon running back along the other side of the stream. The small man put on a burst of speed and cleared a fallen log in a single leap. He was shouting something as he ran, but it made no sense.

"Draak?" Hallon asked, gathering up his pack.

Gringers helped Diak to his feet. "I don't know. Better get ready to move."

Gringers waded the shallow stream. The others followed. Theon reached them moments later, babbling something about Lil-el.

"What about Lil-el?" Gringers demanded, catching Theon by the arms.

"Heard her . . . singing," Theon gasped. "Back there . . . it has to be her. No other draak singers in the . . ."

Bhaldavin didn't wait to hear any more. He turned and started running, passing Hallon and Gringers before either man could stop him. He heard Gringers yell as he sprinted alongside the stream, but he ignored him and kept going, his thoughts focused on Lil-el. He cleared the same log Theon had hurtled and ran on.

"Bhaldavin, stop! Wait for us!"

He heard Gringers's voice, but it wasn't the one he was listening for, and he ran on.

Gringers shed his pack and was running full tilt as he closed on Bhaldavin. Hallon and the others were far behind.

Bhaldavin slowed so suddenly that Gringers almost overran him. He caught Bhaldavin around the waist as he collided with him.

Bhaldavin twisted out of Gringers's hold as they came to a stop. "Something. Over there!" he cried, pointing.

"Where?" Gringers demanded, his glance flicking over the woods bordering the stream.

Bhaldavin was pointing to several clumps of bushes to their left. "There! Look!"

"I see it. Stand still, Bhaldavin. Don't move," Gringers said softly.

Bhaldavin dropped his arm and stared at the creature standing half-hidden near the bushes. The shadows under the trees made it difficult to see clearly, but he was sure he saw a head, a pair of eyes, a nose, and a large mouth with protruding teeth.

The creature moved around behind one of the bushes, dashed between two trees, and paused behind another bush.

Bhaldavin was sure he saw legs and arms, and the creature was either furred or it wore some type of furred clothing.

"It's shaped like a man," Gringers said softly. "Did you see it clearly, Bhaldavin?"

Hallon appeared, striding through the tall grass at the edge of the stream. When he saw Gringers and Bhaldavin, he turned and called to Theon and Diak, who were behind him. "I've found them."

Gringers spun around, hissing to Hallon to be silent. Then he pointed toward the trees.

Hallon set Gringers's pack down on the ground and approached quietly. He stopped when he saw the shadowy figure in the bushes. "What is it?" he whispered.

"It's man-shaped," Gringers answered, keeping his voice down. "And it's curious."

"Could it be someone from Barl-gan?" Hallon asked excitedly.

"What's going on?" Theon called.

Gringers cursed as the shadowy figure ducked out of sight. He turned on Theon as he and Diak approached. "Quiet, you fool," he hissed angrily.

"What did I—"

"There's someone in the bushes. Quiet or you'll frighten him away."

"Someone? You mean..."

Gringers wasn't listening. He moved up beside Bhaldavin and placed a hand on his shoulder. "Do you see him?"

Bhaldavin pointed to a bush just beyond the tree. Gringers took a few steps forward. The shadowy figure moved again.

"Hello," Gringers called, carefully keeping his voice neutral. "You in the bushes, we mean you no harm. Please come out where we can see you."

Gringers's overture was met by silence.

He tried again, moving forward a few more steps. "Hello. Can you understand me?" He raised his hands and turned them palms up. "We come in peace. We won't hurt you."

A cackle of laughter erupted from the bushes, and the shadowy form stepped back, disappearing into the undergrowth.

Gringers lunged for his pack. "Come on! Let's try to follow it."

The others ran after Gringers as he plunged into the woods, weaving in and out between the trees and running a gauntlet of low branches that caught at their hair and clothing, slowing their progress.

Bhaldavin ran behind Theon. He heard Hallon and Diak behind him, but soon the snap of branches and Hallon's curses grew fainter. He lost sight of Theon for a few moments, but followed the path of still-moving branches until he came upon Gringers and Theon standing in a relatively open spot under a large aban tree.

Gringers glanced at him as he approached. "Where are the others?"

"Behind me somewhere. What happened to the —the creature you were following?"

"I lost it." Gringers looked past Bhaldavin and raised his voice, calling Hallon's name.

Hallon heard and answered, and a few minutes later appeared, pushing his way through the bushes, Diak following close behind. The old man looked pale and he was coughing again.

Gringers went to Diak and told him to sit down.

"What now?" Theon asked as Gringers offered Diak a drink of water.

Another strange burst of laughter answered Theon's question. All heads turned. The manlike creature stood watching them from the shelter of another tree. Only its head and one arm were visible as it peeked out of hiding. A thatch of short brown hair covered the top of its head.

Gringers stood up slowly. The creature laughed again and stepped back out of sight. Gringers drew his knife and advanced cautiously. Theon and Hallon flanked him, both moving out and away as they neared the tree.

Bhaldavin and Diak watched as the three moved in on their target. Gringers was the first around the tree. Hallon came around the other side to meet him; then Theon disappeared just as another burst of laughter filled the afternoon air.

Bhaldavin helped Diak to his feet and gave the old man the support of his arm as they went to see what Gringers and the others were doing. They found the three men studying two very clear footprints near the base of the tree.

Gringers looked up. "The footprints belong to the same kind of creature that took Lil-el."

Theon stood up as something moved in the bushes. "There he is again," he cried. "Look! I think it wants us to follow."

Gringers looked in the direction Theon pointed. The creature laughed again and beckoned with one hand. They were close enough now to see that it was dressed in furred vest and leggings.

"Do we follow it?" Hallon asked.

"It's that or go back and try to pick up the trail we were following before," Gringers responded. He looked to Diak. "What do you think?"

"Let's follow it. Go ahead; I'll try to keep up."

Gringers picked up his pack and helped Diak up. "Let's go then. Hallon, stay with Diak, and don't get too far behind."

The man-creature darted away as soon as Gringers and the others headed in his direction. His laughter guided them through tangled undergrowth and up and down narrow river ravines. As the minutes passed, the wild scramble through the woods took on the semblance of a game.

Gringers quickly realized that Diak would not be able to keep up with the pace and deliberately stopped, testing the man-creature to see what it would do.

"Did you lose him again?" Hallon asked as he and Diak caught up.

"Yes and no," Gringers replied. "I believe he's off that way."

Hallon frowned. "We aren't going to go after him?"

"No. We'll wait a few minutes. I want to see if he'll circle back once he realizes we aren't following him."

"And if he doesn't?"

Gringers slapped his cousin's shoulder. "Then we'll have to try to follow his trail. It will be slower, but—"

Theon dug Gringers in the side with an elbow. "He's back!"

Gringers turned and called out. "You, ahead! We will follow you, but not at a run. Do you understand?"

A ripple of insane laughter was Gringers's answer.

"I'm beginning to wonder if following this—man-thing

is wise," Theon muttered. "What if he's just playing with us, leading us in the wrong direction?"

"We've come too far to turn back," Gringers said. "Let's go. We'll keep to a walk and see if our guide stays with us. Diak, how is it with you?"

Diak nodded, saving his breath.

Hours passed. The creature they followed had ceased its strange laughter and now moved ahead of them silently, always carefully maintaining its distance.

As the afternoon waned and shadows began to lengthen, their guide led them out into the open to the edge of a lake. The distant shore was barely visible.

The man-creature walked eastward along the shore, looking back every once in a while as if to make sure Gringers and his band still followed.

Suddenly there was a movement at the edge of the forest. The man-creature was so intent upon those behind him that he failed to see the draak until it was upon him.

"Sing, Bhaldavin!" Gringers cried.

Bhaldavin wasn't sure he was close enough to help, but the beginning notes of "Nar-donva" were in the air as he raced down the lakeshore behind Gringers.

The man-creature saw his danger and leaped aside, barely missing the draak's teeth; then he was down and rolling. He pulled something from somewhere inside his furred clothing, and a second later, a flash of light shot from his hand toward the draak's head.

The draak roared in anger as the light touched it. It threw itself backward, then circled and came at the man-creature again. Another flash of light caught the draak in the chest.

Bhaldavin's song was drowned by the beast's roar of pain.

The light struck once more, and this time the draak had had enough. It turned and dove for the forest, crashing back into the shelter of the trees before the light could strike again.

The man-creature was just getting to his feet as Gringers and Bhaldavin ran up. He raised a small silver-colored box and pointed it at them. With his other hand he made a halting gesture.

Neither Gringers nor Bhaldavin could have named the object in the man-creature's hand, but the meaning of his stance was unmistakable! If threatened, he would retaliate with his strange light weapon.

When Theon and the other two arrived, Gringers ordered them to stand quietly, never once taking his glance from the ragged-looking being standing before them.

The man-creature slowly lowered the box in his hand.

"Give him a bath and cut his hair and he looks just like us," Theon said softly.

"Except for his feet," Hallon added.

The man-creature shifted uneasily under the scrutiny of the men, his splayed feet and long toenails creating the same strange footprints they had been following for the last two days.

"Are you all right?" Gringers asked, carefully spacing the words.

The man-creature looked at Gringers, then finally nodded.

"He understands!" Gringers took a deep breath, trying to keep the excitement from his voice.

"Who are you?" he asked. "Where do you come from?"

There was no response.

"Where are you taking us?"

The man-creature pointed east, then made a gesture with his free hand.

Gringers shook his head. "I'm sorry. I don't understand."

The sign was repeated, but still no one understood.

Bhaldavin stepped forward. Ignoring the weapon that the man-creature raised, he held out his hands. "Please, we look for another who is like me. She has green hair and crystal eyes and she sings to draak. Have you seen her?"

The man-creature took a moment or two to respond; then he nodded.

"Do you know where she is? Can you take us to her?"

There was no response.

Gringers pointed to the box in the man-creature's hand. "What is that?"

The man-creature glanced at a dead branch lying a short distance away. He pointed the box at the branch, and a stream of light shot out to engulf the branch. There was a small crackle of sound, and the branch burst into flame.

"Damn!" Theon stepped back a pace or two.

"Gringers," Diak cried softly. "It's another magic box. It means we've found the men of Barl-gan!"

Gringers was still staring at the branch as if stunned.

Hallon laid a hand on Gringers's shoulder. "He's leaving. Do we follow him?"

Looking up, Gringers saw that the man-creature was already several hundred paces away. For the first time Bhaldavin could remember, Gringers looked indecisive. Bhaldavin adjusted his pack, and without a word to anyone, he started out. If there was even one chance in fifty that Birdfoot knew where to find Lil-el, he was going to follow him.

"Wait, Bhaldavin," Gringers called. "We're coming."

Chapter 22 🦅

TRAVELING AFTER DARK WAS UNWISE BECAUSE THAT WAS the time when both draak and gensvolf left lair and den to hunt. But their guide showed no inclination to stop, continuing on to turn from the lakeshore and lead them back into the forest. When it grew too dark to see, he lighted their way with his strange box. Awed by the light weapon Birdfoot carried, Bhaldavin was careful to keep his distance.

They walked for some time in darkness, wading shallow streams and winding their way down barely perceptible pathways. The land began to rise gradually.

"Gringers!" Hallon cried suddenly. "Diak is down!"

"Damn!" Gringers hissed softly. "You," he called. "You, ahead of us. We have to stop."

Their guide turned at the sound of Gringers's voice.

"He's coming back," Bhaldavin announced. He moved aside as Birdfoot approached with his light.

Diak was clutching his chest, and his face was twisted in agony. The attack lasted only a few seconds; then Diak

222

began to breathe easier. Slowly he opened his eyes. "Gringers?"

"I'm right here, Diak. Don't try to talk. Just relax. Where do you hurt?"

"Chest. Felt like something tore loose."

"Does it still hurt?"

"No. The pain is going."

Bhaldavin looked at Birdfoot while Gringers checked Diak over. It was the closest any of them had been to their guide. A backwash of light from the small box touched Birdfoot's face. His nose was thin, his eyes deeply sunken. The protruding upper teeth made the face appear long. Heavy bushy eyebrows almost connected over the nose. An unpleasant sour smell emanated from him.

Gringers looked up at Birdfoot. "He can't walk any farther tonight. He *has* to rest."

Birdfoot pointed to Gringers and motioned him to pick the old man up.

"You want me to carry him?" Gringers asked. "Where? To some place close?"

Birdfoot nodded.

Gringers nodded to Hallon. "Help me pick him up. Careful."

Birdfoot started walking as soon as Gringers had Diak in his arms. There was nothing to do but follow.

A short time later, Hallon relieved Gringers of Diak's weight, but had carried him only a short distance when suddenly they came to a wall of rock. Birdfoot led them toward a narrow fissure that turned out to be a wedgelike opening in a wall of stone.

"I don't like places like this," Theon complained as they entered the fissure. "What if there's a rockslide? We'd be buried before we could even turn around."

"Quiet!" Gringers snapped. "Just keep moving."

Theon muttered darkly, then fell silent, and kept as close to Gringers as possible.

The fissure widened slightly, and a few minutes later they stepped out onto what appeared to be a stone terrace. They followed their guide to the left and down a half-dozen man-made steps. Birdfoot stopped in front of a wooden door.

A building! The first they had seen on this side of the mountains. Birdfoot's light gave no hint as to the dimensions of the building, but Bhaldavin got the impression of great size. The battered door swung inward on squeaky hinges. The room beyond the door was long and narrow; the stone floor was littered with dry leaves. Four large open windows faced east.

Birdfoot closed the door behind them and walked past, beckoning them to follow him through another doorway and down some steps.

There were wooden benches in the next room and a fireplace with dry fuel stacked neatly for use. Birdfoot quickly built a four-tiered pile of branches and lighted them using his strange box. Once sure that the fire had caught, he stood and stepped away, offering the fire to his guests.

Hallon began to make Diak comfortable with blankets near the fire.

"Is this where we stop?" Theon asked.

Gringers glanced at their guide. "I guess so. Let's see what we have left for food."

"I wonder if Birdfoot is hungry?" Bhaldavin asked softly as Theon helped Gringers look through their packs.

Theon snorted. "Birdfoot! I like that. It's a perfect name for him."

"Keep your voice down," Gringers admonished, glancing at Birdfoot, who had moved back into the shadows.

"Are we going to invite him to eat with us?" Theon asked, whispering.

"Yes. Maybe we can get him to talk to us."

Theon glanced at their guide, then turned back to

Gringers. "Do you think he is like the First Men? I mean, maybe we aren't their descendants if they're all like him."

"Birdfoot, as you call him, is not exactly what I was expecting to find," Gringers admitted.

"Gringers!"

Bhaldavin's cry came from the other side of the room. He was standing in an open doorway looking back at them. "He's gone. As soon as you turned your back, he left. I was going to follow him, but he turned off his light when he saw me."

Gringers picked up a lighted branch. "Theon, you and Bhaldavin stay by the fire with Diak. Hallon and I are going to do a little looking around."

They weren't gone long, but Theon looked greatly relieved when they returned. "Did you find him?"

Gringers settled down by the fire. "No. Just more rooms like this one. All empty."

"Is this Barl-gan?"

"I don't know, Theon. It could be."

"Are we going to stay here the night?"

Gringers dropped another small branch into the fire. "It looks safe enough, and Diak is in no condition to do any more walking right now." He slapped Diak's leg affectionately. "Are you, old man?"

"I'll be all right by morning," Diak answered. "I'm just a bit tired, is all."

"Do you think Birdfoot will be back tonight?" Theon asked.

"We'll keep a watch just in case. If he doesn't return by morning, we'll do some exploring on our own."

Bhaldavin joined the men near the fire. "Gringers, do you think Lil-el is somewhere nearby?"

"I'd say so, yes. Our three-toed friend indicated he'd seen her, so he probably knows where she is now, and since he brought us here, I wouldn't be surprised if his friends didn't bring Lil-el here too. I'm hoping we'll find out tomorrow."

Hallon filled a small pan with water and rigged it to hang over the fire. "I think this *is* Barl-gan," he said, turning to Gringers. "That light box Birdfoot carried is proof that some of the knowledge of the First Men has not been lost."

"It's a wondrous tool," Gringers said.

"More weapon than tool, I'd say," Theon commented.

"It seems to be both," Diak said. "That he didn't use the weapon on us when it would've been so easy for him to do so makes me wonder what he sees in us."

Theon cracked a hait nut and popped the meat into his mouth. "His next meal maybe. Personally, I didn't like the look of Birdfoot's teeth. I'd bet he could crack bone with a single bite, and I don't mean fish or bird bones."

Gringers frowned. "You're gruesome."

Theon gave him a lopsided grin. "Just considering all the possibilities, friend."

Bhaldavin was the last on watch that night. He walked to the open doorway leading to the room above theirs and glanced out through the open windows. Streaks of mint green had appeared in the sky, signaling Ra-shun's return.

He turned back to the shadowy room behind him. It was time to wake the men and continue their search for Lil-el. He was halfway across the room, when suddenly he saw a flicker of movement in the doorway on the other side of the room.

"Gringers, Hallon, Theon. Wake up!"

The three men scrambled to their feet, weapons in hand, just as Birdfoot and his cohorts formed a loose circle around them. Bhaldavin backed up until he stood with the others. He counted seven man-creatures. Three had feet similar to Birdfoot's, the other three had feet more closely resembling a true man's foot, but even they seemed outsized and lumpy.

Birdfoot faced Gringers, his light box pointed at

Gringers's chest. One other held a similar weapon, the other five were armed with long knives.

"Put your weapons down."

The order came from out of the darkness near the lower doorway. "Obey, and you will not be harmed."

A short hunched-over figure moved out of the darkness and limped forward. A huge gensvolf stalked beside him, held in check by a rope around its neck.

A shiver coursed down Bhaldavin's spine as the gensvolf and his master came to a stop beside Birdfoot. He had never heard of anyone taming a gensvolf.

A man's face peered out from under the hooded cloak that covered the figure from head to feet. The man's beard and hair were white; wrinkles about his eyes and mouth spoke of advanced age.

Theon tugged on the back of Gringers's tunic. "Look at his feet," he whispered.

"Normal. I see."

Pale blue eyes regarded Gringers and the others with interest. "Do you put down your weapons, or must we take them from you?" The words were in trader.

Gringers glanced around at the circle of faces. Two of the man-creatures were quite fair to look upon; the others were all deformed in some way: too large teeth, a broken nose, blotchy complexion, a fold of skin that showed the scars of stitching.

The old man touched Birdfoot's hand. A flash of light shot out. Hallon yelled as the light touched his wrist. His sword clattered to the stone floor as he clutched his hand to his chest.

Birdfoot swung the light box back to cover Gringers before the man could even think to move.

"I won't ask again," the old man said.

Gringers slowly lowered his sword point to the floor. "Are we your prisoners?"

"Perhaps. It might depend upon where you come from."

Gringers straightened. "We come from the swamps of

Amla-Bagor over the Draak's Teeth. We look for Barl-gan."

"The Draak's Teeth? What are they?"

"The mountains to the west," Gringers explained.

"There is no way over those mountains. They are impassable."

Gringers glanced at Birdfoot, then looked back at the old man. "I don't wish to argue with you, but we *did* cross the mountains."

"I think you are lying. I think you come from the Wastelands to spy on us."

Gringers shook his head. "No. You're wrong. We didn't come to spy or to take anything from you. We only come to *find*. Among my people there is a legend about the First Men. We call them the Ral-jennob or Sun Travelers. It's said that they came to this world on a great metal ship; that they founded a city called Barl-gan. It is told that they had great medicines that prevented them from getting sick." He pointed to the weapon in Birdfoot's hand. "And that they had magic weapons like that."

Gringers looked at the old man. "I swear, we want nothing from you but the truth behind these legends."

"You want the truth of Barl-gan," the old one said softly.

Gringers's face lighted with excitement. "Yes!"

The old man threw back his head and cackled, a laugh reminiscent of that which had come from Birdfoot. "Death is the truth!" he cried. "The only truth! Death stalks the halls of Barl-gan dressed in robes of darkness and decay. He is a cruel lord. He kills slowly and painfully because he takes away all hope."

The old man stepped closer to Gringers, keeping the gensvolf close beside him. "Lord Death is the truth of Barl-gan, and none can escape him."

"You're just trying to frighten us," Theon muttered.

"Frighten?" The old man had heard Theon's softly spoken words, and he shook his head. "No, I don't try to frighten. I only warn."

He looked up at Gringers, a malicious smile on his wrinkled face. "Well, what will it be? An escort to Barl-gan? Or a run back to the Wastelands?"

Gringers glanced at his friends, then looked down at the light box still pointed at his chest. "We wish to be taken to Barl-gan," he said firmly.

"Then give us your weapons. Only the citizens of Barl-gan are allowed weapons in the city."

Gringers handed Birdfoot the hilt of his sword. "Give them your weapons," he ordered the others, "and gather our things. Diak, can you walk this morning?"

Diak got to his feet. "I can walk, but before we go, may we ask your names?" he said, looking at the old man.

The old man hesitated, then nodded. "A reasonable request. I am Kelsan Watcher." He touched Birdfoot's arm. "This is my grandson, Gils Watcher. The others are Aldi, Enar, Rolf, Davi, Jon, and Lachen. And your names?"

"I am called Diak. These are Gringers, Hallon, Theon, and Bhaldavin. There was one other with us. We became separated several days ago. Her name is Lil-el. Gils hinted that he might know where she was. Is it possible that she's been taken to Barl-gan ahead of us?"

Kelsan's smile widened. "It's possible. I was told that a woman had been found wandering the forest west of Lake Thessel." His glance found Bhaldavin. "Her hair was said to be green, like yours. Is it dyed?"

"No," Bhaldavin answered. "We are Ni."

"Ni. I do not know that word."

"The Ni-lach are known as the Green Ones. They were here on this world before the First Men, or so it is said. Where we come from, Ni and men work together to survive," Gringers said.

"How many of you are there?"

"Ni or men?"

"Both."

Gringers shrugged. "There are probably three to four thousand rafters in Amla-Bagor. Annaroth must hold fifteen to twenty thousand people, and Port Bhalvar and Port Sulta are even larger. I don't know that anyone has ever even tried to take a count."

"He lies!" one of the bird-footed men growled. "There are a few small tribes in the Wastelands, and that's all. He only tries to impress us with—"

"But what if he tells the truth?" another cried. "It would mean that Barl-gan can live again. With new blood we could—"

Kelsan cut them both off. "Enough said. Come. Bring them. Barl-et-Bara will learn the truth from them."

"Who is Barl-et-Bara?" Theon asked.

Kelsan's chin lifted with pride. "Barl-et-Bara were chosen by God to lead us. They are strong, intelligent, and unique as only God could make them. Truth for truth, they will give as they receive. Lie to Bara, and he will know it. Lie to Barl, and he will summon those who serve Lord Death."

Chapter 23 ✎

*B*ARL-GAN WAS A VAST MOUNTAIN CITY BUILT ON TIERS of rock that clung to the mountainsides as a child clings to its mother. It was built at the easternmost edge of Lake Thessel, which was connected to the other lakes farther east by the Selvarn River. The scenes in Diak's box hadn't prepared any of them for the size of the city. The stone buildings were utilitarian in design. Dirt and stone paths led past massive buildings, some of which were actually cut out of the mountainsides; narrow, switchback stairways wound up and down between the different levels, past scrubby fruit trees and garden plots long untended.

Bhaldavin glanced in through an open doorway of one of the stone buildings and thought he saw something slink around in the shadows. He remembered Kelsan's words about death stalking the halls of Barl-gan and moved closer to Gringers, who walked beside him.

"I don't like this place," he said softly.

"You're not alone," Gringers replied. "It's the emptiness. We've been in the main city for over an hour and have yet to see anyone. Thousands must have lived here at one time. What happened to them, I wonder?"

"Gringers! Diak has to stop," Hallon called.

Gringers stopped and turned. Diak's face was chalky white, and he was breathing hard.

"Can't stop now," Kelsan said, coming back from the lead. "Barl-et-Bara waits for us."

"My friend is old and sick," Gringers began.

"No matter," Kelsan interrupted. "It isn't wise to make Barl-et-Bara angry. The old one can be carried. Gils! See to it!"

Birdfoot signaled to two of his men. They formed a chair with their arms and quickly scooped Diak up.

Diak caught Gringers's glance and shook his head. "I'll be all right with them. Go on."

Gringers looked at Hallon. "Keep an eye on him."

"Will do."

Theon caught Gringers's arm as they started out again, following Kelsan up a narrow dirt pathway to the next level. "The more that old man talks about Barl-et-Bara, the more nervous I get," he whispered. "I'm beginning to think it was a mistake to give up our weapons."

"We had no choice," Gringers said. "You saw what they did to Hallon. I've no doubt but that Birdfoot could've killed him with that light weapon if he'd wanted to."

"So what are we going to do?"

"Nothing for the moment. We came to learn about Barl-gan, and I for one do not intend leaving here until I satisfy my curiosity."

"Curiosity could kill you in a place like this, I think."

Theon frowned. "There's something about old Kelsan that rubs me the wrong way, and that's saying nothing about Birdfoot and the others. I've got a bad feeling about this place. It tells me to get out of here as fast as I can."

Bhaldavin felt much the same, but for him there was

no choice of running away, not with Lil-el being held prisoner somewhere in the city.

They continued their upward climb and finally reached a large plateau where stone buildings were sheltered under giant aban trees. A great stone wall defended the plateau; not even the largest of land draaks would be able to damage such a thick wall.

A bird-footed youth and an old woman stood guard at the gate. Both were dressed in furred vests and pants. The old woman's face and scrawny arms were pock-marked and discolored; her toothless grin as they passed made Bhaldavin nervous. He turned and looked back and saw the old woman and boy swing the gate door closed, its unoiled hinges squawking loudly in the morning air.

Theon met Bhaldavin's glance as the lock on the gate *thunked* into place. "Stay close, Little Fish. We don't want to lose you like we did Lil-el."

Gringers started to speak, but was interrupted by sharp squeals of excitement. Suddenly six or seven children swung down from nearby trees. They dropped to the ground and raced toward the newcomers, waving sticks and laughing. They varied in size and age, the youngest being no more than seven. Five were boys, two were girls. Three displayed birdfeet and one a too-large skull.

They ran past Kelsan and his men and bounded in and out around Gringers, Theon, Hallon, and Bhaldavin, their sticks tapping legs, stomach, or buttocks as they shouted and numbered their victims.

Theon instinctively dropped to a fighting stance, but Gringers maintained his poise, the delighted looks on the faces of Kelsan and his men alerting him to the meaning behind the gamelike performance of the children.

"Stand still," he said to the others.

Theon received a harder blow to the legs and lunged after the boy who had chosen him as a target. Gringers caught Theon by an arm and brought him up short.

"Stand still, I said," Gringers hissed softly. "It's only a game."

"Game be damned," Theon snarled. "That hurt."

Kelsan let the children run a few seconds longer, then he clapped his hands twice and told them to behave themselves. He gave Theon a look of disapproval, then waved them all forward.

"Come. Barl-et-Bara waits for you."

Bhaldavin kept a wary eye on the children as they joined the small procession, for they were like no other children he had ever seen. There was something in their faces, in their eyes, in the very way they walked that seemed feral and threatening.

They passed between two uniform rows of trees. There were food gardens beyond the trees in both directions. The few people who were working in the gardens seemed to pay no attention to the arrival of the strangers.

They finally reached the steps of a large stone building that rivaled the aban trees for height. Rising above the building stood four narrow, windowless towers.

"The way this city is built reminds me a lot of Port Bhalvar," Gringers said to Theon as they followed Kelsan up the steps. "The climbing stairways, the terraced gardens. Think of the years it must have taken to build such a place."

"I'm thinking more about the people needed to build it. Where is everyone? I don't like this, Gringers. I still think we should get out of here while we are all in one piece."

"Not yet, friend. If our climb over the Draak's Teeth is to mean anything at all, we've got to have some kind of proof that the legends behind Barl-gan are true."

"Would one of those light weapons be proof enough?"

"It would be a start, but don't get light-fingered too soon. Maybe we can trade for what we want."

"Trade? What've we got to trade with?"

"Diak's box should be worth a few of those weapons, I'd think. Maybe a lot more."

The steps brought them up to a long, narrow porch that ran the length of the building. The doors leading inside stood open. The light in the first room they entered came from the windows facing north, but the windowless rooms beyond were lighted by glowing panels on the ceilings. At first Bhaldavin thought the strange light panels were made of thin sheets of vellum that would allow the outside sunlight to come through, then he remembered the walls of stone rising above the ground floor and knew that there was no way the sunlight could penetrate such stonework.

The hall they walked through was bare except for a series of paintings that were placed at various intervals along the walls. The paintings varied in style; some were portraits, others depicted scenes in and around the cliffside city.

Bhaldavin had seen little of man's artwork and was pleasantly surprised by the depth and color in the paintings. He became so engrossed with one of the paintings that he was left behind.

A poke in the back startled him out of his reverie. He turned to find Birdfoot standing behind him, motioning him to move along. He glanced one last time at the strange but beautiful four-legged creature in the painting and hurried after Gringers and the others, wondering if the animal the artist had painted was a real thing or a dream thing. The sky in the picture had been blue, not mint green, and the flat land with its oddly shaped rock formations—was there ever such a place on Lach?

If men had come from another world, he thought, perhaps what he'd just seen was something from that other world. The idea intrigued him, and he would have given much to stop and take a closer look at the rest of the paintings in the hall.

They passed ten doors off the hall. Three stood open,

revealing rooms that looked cluttered but comfortable. As they passed, several men stepped out into the hallway, their curious glances and excited voices following the new-comers toward the set of double doors at the end of the hall.

Kelsan knocked, and the doors swung open. Birdfoot and his men herded their charges into the room beyond and closed the door on those who had followed.

Gringers and the others looked around the large, windowless room. All they saw was a huge chair sitting in front of a long panel of red drapes on the far side of the room, and a few less-ornate chairs scattered about the room.

Kelsan spoke softly to the old man who had opened the doors. The old man, bent with some kind of crippling disease, whispered to Kelsan, then motioned them all forward.

Bhaldavin saw the old man touch several places on the wall, and instantly the lighted panels overhead dimmed.

"Come," Kelsan said, leading them toward the other side of the room. "Barl-et-Bara will be with us soon. We'll await him over here."

Theon was unable to restrain his curiosity any longer. "Where does the light come from, Kelsan? How do you control it?"

Kelsan glanced up, then back over his shoulder, smil-ing mysteriously. "From the wind towers, of course. But I forgot—the Wastelanders have lost all knowledge of electricity, haven't they? Just as they have lost all knowl-edge of their beginnings. It's a shame your people will not cooperate with us. We could both gain from—"

There was movement behind the drapes. Kelsan stopped speaking and signaled his men. Birdfoot and the rest of his men moved up behind Gringers, Hallon, Theon, and Bhaldavin. The pinpricks of knives were felt by all.

"Stand quietly," Kelsan said softly, "and you will not be hurt."

Kelsan turned and faced the drapes. "All is secure, my lords."

The draperies moved, and two men stepped out of the darkness behind the chair into the dim light.

Theon's eyes started from his head. "It can't be. It's impossible!"

Gringers's indrawn breath of astonishment was matched by an inarticulate cry from Hallon. Diak and Bhaldavin just stared, unable to believe what they were seeing.

Bhaldavin swallowed again and again, fighting for breath and trying to stop the queasiness in his stomach. He blinked and then shook his head, praying that the terrible apparition before him would disappear, for Barl-et-Bara, lords of Barl-gan, were two in one, an impossibility that refused to vanish.

They were tall and strong-looking. From the hips down, they were as one man; from the stomach up, they were two. Their outside arms hung down from their sides in normal fashion, their other two arms were carried about one another's waist in a casual embrace. Their faces were identical. They had straight noses, full lips, and deep-set, dark eyes that glittered with intelligence. Thick black hair framed both faces. The right head went unadorned, the left wore a golden band around its forehead and a single gold earring in its left earlobe. The face to the right was sober, the one to the left wore a scornful smile, as if pleased to know that his guests were startled if not frightened by their appearance.

"These are my lords, Barl-et-Bara," Kelsan announced. "My lords, I bring you visitors. They are named Gringers, Hallon, Diak, Theon, and Bhaldavin."

The head to the left grinned and spoke, his booming voice filling the room. "I am Barl."

"I am Bara," the other head said in a more modest tone. "We welcome you to Barl-gan."

Too stunned to speak, Gringers and the others simply stared.

"Welcome is not exactly as I would have said it, Bara," Barl countered, "until we know where they come from and why they're here."

Bara turned to his brother. "If you had listened to the green-haired woman, you would already know that."

"I listened," Barl snapped. "But that doesn't mean I *believed* all she told us."

"No one can lie to me. You know that. What she said was true. It means that we are no longer alone. Can't you see what—"

"I *see*! More than you credit me with. Now be still. I'm leader this year. Things will be done as I say."

"Barl, would you please listen?"

Barl glared at his other half. "No! Not now! We can talk later, when we're alone."

Theon started to giggle uncontrollably. Gringers grabbed him by the arm. "Quiet! What's gotten into you?"

"He's arguing with himself," Theon sputtered. "I don't believe it. It can't be real."

Gringers didn't like the wild look in Theon's eyes. He shook him. "Stop it. You're going to get us in trouble."

"Trouble?" Theon crowed. "No trouble. It's all an illusion. Don't you see? It's not possible. It can't be real."

"Theon!" Gringers cried, trying to hold on to the smaller man as he backed away. "Hallon, help me."

But before Hallon could move, Barl-et-Bara was there, pushing Gringers aside. "Not real?" Barl yelled. "Filth! Guttershit! Ratface! I'll show you real!"

Kelsan's men moved in to restrain Gringers, Hallon, Diak, and Bhaldavin only a moment or two after their lords attacked Theon.

"No, Barl," Bara cried as Barl pulled Theon from his feet. "Put him down. *Put him down!*"

Crushed up against Barl's chest, face-to-face with a nightmarish being who screamed obscenities at him, Theon gibbered incoherently, flailing and kicking wildly.

Bara caught at his brother's arm, trying to break his

hold. Barl swore and swung his right elbow up and back, catching Bara in the mouth.

"Leave me alone," Barl cried.

Blood dribbled from Bara's lips as he renewed his struggle with his brother. "Barl! Let him go!"

Barl's eyes glittered with malicious contempt. "Is that what you really want, Brother? For me to let him go?"

"Yes."

Barl laughed an ugly laugh, caught Theon up by a leg and arm, raised him high over his head, and hurled him across the floor. "So be it."

The snap of bone was audible as Theon hit the stone floor. His scream of pain left Gringers white with rage. He ceased his battle with the two men clinging to his arms and glared at Kelsan.

"If they are your lords, Kelsan Watcher, I think you have chosen unwisely." Gringers spoke loud enough for all to hear.

Barl-et-Bara looked at Gringers. Barl's face was flushed with triumph. Bara was frowning and wiping blood from his lips.

"Boldly said, stranger," Barl snapped. "Do you also wish a taste of my reality?"

"That is precisely what he wants, Brother," Bara said coldly. "Look at him. He's not afraid of you. He would like nothing better than to have his hands around your neck. And I don't blame him."

Barl frowned at Bara, then looked at Gringers. "A fight? Yes. That might prove very interesting. He looks like he could give us a good battle."

"Not *us*," Bara said. "You fight *him*—you fight alone."

Barl turned to his brother. "You know, I might try that if I thought you'd stay out of it, but I have a sneaking suspicion that you'd fight on his side just to teach me a lesson. I'm right, aren't I?"

"You need a lesson taught you. One in manners."

Barl shook his head. "And you would like to be the

one to teach me? You're too late, Brother. I've had all the schooling I want. I'll leave you to do the studying, thank you. I have more important things on my mind, such as thieving Wastelanders."

Bara turned his head away. "There are moments, Brother, when I wish I never had to see you again."

"You aren't the only one to wish that," Barl snapped.

Silence descended on the room, broken only by Theon's soft moaning.

Barl looked at the crumpled figure and spoke to Kelsan. "Leave the big one"—he pointed at Gringers—"and take the others somewhere and lock them up. We'll talk to them later, one by one."

Theon flinched as Diak and one of Kelsan's men touched him.

"It's Diak, Theon. Come, sit up if you can."

"My arm. It's broken."

"We'll take care of it. Can you stand up? Are you hurt anywhere else?"

"Don't think so," Theon snuffled. His glance darted around fearfully. It touched upon Barl-et-Bara and snapped away.

Diak and the other man helped Theon up and led him toward the hallway doors. Hallon and Bhaldavin were brought along by four others.

Theon looked at Diak as the doors closed behind them. "What's going to happen to Gringers?" There was fear in his voice.

"Barl-et-Bara is just going to talk to him," Diak said.

Tears began to well in Theon's eyes. "Not true. They're going to kill him. They're going to kill us all. That—that monster's not sane." Theon shuddered.

Kelsan's voice came from behind. "Some things are better off not said, Wastelander! Barl-et-Bara are sane, at least as sane as the majority here in Barl-gan, and they are also very dangerous. So be warned! Guard your tongue and make no trouble and maybe—just maybe—they will let you live."

Chapter 24

THEON PACED RESTLESSLY AROUND THE ROOM, MUT-
tering softly to himself. He passed behind Hallon and
Diak, who sat on a cushioned couch they had drawn into
the center of the room. "It's been hours," he said, nervously glancing at the closed door. "Why haven't they
brought him back?"

Bhaldavin looked up from his position on the floor.
Spread before him was an array of picture cards, which
Diak had said were probably used in some kind of game.
He had been studying the brightly colored cards for some
time, moving them around to make eye-pleasing patterns.

"He's probably still talking to Barl-et-Bara," Diak said,
trying to calm Theon's fears.

Theon touched his makeshift cast. "Either that or he's
dead." There was a bleak look on his face. "They can
take us out of here one at a time, kill us, and those left
behind would never know—until it's their turn."

"Are you suggesting we try to escape?" Hallon asked.

"It's better than sitting here waiting to be slaughtered,

isn't it?" Theon grasped at the leather thong about his neck and pulled a hidden knife from the back of his tunic. He held the knife clumsily in his left hand.

"Here," he said, handing the knife to Hallon. "It will be of more use in your hand than mine."

Hallon accepted the knife and turned to Diak. "What do you think?"

"I wouldn't be of much use to you in a fight, nor would Bhaldavin with only one arm, but if you mean to try something, we'd back you."

Bhaldavin met the old man's glance and nodded. He didn't like the waiting any more than the others did, and he was very worried about Lil-el. From what had been said, he believed she was somewhere within the confines of the huge building, *if* she was still alive. After witnessing Barl-et-Bara's attack on Theon, he feared for anyone who came within reach of the strange twins. The thought of standing alone before them made him shiver. The existence of such a creature was beyond his wildest dreams.

Diak had explained that close inbreeding among a relatively small group of people might account for most of the deformities they'd seen among the people of Barl-gan; but even he had to admit that the joining of Barl-et-Bara at the waist was a deformity that almost went beyond the realm of possibilities.

Suddenly the door behind Theon opened. Kelsan Watcher, Birdfoot, and three others entered the room.

"You're next," Kelsan said, pointing at Theon.

"Where's Gringers?" Theon demanded.

"He has been given private quarters," Kelsan answered. "Come. Barl-et-Bara waits."

Theon backed away. "No! I'll go nowhere until you bring Gringers back here."

Hallon, Diak, and Bhaldavin all stood up as Kelsan signaled Birdfoot to collect Theon.

"Stay away from me," Theon cried. "I'm not going anywhere until you prove to me that Gringers is all right."

"He is fine," Kelsan said firmly. "He was taken to—"

"Liar! You've killed him. I know it. Damn you and your misshapen lords. Now, Hallon," Theon screamed and launched himself at Birdfoot.

Birdfoot moved quickly, sidestepping Theon's lunge and slamming his fist down on his back. Diak, Bhaldavin, and Hallon rushed the doorway as Theon hit the floor.

Kelsan shouted, then suddenly a flash of light caught Hallon full in the chest. Head thrown back, he screamed, dropped Theon's knife, and clutched at his chest; then he crumpled to the floor. Bhaldavin tripped over him. Diak halted, eyes wide at the sight of the light weapon pointed at his face.

Kelsan turned on the man who had used the light weapon. He knocked the man's arm down, cursing. "Fool, Barl-et-Bara wants them alive."

"But he had a weapon," the man protested.

"They were supposed to have been checked for weapons." Kelsan glared at his men. "Check them now. Strip them if you must."

While that was being done, Kelsan walked to Hallon's still form and turned him over. He muttered something to himself and stood up.

Birdfoot had Theon stripped to the skin in seconds. He left the arm splint intact. Diak and Bhaldavin were accorded the same treatment. Once assured that there were no other weapons in the prisoners' possession, Kelsan ordered that Theon be taken to Barl-et-Bara immediately.

Theon bent to reach for his clothes. Birdfoot kicked them away and caught him by his good arm. Theon's face was chalk-white as he was pushed through the doorway.

Diak went to Hallon as soon as the door closed. Bhaldavin stood quietly, waiting.

"Oh, my dear boy," Diak sobbed softly. "To have come

so far only to die like that. What have I done to you?
What have I done?"

Bhaldavin dressed, then helped Diak into his clothes.
The old man went to the couch and sat down, his head
dropping into his hands.

Bhaldavin moved around the couch and went to stand
over Hallon's body. He could see where the light had
burned into Hallon's chest. There was very little blood.
He knelt and picked up Hallon's hands; both were charred.
He glanced at Hallon's open eyes and quickly looked
away, suddenly remembering little things about the man,
things that touched him with sadness: his voice, the way
he held his head when he laughed, his quiet presence
around the campfires, the strength in his hands as he
reached out to help the others over the difficult places
while climbing in the mountains.

In that moment he realized that his perception of Hallon
as a mere extension of Gringers had been wrong, that he
had been much more than just Gringers's cousin, that he
had been a stabilizing force for them all.

He looked over at Diak, suddenly wanting to comfort
the old man but not sure how to go about it. To have such
feelings toward men was a revelation for him. He had
spent so many months hating these men for keeping him
prisoner that he had failed to see the tendrils of friendship
silently weaving their bonds around him.

And so you capture me at last, he mused, standing and
moving toward the couch. The love I fought so hard against
has taken me unawares.

Diak looked up, tears tracking his face. "It shouldn't
have ended like this, Bhaldavin. I had such dreams."

Bhaldavin sat down beside the old man. "Among the
People it's said that dreams are growing seed, that without
them we would be no more than a tree or a draak."

Diak wiped at his tears. "But it was *my* dream that
killed Hallon—maybe all of us. I had no right to force it
on all of you."

"I didn't see much forcing," Bhaldavin said gently. "Some dream for themselves. Some dream for others. To share another's dream is not always a sacrifice."

Diak glanced at Hallon's body. "Even when it kills you?"

"Even then."

Diak looked at Bhaldavin; he drew a shuddering breath and released it slowly. "You've changed, Bhaldavin. You've grown patient and wise these past few weeks. And I don't think you hate us anymore, do you?"

"I don't know that I ever really hated you, any of you. I just didn't understand you. And I was angry for a long time. All I could think about was my freedom."

Diak's glance dropped. "Freedom that we all denied you for our own special interests." He looked up. "I wish I had it all to do over again."

"I doubt you would do any differently, Diak. To deny one's dream is to cease to care, and not to care is not to live."

They came for Diak a short time later. He went quietly, without protest. As Bhaldavin helped him to his feet, Diak embraced him. "Until we meet again, my friend."

Bhaldavin remained standing until the door closed behind Diak and his escort; then he went to the couch and lay down, facing away from Hallon's body. He meant to stay awake, to try to form some plan that might gain him freedom, but sleep gradually stole upon him, banishing the spectre of death that seemed to lurk in every corner of the empty city.

Darkness greeted him upon waking, and for long moments he just lay quietly, remembering where he was and what had happened. Standing, he moved toward the wall near the door and felt around until he found the shoulder-high depressions; he pressed and the light panels above were turned on.

He glanced around the room. Hallon's body was gone,

as were Theon's pile of clothes. How long had he been sleeping? he wondered. Why hadn't they returned for him? Perhaps they didn't perceive him as a threat. Or perhaps they just hadn't finished with the old man.

He returned to the couch. Hallon is dead, he thought, but what about the others? Had Barl-et-Bara ordered them all killed after he had finished talking to them? Or were they still alive somewhere in the building?

Time passed.

He got up and tried the door for the fifth time, then turned and paced restlessly around the room. He was growing hungry, and nature was making other demands upon him. He held out as long as he could, then used one of the corners of the room to relieve himself.

He returned to the couch and gathered up the cards he had been studying. With nothing else to do, he began to lay them out.

A small clicking noise startled him. He turned as the door swung open. Barl-et-Bara stood there, their upper bodies filling the doorway.

Bhaldavin rose and backed away, letting the cards fall from his hand. He glanced beyond the twins, but the hall was empty. His heartbeat quickened as the lords of Barl-gan approached.

Barl saw Bhaldavin's fear and smiled wickedly. He signaled with his hand. "Come, it's your turn now, Green Hair."

Bara rubbed at sleep-laden eyes. "Stop it, Barl. You're scaring him."

"Shut up and go back to sleep," Barl snapped at his brother.

"Why don't we both go back to sleep? This can wait until tomorrow."

"I did sleep. While you were talking to that old fossil. He had you mesmerized with his stories about the men who live on the other side of the mountains. I didn't think he'd ever run down."

"You should've stayed awake and listened to him. You might have learned something."

"The Wastelanders have nothing to teach us," Barl said scornfully. "They're ignorant. Little better than the wolves and lizards that scavenge the land."

"They are not Wastelanders."

"You're a fool if you believe that. You with your studies and dreams about the stars. You know as well as I that no one is ever going to come back to rescue us. There are no truths in the old prophecies. They are all lies."

"You speak blasphemy. The gods will return one day and—"

"No!" Barl roared. "There are no gods. There never were. It's time you opened your eyes and faced reality. Barl-gan is dying. We are the last leaders it shall ever have. There is no future for us. The Wastelanders will come here someday, and no one will be left to deny them our possessions. All that we have will be theirs. Everything!"

Bara shook his head. "You're wrong, Barl. Diak says there *are* other men in the world, men who'll take over after we're gone, *if* we can persuade them to come here. And as for the prophecies, tomorrow he is going to show us a gift from the First Men, those who built Barl-gan. He says it shows pictures of the ship that brought them here. It will prove that—"

"That the First Men were gods. Then we too must be gods, for we are their descendants." Barl's booming laugh filled the room. "And if we are gods, then Barl-gan must be heaven. Heaven! Where death and sickness reign supreme."

Barl's laughter was filled with the sound of madness, and it sent shivers coursing down Bhaldavin's spine. Slowly he edged along the wall away from the twins. The open door beckoned.

Barl caught a flicker of movement out of the corner of his eye and turned. His argument with his brother forgotten, he lunged just as Bhaldavin made a run for the open doorway. He caught Bhaldavin around the waist and swung halfway around, almost losing his balance. But Bara put out his hands and braced himself on the back of the couch.

Bhaldavin tried to twist free.

"Grab his legs!" Barl shouted at his brother.

"You have two arms and are bigger than he is. You don't need my help," Bara retorted, ducking to avoid Bhaldavin's fist.

"Bara!"

"No!"

Barl swore and readjusted his hold, one hand going to Bhaldavin's throat. A few seconds later, Bhaldavin was gasping for breath. He tore at the bony fingers choking him, but he was no match for Barl's strength.

"Stop it, Barl. You'll kill him," Bara shouted.

"Shut up!"

"Stop! I'll help you. Damn it, I said I'd help you. Let him go."

The fingers at Bhaldavin's throat loosened, and air rushed into his lungs. The darkness that had threatened to engulf him gradually receded, and he became aware of his surroundings once more. He was being carried through the doorway and down the hall.

He licked at dry lips and tried to speak. His voice sounded raspy. "Where are you taking me?"

Barl stared straight ahead, his lips grim. "To be examined," he said crisply, "as were the others." He let Bhaldavin down. "You can walk the rest of the way."

They came to a set of unlighted stairs leading down. Barl guided Bhaldavin down the steps, keeping a hand at the back of his neck. There was a landing and a door halfway down the stairs. Barl leaned over Bhaldavin's shoulder and opened the door. A touch on the wall, and the room beyond was lighted.

Someone rose from the floor at the far end of the room.

It was Birdfoot, looking surprised and blinking sleep from his eyes. He glanced at Bhaldavin as Barl-et-Bara led him to a long, low table in the center of the room.

"Is all well with the prisoners?" Barl-et-Bara asked Birdfoot.

Birdfoot nodded.

"Good. We have one more for you to look after. I know it's early, but go and fetch Kelsan. We'll prepare this one while you're gone."

Bhaldavin looked at the door Birdfoot had been guarding, relieved to learn that the others still lived. They had to be the prisoners to which Barl-et-Bara had referred.

Gils Watcher left, taking the stairs two at a time.

Bhaldavin eyed the table warily, liking neither the leather straps that lay folded nearly across it nor the strange metal armlike things that hung over it.

"Undress."

Bhaldavin flinched at Barl's command, a bubble of fear rising to choke him. What were they going to do to him? He faced Barl-et-Bara, his glance going from one face to the other. Barl's look was stern, Bara's sympathetic.

Bara nodded encouragement. "Do as you are told. You will not be harmed."

Bhaldavin began to undress, knowing he had no choice. Barl grew impatient with his awkwardness in removing his clothes and stepped forward to help.

Moments later Bhaldavin stood stripped of everything but his boots. Barl pushed him back onto the table.

"See to his boots," Barl ordered.

Bara frowned at his brother, but did as he was told.

Bhaldavin tried to speak as Barl began strapping him down on the table, but his mouth was dry and he couldn't get the words out.

Barl took delight in the fear reflected on Bhaldavin's face. When he had finished with the straps, he put a hand on Bhaldavin's chest and stroked down the length of his body, his strong blunt fingers probing muscles and sensitive places.

"Don't, Barl!" Bara snapped. "He's afraid!"

Bara smiled maliciously. "I can see that. He thinks we mean to kill him." He reached over and touched the stump of Bhaldavin's arm. "Or perhaps it's further mutilation he's afraid of. Is that it, Green Hair? How did you lose your arm? Whoever did it did a good job, you know. Almost as good a job as Kelsan could do."

He leaned over Bhaldavin. "You look rather lopsided with only one arm. Perhaps you'd like us to cut off the other one and return your body to a more symmetrical design?"

"Don't listen to him, Bhaldavin," Bara said. "No one is going to hurt you. All we want to do is examine you, to see if you're healthy and—virile. We have need of—"

"Silence!" Barl growled, turning on his brother. "Our needs do not concern him—at least at the moment."

Barl-et-Bara turned at the sound of footsteps on the stairs.

"I thought this one was to wait until morning," Kelsan said, coming into the room with Birdfoot.

"It could've as far as I'm concerned," Bara said disgustedly. "But Barl woke up and was restless. He—"

"Never mind about me," Barl said. "Just get on with the examination. We'll await your report in our room. Bring him to us when you're finished."

Kelsan waited until Barl-et-Bara left the room before beginning the examination. When he saw the straps holding Bhaldavin down, he muttered something under his breath and loosened them a bit. "Better?"

Bhaldavin cleared his throat, trying to find his voice. "What are you going to do to me?"

"You are to be examined. Relax. It won't take long. I'll explain everything I'm doing so you'll understand and cooperate."

Kelsan was true to his word. The examination didn't take long, but several of the procedures he carried out were painful, and Bhaldavin shivered with relief as Birdfoot released him from the straps and helped him sit up.

Kelsan looked at his grandson as he gathered up the samples he had taken. "Take him to Barl-et-Bara and stay with him. I'll find someone to take your place here."

Birdfoot nodded and assisted Bhaldavin in dressing; then he led him toward the stairs.

Bhaldavin kept track of the number of halls and stairways they passed, thinking that if he escaped and had to find his way back to the place where his friends were being held, he could do so quickly and surely.

When they reached Barl-et-Bara's room, Birdfoot knocked on the door and entered, pulling Bhaldavin along in his wake. The room was deeply shadowed. The only light in the room came from a strange round globe sitting on a bedside table. Floor-to-ceiling draperies covered most of the walls.

The twins were in bed. Barl lifted a hand and signaled Birdfoot to bring Bhaldavin forward.

Bhaldavin's heart beat faster as he came to a stop next to the huge bed. He looked beyond Barl, who was watching him intently, and saw that Bara was fast asleep.

Barl reached out and caught Bhaldavin's wrist. His fingers tightened as Bhaldavin tried to draw back.

"Your eyes betray you, Green Hair," Barl said. "Why do you fear me and not my brother?"

Bhaldavin winced as Barl tightened his hold.

"Is it my voice that frightens you? Surely it can't be my face, because we are the same."

Bhaldavin glanced at Bara.

"Don't look to him for protection." Barl's fingers squeezed, grinding wrist bones. Bhaldavin gasped in pain and fell to his knees, trying to relieve the pressure on his wrist.

"Do you know what I am called by the people of Barl-gan?" Barl said softly.

Bhaldavin shook his head.

"Ah, a response. Good." Barl smiled. "I'm called Lord Death, Green Hair, because I decide who lives and who dies. Bara is too weak to make such decisions; he will have no part of it. So it's left to me. When one is born, or when one comes to us from the Wastelands, they are brought to me. If they are reasonably whole and useful, they live." He glanced at Bhaldavin's armless sleeve. "If they are badly deformed and unable to be of service, they die. Which will it be for you? I wonder."

Barl released Bhaldavin's wrist. Bhaldavin closed his eyes in relief and tried to breathe normally.

"Look at me."

Bhaldavin looked up, wondering if each of his friends had been subjected to a similar ordeal.

"I'm going to ask you a question," Barl said. "Lie to me, and you will die a second later. Tell the truth, and you will live."

Birdfoot caught a handful of Bhaldavin's hair and tilted his head back, exposing his throat. Bhaldavin flinched at the touch of cold metal at the base of his throat.

"Do you understand?" Barl asked softly, smiling.

"Yes."

"Good. This then is the question. Are you or are you not able to control the great lizards that infest this world?"

Lizards? The trader word was new to him, but he realized that Barl had to be speaking about draak. "I can sing draak, yes."

"Draak. Yes, that is what Lil-el called them. And would you sing these draak for me, for the protection of Barl-gan?"

"I would do it, but not willingly."

"So. You would serve us, but not willingly. The other Green Hair said much the same. She also told me that she was mated—to you, I assume?"

Bhaldavin hesitated, then nodded.

Barl looked down at his hands and toyed with the ring on one of his fingers. When he looked up, his steady, unblinking stare made Bhaldavin think of a snake before it strikes.

"There is only one woman of childbearing age among us now. I wonder, would you consider *sharing* your mate with us—for the betterment of Barl-gan? We could, of course, take her without your permission. Still, it is polite to ask."

The enormity of the request filled Bhaldavin with such rage that he forgot the knife at his throat and launched himself at Barl. A painful jerk on his head caught him off-balance. Birdfoot brought the hilt of his knife up and struck Bhaldavin on the back of his head.

Chapter 25

BHALDAVIN WOKE TO A SUDDEN GLARE OF LIGHT. HE opened his eyes, then shut them quickly. He rolled over and sat up; his head ached, and for a moment or two he thought he was going to be sick.

"Bhaldavin."

He turned at the sound of the voice. "Diak?"

"Yes."

He pushed to his feet as Diak shuffled into the room. He avoided looking up at the light panels overhead and quickly inspected the room; it was small, empty, and had no windows. It also had a musty odor, and there was a noticeable layer of dust on the floor.

"Where are we?" Bhaldavin asked.

The old man put out a shaky hand and caught at Bhaldavin's tunic. "Never mind. Come," he said urgently. "We must find the others."

"How did you find me?" Bhaldavin asked as he followed Diak out of the room.

"Not easily," the old man chuckled. Suddenly he began coughing deep, racking coughs that frightened Bhaldavin.

"Are you all right?"

The old man wiped at the spittle on his lips and nodded. "Just tired, Bhaldavin, but there's no time for rest. Not now. We must find the others and free them. Bara fears for their lives."

"Bara?"

Diak started down the hallway checking each door they came to. "I spent a lot of time with Barl-et-Bara yesterday and this morning. I told them about the world beyond the mountains, and just a little while ago I showed them how the life recorder works. Bara was excited about it and wanted to see more of the pictures, but Barl wouldn't let him. He took the box from me and swore it was all a Wastelander trick, a way to take by guile what they'd been unable to take by force. Bara tried to argue with him. Barl told him to be quiet or he'd order me killed."

Bhaldavin glanced down the hallway ahead of them, fearing to see Birdfoot suddenly appear. "How did you get away?"

Diak looked at Bhaldavin and smiled. "Barl touched the crystal with his bare hand. I forgot to warn him. It gave him quite a jolt. Bara even felt it, but he recovered more quickly than Barl. While his brother was unconscious, Bara told me how to leave their rooms without alerting the guard; then he told me to find my friends and leave Barl-gan as quickly as possible. He was sure Barl meant to have several of us put to death."

"Did Bara say anything to you about Lil-el?"

"No. Why?"

Bhaldavin quickly told Diak about his interview with Barl and his fears for her safety.

"We must find her quickly, and the others, before Barl calls for them again," Diak said.

There were so many rooms off the hall that Bhaldavin and Diak split up, each taking a side of the hall. There seemed to be no rhyme or reason to the placement of prisoners. Diak found Gringers first, and with his help they soon located Theon.

"That leaves Lil-el," Gringers said, as Theon stepped out into the hallway. "Let's keep looking."

Theon looked haggard, and his eyes had a haunted look that worried Bhaldavin. "I don't think Lil-el is down here," Theon said. He stood with his back braced against the wall, as if he didn't trust his own legs.

"What makes you say that?" Gringers demanded.

"I heard voices just a little while ago. One was Lil-el's. She was arguing with someone as she passed my room. I called out to her, but I don't know if she heard me."

"I heard nothing."

Theon shrugged. "I'm sure it was her voice. She passed heading that way, I think." He pointed to the flight of steps leading back up to the floors above.

"You said she was arguing. With who?"

"I don't know. It might have been Kelsan, but I'm not sure."

Bhaldavin looked at Diak, a bubble of fear choking him. "Barl!"

"What about Barl?" Gringers snapped.

Bhaldavin quickly told them about his appearance before Barl-et-Bara. "I think he means to"—Bhaldavin almost choked on the last word—"mate with her."

"Rape her, you mean," Theon growled.

"And he'll do it, I'm afraid," Diak said, "unless Bara can stop him."

"Would he?" Gringers asked.

Diak shook his head. "I don't know. The brief time I've been with them, I got the impression that Bara often gives in to Barl's demands. He might protest if Lil-el seemed an unwilling partner, but whether or not he could stop Barl from doing what he wants—I don't know."

Gringers caught Diak by the arm. "Could you find your way back to Barl-et-Bara's room?"

"Yes, I think so."

"All right. Then we go there first."

"Unarmed?" Theon protested.

"We'll have to try to get hold of one of those light weapons if we can."

"More than one," Theon said.

Gringers walked Diak toward the stairs. "When we first arrived in Barl-gan, I had hoped we could set up some kind of peaceful agreement that would allow us to stay here and learn about the First Men. Now I'm convinced that as long as Barl-et-Bara are in command, we'll see nothing but death or slavery."

Theon grabbed at the back of Gringers's tunic. "What are you saying? That we should take over?"

"Why not? All we'd have to do is get rid of Barl-et-Bara."

"You're crazy! I say we get the hell out of here. This place has nothing we want."

"How do we know? We haven't had a chance to look around yet."

"Gringers! Staying here is suicide. We've already lost Hallon. Who'll be next? Please, let's just get out of here while we're still able to. You wanted proof that Barl-gan exists. One or two of those weapons would be proof enough."

"I want more than proof, Theon, I want knowledge. And the only way to get it is to stay here and search for it."

Theon shook his head in disgust. "If we kill Barl-et-Bara, those who are left will kill us."

Gringers turned on Theon as they reached the top of the stairs. "I said nothing about killing the lords Barl-et-Bara. I was thinking more about *controlling* them. If we could get them in a position where their own lives were at stake, I think we could bargain for what we want."

Bhaldavin cared nothing about Barl-et-Bara or the knowledge of the First Men. "What about Lil-el?" he demanded, glaring at Gringers. "You once told me that you loved her. If you do, then help me find her. Quickly!"

Gringers swallowed angry words and took a deep breath. "I'm sorry, Bhaldavin. You're right. Lil-el comes first. Come on, Diak, show us the way."

Diak led the way back to the main floor where Barl-et-Bara had their rooms. He paused when they reached the main hallway. They could hear voices coming in their direction.

Gringers signaled Theon forward and the other two back. Bhaldavin obeyed reluctantly. Every moment of delay meant more danger for Lil-el.

The voices grew louder.

Gringers and Theon crouched along the wall, waiting for the right moment. When it came, Gringers lunged up from his position and caught the first man around the chest, pinning his arms to his sides as they fell. Theon was only a step behind, but the second man had time enough to draw his weapon before he was knocked back against the wall across from the stairwell. A flash of deadly light shot over Bhaldavin's head as he threw himself into the battle behind Theon.

Theon dragged the man down to the floor, cursing as his splinted arm got in the way. The light weapon flashed once more, then Bhaldavin was there, pinning the man's arm down to the floor with his knee and wrenching the light box away. Theon hit the man in the face several times before he stopped struggling.

Diak shouted a warning.

Bhaldavin turned to see someone running toward them from the other end of the hall; the man was yelling for help and firing another of the light weapons as he closed on them.

Theon cried out as a shaft of light grazed his leg. Gringers stood up and used the man he held as a shield.

"Get behind me," he shouted and began backing toward the door that Diak had indicated would lead them to Barl-et-Bara.

Bhaldavin pressed the button on the light box he held, pointing it down the hallway. He was rewarded by a flash of light. The man running toward them skidded to a halt and dove into one of the rooms off the hall.

Birdfoot and several other men appeared. Bhaldavin used the light weapon again, and they also ducked for cover. Theon limped toward Bhaldavin and reached for the light box.

"Here, let me have that. Follow Diak!"

Bhaldavin turned and saw Diak disappearing into a room off the hall. He handed the light weapon to Theon and hurried after the old man.

Theon backed down the hallway, covering Gringers, who pushed the man he held away from him and stepped into the room behind Bhaldavin. Theon was only a few steps behind. Once into the room, he slammed the door, found the lock, and snapped it shut.

Diak turned on the lights and started across the room. "This way, quickly," he said softly, moving toward a door to the left. "They were in this room when I saw them last."

Gringers, armed with a knife now, stepped around Diak and tried the door. It wasn't locked.

"Careless," Gringers muttered softly.

"They're too few to guard every door," Diak explained, "and they're not used to guarding prisoners."

The room they entered was dimly lit. Bhaldavin paused beside Gringers, his eyes adjusting to the darkness. He heard someone curse softly and saw movement in the bed on the other side of the room.

Bhaldavin started across the room. He felt Gringers right behind him. Suddenly he saw the flash of a naked leg; then he heard Lil-el cry out.

Gringers and Bhaldavin moved as one. They reached

the bed and saw Lil-el lying beneath the twin lords struggling to free herself from Barl's embrace. Barl yelled as
Lil-el bit down on his arm.

Bara turned, saw Bhaldavin and Gringers, and shouted
a warning to his brother, but the warning came too late.
Gringers leaped on Barl's back and caught him around
the neck, pulling the twin halfway off Lil-el.

Bara, who seemed to have been holding himself away
from the proceedings as much as was possible, saw the
knife in Gringers's hand as it plunged toward Barl's chest.
He lunged forward and blocked the thrust by capturing
Gringers's wrist.

"Theon, help!" Gringers cried as he and the twins slid
out of bed onto the floor.

Bhaldavin grabbed Lil-el by an arm and pulled her off
the bed as Theon darted around the large bedposts to help
Gringers. He raised the light weapon, but he hesitated to
fire into the tangle of bodies that thrashed around on the
floor.

Barl was screaming for his guards, but Gringers found
Barl's throat and squeezed, cutting off his cries. Bara tried
to pull Gringers away from Barl and finally managed to
break Gringers's hold. Barl-et-Bara moved in concert then
as they rolled over with Gringers caught between them
and got to their knees.

Barl found the knife Gringers had dropped and raised
it to strike.

"No, Barl!" Bara cried, still holding Gringers.

"I'm going to kill him. Kill them all!"

Theon stepped closer, aimed the light weapon at Barl's
head, and fired.

Barl never made a sound as he folded over; the knife
he held clattered to the floor.

Suddenly the door to the audience chamber banged
open. Theon turned. A flash of light came from beyond
the doorway and caught him in the side. He gasped in
pain and fell to his knees. Another spray of deadly light

passed over his head. He lifted his light weapon and fired at the three figures that burst into the room.

Birdfoot was the first to go down. The man to his right took the second hit and fell rolling. The third man turned and dove for cover, returning to the audience chamber.

Gringers pushed away from Bara, the stink of burned flesh strong in his nostrils. Bara ignored him and leaned over his brother, calling his name.

Another flash of light came from the other room. Theon retaliated. Birdfoot rolled to safety behind a nearby couch. The other man lay where he had fallen.

The sound of angry voices came from the audience room. Gringers cast a frustrated glance at Barl-et-Bara and shook his head. Any chance of controlling them was gone now. All they could hope for was to get out of Barl-gan alive.

Diak pushed Bhaldavin and Lil-el toward the side door. "Out! That way! Back the way we came. Hurry! Gringers, get Theon, and let's get out of here!"

Gringers helped Theon up. "Can you run?"

Theon shook his head.

Gringers took the light weapon and caught Theon around the waist. He fired the weapon again and again as he helped Theon toward the side door.

Bhaldavin turned and watched the two men run through a barrage of light flashes coming from the other room. He saw Bara rise to his feet, his arms around his brother's body. Barl's head lolled forward onto Bara's shoulder, obscuring the charred hole in his right temple. Standing naked in the flickering lights, Bara looked out over the top of his brother's head and followed Gringers and Theon's escape. There was no anger on Bara's face, only a look of infinite sadness.

Lil-el clung tightly to Bhaldavin's arm as they followed Diak back out into the main hallway. She was naked and shivering, and the haunted look in her eyes made Bhaldavin feel sick. "Lil-el, are you all right?"

She nodded, but wouldn't look at him.

Diak motioned them to hurry. "Quickly. Before some-one comes."

They followed Diak's lead, leaving Gringers and Theon to bring up the rear. Twice in the next few minutes they were cut off from escape to the outside. They were left finally with no choice but to climb.

Their run through the maze of hallways and rooms of the upper floors became a nightmare. Gringers finally took the lead and tried to lead them back down to the ground floor, but they were met by deadly flashes of light wielded by a wounded Birdfoot and several others who continued to harry them from hallway to hallway, floor to floor.

Gringers, carrying Theon over his shoulder, used the light weapon to keep their pursuers at a distance. They reached yet another flight of stairs leading up. Gringers ordered them to climb.

"But we must go down," Diak protested.

"Climb!" Gringers yelled. "Maybe I can hold them off at the top of the stairs. Theon, can you walk a little?"

"Put me down. I'll try."

While the others started climbing, Gringers stayed at the bottom of the steps and used the light weapon to discourage anyone from closing in.

Diak was almost to the top of the stairs when suddenly he sagged to his knees. Bhaldavin and Lil-el came up behind him and helped him up. He was gasping for breath and clutching at his chest.

Together they got him up the last few steps; then he collapsed to the floor.

Theon limped up the last few steps, glanced down at the old man, and swore softly to himself.

"Keep moving!" Gringers yelled, running up the stairs two at a time. "We've got to . . ." His words trailed off as he saw Diak on the floor. "What's wrong?"

"It's another attack," Bhaldavin said, moving aside as Gringers knelt beside Diak.

"Damn! That's all we need."

He looked up at Bhaldavin. "Go down the hall and find a room with only one door, a place where we can defend ourselves. Hurry! Theon, can you walk a little farther?"

Theon nodded and started after Bhaldavin and Lil-el, leaving Gringers to carry Diak.

Bhaldavin found a suitable room and helped Theon inside and to a chair; he then stripped off his tunic and gave it to Lil-el. She thanked him softly and quickly slipped it over her head.

Gringers laid the old man on the bed to the right of the doorway and turned. "Bhaldavin, lock the door."

Bhaldavin did as he was told, then turned to Lil-el. "Are you all right, Lil-el?" he asked her gently, pulling her close.

This time her eyes met his. "Just scared."

"Did he—they—hurt you?"

"No. But if you hadn't come . . . Oh, Bhaldavin, just hold me! I don't think I've ever been so frightened in my life. I was so afraid I'd never see any of you again."

Bhaldavin started to say something, but suddenly someone outside tried the doorknob. He released Lil-el and pulled her around behind him. "Gringers!"

Gringers turned and was across the room in five quick strides. He motioned to Bhaldavin and Lil-el to back out of the way.

"I'll kill the first man through that door," he roared.

The doorknob snapped back, and out in the hall there were sounds of voices; moments later there was silence.

Slowly Gringers backed away from the door. "Theon, get over in that far corner. Put that couch in front of you. Bhaldavin, you and Lil-el join him."

"What about Diak?" Theon asked, rising slowly. "You want some help with him?"

Gringers didn't respond for a moment, then he turned. "He's dead," he said bleakly. "His heart finally gave out." He tossed the light weapon onto the bed beside Diak. "He's as dead as this weapon."

Chapter 26 ✎

GRINGERS PACED RESTLESSLY AROUND THE ROOM. HE
paused briefly at the side of one of the windows and
glanced down at the three men stationed on the terrace
below. As long as it was light outside, there would be no
escape that way. Even in darkness it would prove dangerous.

Bhaldavin watched Gringers move over to where Theon
lay on the floor. He glanced at Lil-el, who had fallen asleep
leaning against his shoulder. Carefully he eased her down
onto the couch and stood up.

Hours had passed since Kelsan had come to their door
to demand their surrender. Gringers, grieving over Diak's
death, had told him in no uncertain terms just where he
could go with his demands, and had even threatened him
with his useless light weapon.

"How is he?" Bhaldavin asked softly.

"Not good," Gringers replied. One hand went to Theon's
forehead. "He's got a fever, and we've nothing to tend
his wounds with."

Theon stirred at Gringers's touch. His face was flushed, and it seemed hard for him to focus on anything. "Gringers?"

"Right here, Theon."

"I feel rotten."

"I know."

Theon licked at dry lips. "Could I have something to drink?"

Gringers looked up at Bhaldavin through anguish-filled eyes. He turned back to his friend. "There is nothing to drink, Theon, but—maybe I can get you something."

Theon caught Gringers's arm as he started to rise. "No. Don't do anything foolish. It's all right. I don't need anything. Gringers?"

Gringers settled back down. "Yes."

"Am I—going to die?"

Gringers caught at Theon's hands. "No, you're not going to die. Not of a couple of small burns."

Theon tried to smile. "That's good to hear. I thought— I thought maybe—it was my turn next."

Gringers tried to say something, but couldn't. He swallowed and cleared his throat. "Theon, please don't give up. I swear, I'll get you out of here alive."

"Sure about that?"

"I'm sure!"

Theon noticed Bhaldavin. "Little Fish. How's Lil-el?"

"She's asleep."

"Good. That's good. Gods, Gringers, but I'm thirsty."

Gringers cursed softly and again started to rise, but Theon held on to his arm.

"No! Don't go! I've got something I want to tell you."

"What?" Gringers asked gently.

"I—I want you to know that I didn't come to Barl-gan for any treasure." His glance locked on Gringers. "I came because—I wanted to be with you, because I—"

"I know why you came, friend. I know." Gringers

squeezed Theon's hand. "Now hang on, and don't give up. Everything's going to be all right."

Theon closed his eyes. "Wish I could believe that."

"Believe it!"

Gringers rose and caught Bhaldavin's arm, pulling him toward the center of the room. "I'm going out into the hall empty-handed," he said, keeping his voice down. "I've got to see if I can get some help for Theon."

"It would be better for me to go. If they tried to break in, I couldn't do much to stop them."

"No! I'm going."

Bhaldavin started to argue, but was interrupted by a sudden knocking on the door.

"Who is it?" Gringers demanded loudly, moving toward the door.

"It's Kelsan. Open the door. We must talk. I'm unarmed."

Lil-el woke up, eyes wide in alarm. "What's happening?"

"It's Kelsan again," Bhaldavin answered. "Stay where you are."

Gringers glanced at Bhaldavin and motioned him back out of the way. He slid the bolt on the door and opened the door a crack. "Are you alone?"

"Yes," Kelsan replied. "I've sent the others back down to the lower floors. Please, let me in. I have to talk with you!"

Gringers opened the door, took a quick look into the hall, and stepped back, allowing Kelsan to enter the room. Bhaldavin relocked the door as Gringers checked Kelsan for weapons.

"All right," Gringers said. "What do you want?"

"Lord Bara has sent me to ask you to come to his room." Kelsan glanced around. "All of you."

"Why?"

Kelsan straightened up as much as possible. "Lord

Bara is dying. He wishes to talk to you—about the future of Barl-gan and its people."

"And us? Are we included in this future?" Gringers demanded.

"I would say yes, though my lord Bara did not confide in me."

"You want us to leave this room, go downstairs, and talk to Lord Bara, whom you say is dying. How do we know we're not being led into some kind of trap?"

"I'm here to act as a hostage. If anyone attacks you, you may kill me first."

Gringers hesitated only a second or two, his glance going to Theon. "All right. We'll come, if someone will see to my friend's wounds."

"May I look?"

Gringers nodded. Kelsan crossed the room and knelt beside Theon, who had fallen into fitful sleep.

"He needs attention quickly," Kelsan said, rising a moment or two later. "Can you carry him?"

"Yes."

"It would be best if you all come together." Kelsan glanced at the bed. "Wake the old one, and we'll go."

Gringers passed Kelsan and bent to pick up Theon. Theon moaned softly as Gringers readjusted him in his arms. "Unlock the door, Bhaldavin. You and Lil-el walk beside Kelsan and see that he doesn't try to escape."

Kelsan again looked at Diak's still form on the bed.

Gringers headed for the door. "He's dead," he said softly.

Gringers, Lil-el, and Bhaldavin sat in chairs next to Lord Bara's bed. Theon lay behind them on a low pallet, his wounds cleaned and carefully bandaged, his eyes closed in sleep.

Kelsan and his grandson, Birdfoot, stood at the foot of Lord Bara's bed. Birdfoot's arm was cradled in a shoulder sling.

Lord Bara's glance touched upon each of them. His face was pale, but his dark eyes glittered with his fight for life. A heavy red coverlet lay across Barl's upper body and head. Bara's glance strayed to his dead brother. He turned away and drew the sheet up higher over his bared chest.

Eyes downcast, he began. "I'm sorry that things happened as they did. I want to apologize to all of you for my brother—and myself. To you first, Lil-el, because I was weak and because I wanted you as much as Barl did. I knew what we were doing was wrong—but I couldn't stop us."

He looked up and reached out a hand to her. "I beg your forgiveness. I don't want to die with you hating me."

Lil-el glanced at Bhaldavin, then took Bara's hand. "There's no hate between us, Lord Bara, not anymore."

He squeezed her hand and let it go. He looked at Gringers, Bhaldavin, and then down at the pallet where Theon lay. "And to the rest of you, I also extend apologies. You were not treated as proper guests. I gave in to Barl's mistrust and let him have his way with you, even though I knew you gave us nothing but the truth."

Bara's glance fastened on Gringers. "I regret Diak's passing. I so enjoyed the hours we spent talking, and I had so much more to say to him, things that now must be said to you, if you'll listen."

Gringers glanced at Kelsan and Birdfoot. "We'll listen, but before you go any further, I want to know if we're free to leave Barl-gan in peace when we are finished here."

Lord Bara looked at Kelsan. "They are free to go—or stay if they wish."

Kelsan nodded.

Lord Bara held out a hand. "Give me the box, Kelsan."

Kelsan went to a nearby table, picked up Diak's magic box, and returned to hand it to Lord Bara.

"This belongs to you," Bara said, passing the box to Gringers. "You and Diak were right in believing that it came from Barl-gan. I've seen only a small portion of the living pictures it contains, but in those scenes I recognized certain places in the city as they must have looked when Barl-gan was new. Whoever took this unusual machine from here must have departed long, long ago. For what reason, we shall probably never know. Perhaps he was unhappy with the way Barl-gan was being ruled; or perhaps he was just restless and wanted to see more of this world. There's also the possibility that he was sent out to find other places where men could live without being threatened by the huge lizards that infest this world.

"In the oldest of our written records, there is mention of such expeditions. One went north overland; another went east by ship through the Niev chain of lakes. If anyone ever tried to climb the escarpment, that which we call the Western Wall, it was never set down."

"The Sarissa claim to have come to the Enzaar Sea by ship," Gringers offered.

"Some of our people, probably," Bara said. "One wonders why they never tried to return. Perhaps the passage was too difficult to attempt more than once."

"They're an arrogant lot," Gringers said. "It would be my guess that once they founded Annaroth, their own city, they decided to keep what they'd found for themselves."

Gringers glanced at Kelsan, then back to Bara. "Tell me, ever since we came here, Barl insisted upon calling us Wastelanders. Who are they? Another lost expedition?"

Lord Bara took a deep breath and released it slowly. He looked tired.

"No," he answered. "Some are, or were, common criminals; others are simple wanderers. But the majority of them are the descendants of citizens of Barl-gan, people who fled the sickness that purged the city hundreds of years ago and left her as you see her today. Our numbers have dwindled rapidly since the sickness. The inbreeding has become so bad that in the last two hundred years, three-quarters of the children born are sterile, and many are deformed either physically or mentally.

"Looking at you, Gringers, I know now what we should be and how far we've strayed from our original design. Kelsan has told me that new blood is all that will save us from extinction, but even now I think it may be too late. There are so few of us left."

He paused. "Do you think it possible to bring more of your people here to Barl-gan, to help us keep the city alive?"

Gringers's glance dropped to his hands; then he shook his head. "I don't think so, not the way we came. It's too dangerous. We'd have to find another way. It might be better for those who are left here to think about leaving Barl-gan, to find lives for themselves elsewhere, perhaps among the Wastelanders or with those who live around the Enzaar Sea."

Lord Bara frowned. "No. They wouldn't be accepted. Anyway, someone must stay here to take care of the star beacon or the gods will never know how to find us."

"What gods?" Gringers asked.

"*The gods*, the gods that brought us here, of course," Bara said petulantly. "According to the prophecies, the gods will return one day and take us back to the world from whence we came, a beautiful world where the sky is blue and the land is free of savage beasts, a world of peace and harmony, where we'll all be greeted as lost brothers found."

"What is a star beacon?"

"It's how we speak to the gods." Bara looked at the magic box in Gringers's hands. "It's a machine like that, but much larger. It's housed in the northernmost wind tower. Care of the beacon is passed down from generation to generation."

Bara looked at Kelsan and Birdfoot. "These two are the last of the Watchers." He looked back at Gringers.

"At the moment there is no one in Barl-gan to whom Kelsan or Gils can pass on the knowledge they possess, someone who can learn and remember for longer than a few days at a time."

"You're telling us that you speak to your gods through a machine?" Gringers asked, a disbelieving tone in his voice.

"Yes."

"And they answer you?"

A crafty smile touched Bara's face. "There's only one way for you to find out the answer to that question."

Lil-el leaned over and whispered in Bhaldavin's ear. "He's mad! He wants Gringers to stay and replace him."

"I know," Bhaldavin responded softly.

Gringers heard their whispers and turned. "Something wrong?"

Lil-el straightened in her chair, a determined look on her face. "You wouldn't be happy here, Gringers."

"There's much to learn in a place like this," he countered. "Things that might benefit both of our peoples in the long run."

"Perhaps," Lil-el conceded. "But I would caution you before you decide. Look around you. What has the knowledge of the First Men gained these people?"

"What do you think, Bhaldavin?" Gringers asked. "Should we stay?"

"You can stay," Bhaldavin answered, "but I have no wish to."

Gringers looked at Lord Bara, indecision in his eyes.

"Stay, Gringers," Lord Bara urged. "Stay to rule Barl-gan."

"And wait for your gods' return?" Gringers said.

"Yes."

Gringers frowned. "I know nothing of your gods, Lord Bara, but if those you wait for *are* gods, as I understand the term, I would think they could find you with or without your beacon."

"Does that mean you won't stay?"

Gringers shook his head. "I didn't say that. I might stay—for a while."

Lord Bara shivered convulsively and closed his eyes. When he opened them again, death's shadow hovered near. "Stay if you wish, or go," he said softly. "It won't matter to me much longer either way. The cord that linked me to Barl and us to this body has been severed, and weakness steals upon me."

Bara turned and drew the blanket back from his brother's face. Barl's eyes had been closed and his hair combed down over the hole in his temple.

"He goes before me," Bara said, "alone for once in his life. He loved me and hated me at the same time and was always angry that we had to share this body. I pray he's happy now. May he be granted his own body the next time around."

Bara died quietly a few hours later. Unable to sustain blood and oxygen to both his own and his brother's body, he simply went to sleep; his last words to Kelsan concerned the place he wanted their body to be buried.

Bhaldavin and Lil-el walked down the pathway to the main gate, where Gringers and Theon waited for them. Bhaldavin paused and glanced back at the great stone building that housed the last of Barl-gan's citizens. The four wind towers stood tall and sheer in the morning sun, lonely sentinels from the past. A few tendrils of fog drifted around the towers, defying Ra-shun's power to clear the air.

Lil-el touched Bhaldavin's arm. "Having second thoughts?"

"About leaving?"

"Yes."

He shook his head. "There's nothing for me here and— I have a promise to keep."

"A promise?"

"To my brother, Dhalvad. It's been fifteen years since I left him behind. It's time I try to go back to the Deep to find him—if he still lives." He caught her hand. "You'll come with me, won't you?"

"You know I will."

"It may take us a while to find a way around the Draak's Teeth."

"We'll find a way," she assured him. "I only wish that Gringers and Theon were coming with us. I hate the thought of leaving them here alone."

"I'm not as worried about them as I am about the star beacon and Bara's 'gods.' Who were the Ral-jennob really? Were they gods or were they men?"

"Does it matter now?"

"It might, if Bara's star beacon really works. What if his gods do decide to return someday to Lach? What will it mean to our people?"

She leaned close. "You worry too much, Bhaldavin. If in two thousand years, Bara's gods haven't returned, either the star beacon isn't working properly—or the Ral-jennob aren't listening."

"Perhaps. Still, it might not be a bad idea to destroy the beacon just to make sure."

"Destroy the beacon, and Bara's people have nothing to live for," Lil-el chided gently. "Leave them their dreams, Bhaldavin." She took his arm. "Come, let's go say good-bye to Gringers and Theon."

Bhaldavin cast one last glance at the wind towers and knew Lil-el was right. Barl-gan's few remaining citizens had a right to their dreams.

Lil-el and Bhaldavin continued down the path and through the open gates. Gringers and Theon waited for them on the steps outside. Theon looked pale, but he smiled as they approached.

Gringers gave Lil-el a hug and then helped her with her pack. Theon hugged her too and told her to take care of herself.

"Are you both sure you won't stay?" Gringers asked Bhaldavin.

"No."

"Which way will you be going?"

"East along the lakes," Bhaldavin said. "Then south, I think."

Gringers smiled. "Not going to try the Draak's Teeth again?"

Bhaldavin matched his smile. "No, I think not. Once is enough. How long will you stay here?"

Gringers shrugged. "Until I have what I came after."

"And then?"

"I don't know. Maybe we'll visit the Wastelanders for a while. See what they have to offer."

"Not afraid of traveling alone now, without a draak singer?"

"A little, yes, but we'll have one or two of the laser guns, and if we're careful with them, they should last awhile."

Gringers extended a hand. "Do we part as friends, Bhaldavin?"

Bhaldavin nodded and took Gringers's hand. He was startled as Gringers pulled him into a hug.

"Take good care of her, Bhaldavin," Gringers whispered. "And yourself. And here," he said, stepping back. "The crystal we promised you."

Bhaldavin took the cloth-wrapped crystal and uncovered it. It glowed with a green luminescence that warmed him and made him remember its promise of friendship. He carefully rewrapped the crystal and put it in his tunic pocket.

"Thank you, Gringers. I thought you'd forgotten."

Theon limped forward. "My turn. Well, Bhaldavin, it's been a long haul for us, and I'm sorry it's come to a parting of the ways. I'm really going to miss you."

He called me Bhaldavin!

Theon grinned and caught Bhaldavin by the shoulders.

"We're going to be here awhile, so if you change your mind and decide you'd like to join us in our wanderings, don't be bashful. You know we'd like nothing better than to have two draak singers back with us."

Bhaldavin returned Theon's rough embrace, surprised to discover the pressure of tears behind his eyes.

He turned away and held out a hand to Lil-el. "Ready to go?"

She nodded and together they started down the steps.

Epilogue ✍

"I'D HOPED THEY WOULD STAY WITH US," GRINGERS SAID sadly, his glance following the two Ni as they disappeared into the lower city.

"They'll be back," Theon said.

"I don't know. Bhaldavin has wanted his freedom a long time."

"He'll be back."

Gringers looked at Theon. "What makes you so sure of that?"

Theon reached into his pocket and drew out a crumpled piece of cloth. He carefully unwrapped it and held it up for Gringers's inspection. The fire stone winked brightly in the sunlight.

"When he realizes it's missing, he'll come back looking for it."

Gringers threw back his head and laughed aloud. "Put it away, you scoundrel, and pray that you're right, because I love those two and don't want to lose them now!"

About the Author

Marcia Joanne Bennett was born on June 9, 1945. Raised in a rural community, she has spent all but a few of her working years in central New York State.

After graduating from Albany Business College in 1965, she spent the next seven years in banking.

Several years ago she established a small craft shop in her hometown. While running the shop she began writing, a hobby that quickly became an addiction. Her other interests range from reading, painting, and basketry to astrology and parapsychology.